THE WATCHER CHRONICLES · BOOK TWO

S.J. WEST

Sandra J. West

LIST OF BOOKS IN THE WATCHER SERIES

<u>The Watchers Trilogy</u>

Cursed

Blessed

Forgiven

<u>The Watcher Chronicles</u>

Broken

Kindred

Oblivion

Ascension

<u>Caylin's Story</u>

Timeless

Devoted

Aiden's Story

<u>The Alternate Earth Series</u>

Cataclysm

Uprising

Judgment

The Redemption Series

Malcolm

Anna

Lucifer

Redemption

The Dominion Series

Awakening

Reckoning (Spring 2016)

OTHER BOOKS BY S.J. WEST

The Harvest of Light Trilogy

Harvester

Hope

Dawn

The Vankara Saga

Vankara

Dragon Alliance

War of Atonement

Kindred

CHAPTER ONE

As I stare speechlessly at my father standing on my porch, I feel like the world has become a surreal place, where my greatest wish is colliding with my worst nightmare. The familiar golden glow of his aura surrounds him like a halo of warmth, and I instantly feel like a child again, yearning to be comforted by the love only a father can give to his daughter.

My dad stands with his hands clenched at his sides, staring at me with an uncertain look on his face, like he isn't sure if I'm going to hit him or hug him.

I propel myself into his arms, not caring in that moment where he's been the last fifteen years. I'm just thankful that he's with me now when I need him the most. My heart feels like a battleground, trying to survive dueling emotions: the joy I feel being in my father's arms versus the utter devastation I feel from Mason's departure from my life. Just as I've lost one man I love, I regain another.

My dad holds me so tight I feel as though he never intends to let me go, and that suits me just fine. I'm not sure how long we stand there just holding each other, thankful our long exile from one another is finally over. Eventually, I force myself to pull away because, more than anything else, I want to see if his eyes still hold the kindness and love I remember from my childhood.

His gleaming hazel eyes tell me everything. He's missed me. He loves me. And he wants to help me. As I look at him, I'm amazed to find that time hasn't touched him. He's even dressed in the same black coat and grey scarf he wore the night the Tear first appeared, like he's been preserved in a capsule for the last fifteen years. His wavy brown hair is neatly combed, and a day's growth of stubble covers the lower portion of his face. My father isn't classically handsome. I suppose, to some, he appears rather normal looking, but he's always been the standard by which I've judged all other men. He's still the most handsome man I know.

"Where have you been?" I ask, a question that is long overdue for an answer.

"Why don't we go inside?" he suggests. "I'll answer all of your questions, but we should probably talk about what's made you so upset first."

I take my dad by the hand and lead him inside my home. Once we reach the living room, I sit down on the couch and reluctantly let his hand go so he can take off his coat and scarf. He sits down beside me and reaches for my hands again, seeming to need the close contact as much as I do.

"Now," he says, looking me in the eyes, "why were you so upset when you answered the door? It looked like you were expecting someone in particular to be there."

With the reminder of Mason's goodbye to me, a fresh set of warm tears blurs my vision. My dad pulls me to him, and I rest my head on his shoulder like I used to when I was a child, needing his comfort and strength.

"The man I love left me," I say.

"Why?"

"Because he's a noble idiot."

My father chuckles quietly. "Well, he left you; so I know he's an idiot," he agrees wholeheartedly, "but why do you say noble?"

I pull away from my father and ask, "How much of my life do you know about?"

I watch as his eyebrows knit together.

"I know almost everything, Jessi," he says, and I can tell by his expression that he didn't like all that he saw. "I was shown before I came so I can help you work through things."

"Shown?"

"God showed me what you've been through between the time I left up until you and Chandler killed Baruch tonight. So, I take it Mason left you because he didn't want you to be placed in danger because of him?"

I nod.

"You understand it's not you he left, right?"

I shake my head, listening intently for my father's wisdom.

"Jessi, he loves you enough to leave you so his enemies can't use you or hurt the other people in your life who you love. If anything, that should show you how much he truly *does* care about you. I've watched the two of you together, and there were times when you weren't looking that he allowed himself to look at you with so much love I knew he would never hurt you."

"But he *has* hurt me."

"He loves you. And you love him, right?"

I nod.

"I didn't make you to be someone who stands on the sidelines and watches things happen. I made you to be a fighter, someone who doesn't let anything stand in her way when she knows what needs to be done. Fight for him, Jessi. If you truly do love him, make him see that leaving you isn't the answer. If there is anyone in this world, who can force him stop using his guilt as a shield to hide behind, it's you."

"But what if he's right?" I ask. "What if I'm being selfish by placing our relationship ahead of the safety of the other people in my life?"

"You're making your own enemies," my father tells me, his tone ominous. "If anything, the two of you need to stand by each other's side because you're stronger together than you are apart."

"I don't suppose you could talk to him for me?" I ask, not really thinking my dad will, but silently hoping.

My father shakes his head. "No, that's a talk you need to have with him personally. I don't think Mason will listen to anyone but you."

I take a deep breath because I know he's right. I feel a new determination to make Mason see how his plan does nothing but hurt us both.

"Now that that's settled," my dad says, "I should answer your question about where I've been."

I feel myself holding my breath, awaiting his answer.

"I've been in Heaven since the Tear first opened."

I feel my face scrunch up in confusion. Had Nick been right in his first assessment of my dad?

"Are you a ghost?" I ask.

My dad smiles, like what I've said is funny. "No; I'm not even human, Jessi."

Now I'm really confused.

"What are you?" I ask, realizing I'm asking him the same question Mason asked me when we first met. Am I about to learn the answer to that very important question?

My dad sighs heavily, as if the answer will be a long one.

"First off, I want you to know I love you very much."

I sit up straight and stare at my dad.

"You're scaring me," I tell him. "I feel like you're preparing to tell me something I'm not going to like hearing."

My dad smiles. "Still a smart cookie, I see."

"Are you about to tell me something bad?"

"No, I don't think so; just unexpected." He tightens his hold on my hand, and his gaze wanders to look at our joined hands. His eyes focus on the arm with the cast.

"I forgot about your wrist," he says, taking my injured wrist in his hands.

The natural golden glow that surrounds him suddenly grows brighter around his hands. I feel a warm, tingly sensation surround my broken wrist, and the pain there slowly ebbs. I hear my cast crack, and realize my dad has just broken it in half down the middle. He pulls the cast off my arm and sets it on the coffee table.

"Try moving it," he suggests.

I move my hand up and down, testing my wrist's ability to perform the simple action. I have free movement, and no pain.

"How did you heal me?" I ask.

"It's because of the special connection we share," he says, taking my hands into his again, "and because of what I am."

"Which is?" I ask cautiously, bracing myself for the answer.

"I'm a Guardian from the Treasury of Souls, the Guf. I believe Michael told you about the Guf when you first talked to him."

"Yes, he told me about going there to find volunteers to meld with the archangel souls. But you being an angel doesn't make any sense. I don't have any angel DNA. Allan and Angela tested me when I first joined Mason's group."

"No, you don't have any angel DNA, Jessi."

I stare at my dad, waiting for him to explain further, but he doesn't. He looks at me expectantly, like he's waiting for the information to sink in so I can form my own conclusion.

"You're not my real father, are you?" I finally say, the realization of what my dad isn't saying finally unfolding in my mind.

"I'm not your biological father, but I did help create you."

I feel totally confused and upset by what he's trying to tell me, but, apparently, I don't have to tell him that, because he continues to explain.

"The Guardians of the Guf are charged with making new souls. Every once in a while, God will ask us to make a special soul for a particular purpose. He came to a hundred of us and asked us to mold the most perfect souls we could. Out of those hundred souls, seven of you volunteered to meld with the archangels' souls. But your soul was a special case."

"What do you mean?"

"God allowed me to do something with your soul no other Guardian had been allowed to do before then or since. I was asked to infuse your soul with part of my own. He didn't tell me at the time why I needed to create a soul like yours. But I've come to my own conclusion about that. I think he knew your soul needed to be strong enough to endure everything you've had to deal with so far in your life, and one that can stand up to Lucifer and do what needs to be done to defeat him. So, I may not be the father who gave you half your chromosomes to make your physical body, but you do have part of my soul inside you."

"So where is my biological father?"

"He died years ago, before you were even born."

"How?"

My dad, at least that's the way I still think of him, even with the information he's just given me, shifts nervously where he sits.

"Your father and mother were troubled teenagers, Jessi. When your mom met your dad, she was just coming out of the foster care system, still a kid really, and he was the son of a wealthy man who gave her anything she wanted. They each had demons to work through, and them being together was just an accident waiting to happen. Your father was a drug user, and your mother found it to be a good way to run away from her past. He ended up dying from an overdose, leaving your mother pregnant with you, and basically by herself. That's when I was sent to her."

"Sent to her?"

"I was allowed to help give your mother a decent life while she was pregnant with you. Those years with your mom and you are still the happiest of my life. I wanted to stay with you, but knew that was just me being selfish."

"Selfish?" I ask, not understanding. "If you wanted to stay with me, why didn't you?"

"That's a complicated answer," my dad says. "First, you should know that, even before your soul and Michael's soul melded in the Guf, God came there to have a talk with you."

I'm brought up short by this revelation. "What did we have to talk about?"

"I don't know the specifics, but I do know he warned you what would happen when the Tear appeared, because He told me that part too."

"So you always knew you would be going back to Heaven that night?"

"Yes."

"Did you know He would take my mother too?"

"Yes."

I pull my hands out of my father's grasp, because I suddenly feel the sting of betrayal.

"How could you do that to me?" I ask, not hiding my growing resentment. "How could the two of you just agree to abandon me like that?"

My father looks hurt by my choice of words, but how else am I supposed to see it?

"It was something you agreed to let happen, Jessi," my dad says, not using the information as an excuse, just stating a fact. "There wasn't anything I could do to change the path your life was supposed to take. We had to leave in order for you to become obsessed with finding us. That night was the catalyst for everything that followed, and it's what brought you to this point in your life. If we hadn't, you would have never joined the Watcher Agency. It's something that had to happen, in order to set you on the correct path."

My destiny.

My destiny could take a flying leap over a high cliff, for all I cared.

"Where is she? Where is my mother?" I demand.

"I don't know."

"You don't know, or you're just not allowed to say?" I ask, letting my irritation show.

"I swear to you, Jessi, I don't know. If I did, I would tell you, whether I was allowed to or not."

"Do you know what happened to her? Do you know anything?"

"The only thing I was told was that she would be given another life."

"Did she agree to leave me, or was she just taken away?"

I see my dad's jaw tense, like he doesn't want to say his next words. "She agreed to go."

I close my eyes and feel my heart burn inside my chest as the realization of my abandonment hits home. Lucifer had it right all along;

my parents did abandon me. My father may not have had a choice because of God's involvement, but my mother willingly left.

"So she agreed to leave me," I say, letting the words hang in the air as my tears fall freely.

"Your mother had a hard life," my dad says. "I can't tell you why she agreed to leave, because she never told me. I asked her once, but she refused to say. During the time I was allowed to stay with you both, I got the feeling she didn't feel like she could be a good enough mother to you because of her past. That's why she chose Mama Lynn to be your mother."

I open my eyes and stare at my dad.

"What do you mean she *chose* Mama Lynn?"

"God came to her and showed her a few people He knew would become foster parents to the Tear children. As soon as your mother met Mama Lynn, she knew you would have a good mother to raise you. It was important to her for you to have someone you could rely on. I don't think she ever felt like she was strong enough to raise someone who would end up saving the world one day."

"Why does it seem like the people who supposedly love me never want to stay with me? Why do they keep leaving because they think it's the best thing for me, when it's the complete opposite?"

"People are complicated, Jessi. We all do the best we can, but that doesn't mean we don't make mistakes. But you should never doubt that your mother loved you. She just wanted you to have a better life than she did. She didn't feel like she could raise you the way you deserved to be."

I stand up and start to pace out my agitation in front of the unlit fireplace.

"It's just like Mason," I say. "He left to protect me. Mom left because she didn't think she could be a good enough mother to me. You left because you wanted me to reach my destiny. Who's going to be next? Mama Lynn? Faison?"

My dad remains silent, letting me work through the information he's just given me on my own, because it's the only way I'll ever come to terms with it.

I stop pacing and turn to face my dad. "So, why are you here now? Why did He let you come back?"

"Because you're set on the path to your destiny, and He felt you needed my comfort tonight. Let me help you," my dad begs. "I love you, Jessi."

I feel my agitation and anger fade away as I look at the earnest expression on my dad's face. I do need him tonight. Of all the nights in my life, this is the one when only the comfort of my father will help heal my heart. I walk back to the couch and let him fold me into his arms.

"How long can you stay?" I ask.

"Until you fall asleep."

"What if I stay awake forever?"

He chuckles, and I know he's pleased with my suggestion. "Don't worry, Jessi. You can call me to come to you anytime you want."

"How?"

"All you have to do is say my angelic name when you need me."

I pull away and look into his kind hazel eyes. "What's your angelic name?"

"Zeruel. If you need me, just close your eyes, picture my face in your mind, and say my name out loud. I'll hear you."

"You promise you'll come?" I ask, my voice sounding childlike.

"I promise, Jessi. I'll come."

I sit there silently, enjoying the warmth emanating from my dad.

"Were you the only Guardian allowed to come to Earth?" I ask.

"No, the seven of us who made the vessel souls were allowed to stay with each of you for the first seven years of your life. After that time, we were ordered to return to Heaven. We all did, except for one of us. We just assumed God sent Remiel on another mission somewhere else. The seven of us were responsible for hiding your crowns so you could find them when the time was right."

I pull away from my dad and ask, "Do you know where the other crowns are?"

"No, I was only in charge of the one you were supposed to find. None of us told the others where the crowns were hidden. It was against the rules."

"What about the talismans? Do you know what Chandler's is supposed to be, and where it is?"

My dad shakes his head. "No, I'm sorry. I don't know. But you'll figure it out."

I lay my head on my dad's chest, smiling faintly when he tightens his arms around me.

The slow beating of his heart lulls my troubled mind, and his warmth relaxes my body to a point where sleep is inevitable.

I find myself once again in my father's study. Michael is standing by the only window in the room, with the sun shining through the sheer curtains behind him, giving him an ethereal glow.

"I wasn't sure you were going to speak to me again," he says.

"Me neither," I admit.

"Have you forgiven me yet?"

"There was never anything to forgive." I sigh. "Apparently, my soul knew what it was asking for. It wasn't your fault."

"I'm glad to see Zeruel was allowed to come back when you needed him."

"Me too."

There's an awkward silence between us, now that I know the truth of things.

"I can come to you now," he tells me.

"What do you mean?"

"The neural connections I told you about have been made. If you want to see me when you're awake, just think about me, and if I need to tell you something, I can come to you too."

"Will I be the only one who can see you?"

"Yes," a lopsided grin appears on Michael's face. "I'm still inside your head, not physically real."

"I've been warned Lilly will want to talk to me about you."

Michael's gaze drifts to the floor at the mention of his daughter. "Yes, I know."

"What do you want me to say to her?"

"I'm not sure yet," he says, looking back up at me. "I guess we'll just have to see what she wants to say to us first."

"So I guess my next move is to find Chandler's crown, talisman, and the next vessel?"

"And prove to Mason that you're supposed to be together, not apart."

I shake my head, because I have absolutely no idea how I'm going to manage such a feat. "I'm afraid that will be the toughest one to accomplish."

"I don't think it will be as impossible as you think. You'll prove to him that you belong together. I know you will."

"Yes," I say, because any other outcome is out of the question, "I'll find a way. I have to."

Kindred

CHAPTER TWO

When I wake up the next morning, my dad is nowhere to be seen. I hadn't expected him to be there, and a small part of me is thankful he's giving me time to digest everything he revealed to me the night before. My mind is still reeling from all the information he dumped into it. I lay in bed for a while, thinking over everything, and eventually allow my thoughts to wander into dangerous territory to think about Mason. Just the thought of him makes my heart ache to a point where I'm not sure it will keep beating on its own.

My dad's advice was to fight for Mason, but how do you fight for someone who doesn't want you to? Or did he? I simply didn't know, but I did know I had to follow what my heart was telling me to do. I would find a way to prove to him that we belonged together, even if it killed me. At least death wouldn't hurt this bad.

My cell phone starts to buzz on my nightstand, and I quickly reach for it, hoping it's a call from Mason. Unfortunately, it's Isaiah.

"Hello, Isaiah," I say without much enthusiasm when I answer.

"Good morning, Jess. Are you all right?"

I hear the concern in Isaiah's voice, and can tell without him even having to say it that he knows what happened between Mason and me the night before.

"Not really," I confess, not having the will to pretend otherwise. "My father came to see me last night after Mason left."

There's complete silence on the other end of the line.

"I'll be right over," Isaiah says.

"Wait!"

"Why?"

"Give me thirty minutes," I tell him, sitting up in bed, rubbing the sleep from my eyes. "I just woke up. At least let me take a shower and get dressed before you come over."

"Ok. I'll be there in thirty minutes."

When I get off the phone with Isaiah, I quickly hop in the shower and get ready for my day. I immediately know I want Chandler to hear what I have to say about my dad. Plus, I want to check on him anyway, to make sure he's all right. After being so brutally assaulted by the Watchers the night before, I feel a need to make sure he isn't only physically well, but mentally stable. It will also ensure I only had to repeat what my dad told me once.

True to his word, Isaiah knocks on my front door exactly thirty minutes later… gotta love Watcher punctuality.

"Would you mind taking me to Chandler?" I ask him, putting on my leather Watcher jacket. I'm wearing my uniform because I have no way of knowing what the day will bring, and wearing my pistol on my thigh brings me comfort and a sense of security. "I would rather not have to repeat the same story twice."

"Mason took him back to his penthouse suite in New York this morning," Isaiah informs me.

I nod. "Good. It's better than the villa. At least I don't have to worry about running into Mason yet."

"Jess…"

I look up at Isaiah and see the concern he holds for me in his eyes. "Mason told me what happened last night. Would you mind me asking if you truly do love him?"

I'm surprised Mason told Isaiah about my declaration of love, but I see no reason to hide the fact.

"Yes, I do love him, and I don't intend to let him hide from me, Isaiah, no matter how noble he might think he's being. You can tell him that for me if you want."

Isaiah smiles. "Good. I was hoping that would be your attitude. Sometimes Mason can't see the bigger picture until someone slams it in his face. It's his feelings for you that make him want to protect you, no matter the personal cost."

"I know," I say, resigning myself to the fact that the man I love is, indeed, a noble idiot. "I just have to prove to him that leaving me doesn't solve anything."

"If you need my assistance, let me know. I will do whatever I can to aid you in helping him see the error of his ways."

I grin at Isaiah as I realize I have my first official ally in my quest to get Mason back.

"Thanks. I might just take you up on the offer as soon as I figure out what to do next."

"I feel I should warn you, though. Mason is very stubborn. Once he gets an idea in his head, it's hard to change his mind."

"You know who you're talking to, right?" I ask, slightly amused by Isaiah's warning. "There's no way he's more hard-headed than I am. I pretty much own the monopoly on being stubborn."

"I can't argue about that," Isaiah agrees, smiling. "You are the most stubborn human I know."

I smile back. "I will take that as a compliment. Now, take me to Chandler, so I can tell you both what my father told me."

Isaiah phases us, and I find myself standing outside Chandler's bedroom door. Isaiah knocks on the door, and I hear Chandler call for us to come in.

When Isaiah swings the door open, I see Chandler sitting up in his bed, pillows propping his back up against the wall behind him. He's bare-chested, and the white down comforter on his bed is covering him from the waist down. He immediately smiles when he sees me, and I instantly feel our close connection kick in, bringing me some much-needed comfort after the night I just had.

"How are you feeling this morning?" I ask him, preceding Isaiah into the room and walking over to sit on the bed.

A large white bandage covers the side of his neck where the Watcher bit him the night before. I grimace a little inside, but try to hide my sympathetic pain from him.

Chandler takes one of my hands and squeezes it. "Better, now that you're here. And don't worry; it looks worse than it feels."

If people didn't know about the special bond between Chandler and me, they would probably think we are lovers, the way we act when we're together. But our relationship is more like that of a brother and sister; no romance, just a deep inseparable bond.

"So Mr. Moody didn't seem in a very good mood this morning," Chandler tells me, cocking his head to the side. "What happened when you left me last night?"

I tell Chandler what Mason did the night before.

"If I know you," Chandler says, "you're not going to let him get away with that."

"No, I'm not," I reply. "Did he say anything about me to you this morning?"

"When I asked where you were, he said he didn't know, but presumed you would be at home. He didn't seem in a very talkative mood, so I didn't push it."

"Well, that's not the only thing that happened last night." I take a deep breath. "After Mason left, my dad came to see me."

Chandler's eyes open so wide at this news, I almost laugh.

"My God, Jess, what happened?"

I go on to fill Isaiah and Chandler in on my dad's revelations from the night before.

"As far as I know," Isaiah says, "a Guardian of the Guf has never been allowed to father a child."

"I'm not sure what he did would qualify as fathering," I say.

"That's exactly what he did," Isaiah retorts, like I should know better. "He may not have created the body you have, but he gave you something far more valuable. The Guardians are chosen because of their wisdom, strength, and willingness to protect at any cost. He shared with you the most important part of himself, Jess. If that's not being a father, then I don't know what is."

I sit there, silently considering what Isaiah has just said. I realize he's right. My dad did give me the best parts of himself. He made my soul, the part of me that's always pushed me to do better, be stronger. If not for that very important piece, I wouldn't be the person I am today.

"Either way," Chandler says, "you finally got him back."

I nod. "Yeah, I did."

"Did he say why he was allowed to come back now?"

"He said God told him it was time for him to re-enter my life. I was so upset when Mason left, I guess He thought I needed someone to help me through it and realize what my next steps should be."

"Did he say anything about your mother?" Isaiah asks.

I look at Isaiah. "Only that he didn't know where she was."

Isaiah nods, like he expected my answer. "Joshua is still searching for her. It's only a matter of time before we locate her for you."

Silently, I debate with myself as to whether or not I actually want her found. Knowing that she gave me up, even if it was so I could have a better life, doesn't make me want to find her anytime soon. I have spent most of my life looking for a way to be reunited with my parents. Now I have my father back, but did I really want a mother who could so readily hand me over to a complete stranger? Would a woman like that even want to see her daughter again? My grand fantasy of having a joyous family reunion crumbled the moment my dad told me why she left the night the Tear opened. I'm not even sure I want to find her anymore.

"Speaking of Joshua," I say, "has he located Chandler's crown?"

"Yes," Isaiah tells us. "We're simply waiting for Chandler to recover enough to go get it."

"Where is it?" Chandler asks.

"It appears to be inside a tree on your parents' old property in Georgia."

Chandler looks confused for a second, but then he smiles. "I bet I know which tree." He looks at me. "I used to have this massively cool tree house when I was a kid."

"Why am I not surprised?" I say with a roll of my eyes, just further proof of Chandler's charmed, over-privileged life.

"I played in that thing all the time when I was a kid."

"Chandler, do you remember anyone special in your life when you were younger; someone who was only around until you were about seven-years-old?"

"Nanny Simone," Chandler answers without hesitation. "God, she was gorgeous. I remember just staring at her when I was a kid, thinking she must be an angel."

I smile. "Well, you were right."

"Really?" Chandler says, sitting up straighter, clearly excited by this news.

"My dad said we were all allowed to have the Guardian who made us, for the first seven years of our lives."

Chandler's forehead crinkles as he thinks about what I've said. "You know, she did seem to just up and disappear right after my seventh birthday party. I remember being upset about her leaving, but I don't remember being told why she left. I'm not sure my parents knew the reason either. It was like she was there one day and gone the next."

"Our Guardians didn't have a choice about leaving, from what my dad said. They had to go back to the Guf."

"Do you think I'll be able to see her again? I swear she ruined me for life. I can't even look at women without comparing them to Simone. Maybe that's why I've never been able to fall in love."

"Trust me," I say, "falling in love isn't all chocolates and roses. Maybe you should be happy you haven't yet."

Chandler squeezes my hand. "Don't say that, Jess. I would give anything to feel the way you do about Mason."

"Even if it makes you feel like your heart is a lump of hot twisted metal burning a hole inside your chest?"

"Even then," he smiles sadly. "If I could have that sort of connection with someone, it would be worth the heartache to me."

Chandler looks like he wants to say more, but hesitates.

"Go on," I urge him. "Say it."

"It always seems like things happen for a reason," he says. "Do you think maybe you're supposed to be with someone else instead of Mason? That maybe this has happened to free you to fall in love with another person?"

"No," I answer bluntly, "I don't. Why would you even ask such a question? Can't you use your power to sense how much I love him?"

"Yes," Chandler says, squeezing the hand he still holds. "I can."

My phone begins to vibrate in my jacket pocket, and I quickly pull it out to see who's calling. It's Mama Lynn.

"Hey, Mama Lynn," I say when I answer.

I hear Mama Lynn sniff on the other end. "Jess, can you come home?"

She breaks down into sobs, and I know what's happened.

"Has Uncle Dan died?" I ask.

Mama Lynn's sobs grow louder, but she finally gets out a, "Yes."

"I'll be right there."

I hold the phone in my hand and just stare at it. I knew this day would come, and all I can think about is Uncle Dan's soul. What torturous things were Lucifer and those under his command doing to Uncle Dan in Hell? In my mind, I can still see Uncle Dan's skeletal face twisted into a mask of fear after Lucifer told him he would suffer a million- fold for what he did to me as a child. I just can't quite decide if I feel sorry for what he's going through now, or happy that he's finally getting what he deserves. I decide not to dwell on it, because the torture of his soul isn't something I can control. Whatever Lucifer does to Uncle Dan is too far out of my reach to have any influence over. The monster of my childhood is finally out of my life for good, and I can't help but feel relieved by that fact.

I stand up, but Chandler keeps a hold of my hand, not letting me go yet.

"Let me come with you," he says.

I shake my head. "No, you stay here and rest. I can handle this."

"Then at least let me know when the funeral is," Chandler begs. "I want to be there for you, Jess."

I know I should tell him not to come, but a part of me desperately wants him there. If I can't have Mason by my side for comfort, Chandler is the next best thing.

"Ok," I agree. "I'll call you later and let you know the details about the funeral. I need to head back now, though, and take care of

Mama Lynn. I'm sure she's not in any condition to make the funeral arrangements."

"I'll be waiting for your call."

I have Isaiah take me home. Once he leaves to tell Mason what I learned from my father, I head over to Mama Lynn's house, bracing myself to deal with her grief.

CHAPTER THREE

As I sit between Mama Lynn and Faison by the gravesite, I feel one of Chandler's hands gently squeeze my right shoulder, letting me know he's there if I need him.

We decided only to have a grave-side service for Uncle Dan. Mama Lynn said her brother didn't have many friends, and she was right. There are only a handful of people from Cypress Hollow present plus us, his only family.

I reach up and place my left hand over Chandler's, which remains steadfast on my shoulder. The feel of his hand under mine helps bring comfort to my soul as Pastor Cary drones on about how Uncle Dan will be missed by his family and friends, and what his legacy on Earth is. I tune him out because I don't need to hear the perfunctory speech, which is meant to bring comfort to those like Mama Lynn, who might actually feel like his death is a loss to the world.

My eyes are drawn past the glossy wood casket to my first waking vision of Michael. He's standing two rows down from Uncle Dan's plot in the old churchyard. I see him pointedly look to his left, and I instinctively follow his gaze.

I feel my heart begin to beat, as if a thundering herd of elephants has invaded it when I see Mason standing at the far corner of the graveyard, half hidden by a tall tombstone with an angel of mercy crouched on top of it. His eyes are narrowed on me. He doesn't look away when our eyes meet, and all I want to do is jump up from my seat and run to him. I feel his worry over me like a physical presence between the two of us. His eyes hold a longing to bring me comfort, and all I want to do is go to him and accept it. Our eye-contact never wavers as the funeral service continues and comes to an end.

Our neighbors form a line in front of us to bestow their condolences. I briefly lose sight of Mason when Sadie bends down to give me a kiss on the cheek, telling me how sorry she is for my loss. By the time I'm finally free to stand, I look over at the spot where Mason was and see that he's already phased away.

"Was I imagining things, or was Mason standing over there during the funeral?"

I turn to Chandler, who is still standing behind my chair.

"You weren't imagining things," I say, my heart feeling heavier now with Mason's sudden departure. Why did it seem like he was always leaving me?

"Jess," Mama Lynn says, standing from her seat beside me, "the ladies of the church prepared a lunch for us. Do you have time to stay and eat, or do you need to get back to work right away?"

I put an arm around her shoulders. "Of course I have time. Come on. I know Ms. Margaret probably made us her famous fried chicken."

"Well, you better come on, too, Chandler," Mama Lynn says, trying her best to still be the epitome of Southern hospitality, even while she's grieving. "I can't let you go without at least having lunch with us."

I was surprised by Mama Lynn and Faison's reaction to Chandler's presence. When I told them he was coming to the funeral, Mama Lynn said she was happy I would have a friend there to comfort me, and Faison didn't hound me too much for information about the extent of my relationship with the most sought-after bachelor rock star in America, if not the world.

I desperately wanted to tell them about my reunion with my father, but knew I couldn't. I couldn't tell them anything, which made me realize I was being forced to lead a double life now. Since becoming a Watcher agent, they had become accustomed to my silence about work. But now, that part of my life was leaking into my personal life, and it was becoming almost impossible to keep the two separate.

After lunch, I tell Mama Lynn I need to get back to work. She isn't too surprised, and just seems thankful I took off so much time to be with her, and to handle the funeral arrangements. She tells me to be careful and to call her later. Faison takes me off to the side while her fiancé, John Austin, attempts to have a conversation with Chandler, but I can tell he is completely star-struck by my new friend. What normal person wouldn't be? It's not like Chandler even looks remotely like he belongs in Cypress Hollow. With his designer suit and rock star looks, he doesn't exactly blend in well with the general population.

"I saw Mason," Faison says to me. I told her the previous day what happened between Mason and me, without going into too much detail about the Watcher attack, the impetus of Mason's departure.

"Yeah, he was at the cemetery."

"Are you all right, Jess? Is there anything I can do to help?"

I shake my head. "Not really. Just take care of Mama Lynn for me, so I don't have to worry about her. I'm going to be busy with work for a while, so I'm not going to have a lot of free time to be with you guys."

"Can you tell me anything about what's going on? Maybe it would help if you could talk to me about it."

I sigh. "I really wish I could, but I'm sworn to secrecy. You know that."

Faison smirks at me. "Yeah, yeah, Watcher business. So, do you know what they are now? The Watchers?"

I almost nod, but don't. "I can't answer that. If I did, I would have to kill you afterward."

Faison sticks her tongue out at me. "Fine, keep your secrets. Go on with your new boyfriend and save the world."

"New boyfriend?"

Faison tilts her head towards Chandler. "I see the way you two are together. You don't have to be a genius to see something is going on between the two of you."

"It's not like that," I say, not liking the idea of Faison assuming Chandler and I are anything but friends. "I can't fully explain the relationship Chandler and I have to you, but I don't have any romantic feelings for him. I love Mason."

"Then I'm completely confused," Faison confesses. "I watched the video of him singing to you at his Madison Square Garden concert, and, from the way he was looking at you while he sang, it looked like he felt something deeper than just friendship."

I shake my head. "We do have a connection, but it's more like brother and sister, not boyfriend and girlfriend. Trust me; it's completely asexual."

Faison shrugs. "If you say so, but that's not the way the world is seeing it."

"What do you mean, the world?"

Faison pulls out her cell phone from her purse and goes to a celebrity gossip website. On it, I see a picture of Chandler and me at the concert, on stage. The title of the story is *Chandler Cain Finally Finds Love…with a Watcher Agent.*

I shake my head, completely dismayed by this new revelation. I immediately wonder if Mason has seen this tabloid gossip, and hope he knows how untrue it is.

"Don't believe everything you read on the Internet," I tell Faison.

I call Isaiah and have him come to the church to pick Chandler and me up.

"I want to go get my crown now," Chandler tells us.

"Are you sure you wouldn't rather go back to your apartment and rest for a while?" I ask, concerned he might be pushing himself too hard too soon.

"No, I want to go get it. The sooner I have that part, the sooner I'll be able to find my own fiery sword."

"You do realize," I say, "that we're all supposed to get a talisman that fits us. I hate to be the bearer of bad news, but I don't see a fiery sword in your future, my little rock star."

"Well, it's gotta be something wicked cool, right?" Chandler beams. "Either way, I need it to help me develop my powers. If I have it, maybe it'll make it easier for us to find the third vessel."

"Yeah, I've been thinking about that," I say, looking over at Isaiah. "Do you think Mason would let us use his villa? Chandler and I have already tried to connect with the next vessel at his apartment, but the mood just didn't seem right. I would like to try it at the villa, since that's where it worked for me the first time."

"I will ask," Isaiah says cautiously, "but I can't promise anything."

Secretly, I'm hoping this might also present an opportunity to find a moment alone with Mason. Maybe if I force him to at least be in the same house with me, he'll have to listen to what I want to tell him.

"First," Isaiah says, "let's go to Chandler's childhood home to retrieve his crown."

Isaiah places his hands on my and Chandler's shoulders. We instantly find ourselves standing on the street of a very normal-looking subdivision of upper middle class homes.

"Wow," Chandler says, staring at the house across the street from us. "I haven't been back here in ages."

"You're only twenty-one," I say. "It can't have been ages."

"You know I got my big break when I was fifteen," he says, reminding me of the timeline of his life. "When my first album went platinum, I bought my parents a house in Los Angeles, so they would be close to me out there. We sold this house."

"I have already spoken with the new owners," Isaiah informs us. "They were extremely gracious, and said we could have free rein of the backyard where the tree is."

Isaiah places his hands on our shoulders again, and we find ourselves standing in front of a massive oak tree. The tree house built within the thick limbs of the mighty oak makes it look like a miniature apartment complex. There are two large, house-like structures perched on either side of a wide expanse connected by a plank wood and a rope bridge.

Out of the corner of my eye, I see Isaiah pull out his cell phone. He begins to scan the area, much like Mason did once upon a time, and I know he's using the same radiation detection app to pinpoint the exact location of the crown. We watch as Isaiah walks to the back of the tree. He kneels down to the ground and begins to move an old pile of leaves away from the base of the trunk. There is a natural hole there between the ground and the trunk. Isaiah gives me his phone to hold while he reaches his hand into the hole. The hole is deeper than it appears, because Isaiah ends up having his arm inside it up to his shoulder. Eventually, he pulls out the same type of metal box my crown was found in.

Setting it on the ground in front of him, Isaiah releases the catch and lifts the lid.

Sitting within the box is a pristine silver crown similar to the one I have, with the same intricate fluid markings I know will tell us the name of the archangel the crown belongs to.

"Wicked," Chandler says, kneeling beside Isaiah, staring at the crown.

"Pick it up," I urge him.

Chandler places his hand above the crown and quickly pulls it out.

"Why does it feel like a live wire?" he asks. "Is that normal?"

"Yes," I tell him. "It won't hurt you. It just knows you're here."

Chandler reaches inside the box again and wraps his fingers around the base of the crown, pulling it out easily. Just as mine did, Chandler's box disintegrates into dust.

"I don't care what you say, but *that* was wicked cool," Chandler says of the box's magical disappearance.

Chandler stands back up, holding the crown out in front of him.

"So, what now?" he asks. "How do we find my talisman?"

"We should probably find out the name of the archangel the crown belongs to first," I say, turning my attention to Isaiah. "Will Lilly be able to help us again?"

Isaiah's face looks pinched at my question. "I was asked to bring Chandler when he had possession of his crown, but only him."

I nod. "I understand. She's still not ready to see me yet."

"No, she isn't," Isaiah confirms. "She asked me to tell you not to take it personally, but she needs a little more time to think about what she wants to say when she finally does meet with you again."

"Then, can you take me back to my house while you guys go see Lilly?"

When Isaiah phases us to my home, Chandler gives me a peck on the cheek.

"Be back soon," he tells me, before Isaiah phases him to Lilly's home.

I walk up to my front porch and sit heavily in one of the rocking chairs. Closing my eyes, I try to let the events of the day ebb away.

"How are you doing, Jessica?"

My eyelids fly open, and I see Lucifer standing in front of me, leaning against the porch railing, watching me with hooded eyes.

He's dressed in a pair of form-fitting blue jeans and a red t-shirt which looks a size too small, obviously meant to accentuate the muscles on the upper torso of the body he inhabits. His straight blond hair brushes his shoulders, and there's a day or two of stubble covering his jaw, giving him a ruggedly handsome look.

"As well as can be expected," I answer, wondering why he's come to see me, today of all days.

"I would have thought you would be relieved, knowing your uncle is finally where he belongs. I placed him in the special care of one of my best torturers."

"I don't want to know what you're doing to him," I say.

Lucifer cocks his head to the side. "Aren't you the least bit interested in knowing the price he's paying for what he did to you?"

"No."

"I find that curious," he says, crossing his arms over his chest, studying me with a critical eye. "Why not?"

"Because he's dead and no longer a concern to me. If you don't mind, I would like to keep it that simple."

"What if I gave you a choice?"

"What do you mean by a choice? A choice between what?"

"A choice of the type of torture your uncle will suffer."

"You've lost me."

"I can keep your uncle where he is, or I can send him to the Void."

"What's the Void?"

"Some people call it purgatory. It's pretty much what the name indicates: a void of space where nothing exists, except lost souls that haven't earned a place in either Heaven or Hell. Your uncle would never find peace there, but he wouldn't suffer an eternity in Hell, which is far worse, I assure you."

"Have you lost your mind? Why are you placing the responsibility of how he suffers on me?" I ask, not seeing the point in him giving me such a choice.

Lucifer shrugs. "I'll let you think about it for now. But don't take too long to decide. There will come a time when it won't matter where he is."

"What do you mean?"

"At some point, his mind will break, and it won't matter where he is. He'll become completely insane. At that point, either place will be a living nightmare for him."

Lucifer continues to study me as I remain quiet in my indecision.

Silently, I'm fuming. I don't want to be given a choice. What the hell is he thinking? I have to remind myself this is his nature. This is what he does. He tortures people. He might look like a good guy, and act like he wants to be my friend, but deep down he will always feel a need to present me with impossible choices, none of them good.

Finally, Lucifer uncrosses his arms and places his hands in his front pockets, looking more casual, like he's an old friend who has come over to have a normal conversation.

"If you don't want to talk about your uncle, perhaps we can talk about that sword I saw you with the other night."

I swallow hard. "What about it?"

Lucifer grins. "How did you obtain Jophiel's sword?"

This time I cross my arms over my chest. "Wouldn't you like to know?"

Lucifer's grin grows wider. "Yes, I would. Why don't you tell me?"

"Can't."

"No," he says, his deep blue eyes narrowing on me, "you simply won't."

I shrug. "Same difference. We're not on the same side in this fight."

"Are we fighting?" Lucifer looks amused. "And here I thought we were becoming friends."

"I don't think you're capable of having friends."

"Possibly not." Lucifer shrugs his shoulder, as if it doesn't matter to him one way or the other. "A person in my position has very few people he can trust."

"What about Asmodeus? The two of you looked pretty chummy together."

"Asmodeus is simply a subordinate, nothing more. He's too preoccupied with his own particular specialty to be someone I can talk to."

"And what exactly is his specialty?"

"Hasn't Mason told you yet?"

My eyes drop from Lucifer's face at the mention of Mason's name.

"Oh," Lucifer says knowingly, "I see. He's left you, in some noble sacrifice, has he? Thinks you'll be safe from his enemies if he proves to them he doesn't care about you anymore?"

"Astute observation," I grumble.

"Mason and his never-ending guilt. It's his Achilles' heel, you know. He lets it control him far too easily, makes it rather unchallenging to know how to push his buttons when I want."

"He has a conscience, unlike some people I know," I say, feeling the need to defend the man I love from the devil's condemnation. "Can you feel anything besides hate?"

Lucifer's face softens as he continues to look at me.

"I feel something for you," he admits. "I just don't know why yet." He pauses as he stares at me, trying to figure me out. "Can or would you tell me why I feel so drawn to you?"

"Wouldn't that just spoil your fun?" I ask, having no intention of telling him about Michael. It's the one thing I have that Lucifer wants, and I need to keep him coming to me until we figure out what his plans are.

Lucifer doesn't answer my question. He asks one instead.

"After Mason took you home after Baruch's attack, I felt your pain again," he tells me. "I was otherwise engaged at the time, or I would have come to see what was wrong. I assume that's the moment

Mason left you. But the pain seemed to subside into something you could bear rather quickly, why?"

"I can't tell you that," I say, not wanting him to know about my father coming to visit me. It would be one more clue added to what he already knows in solving what I am.

"Hmm, you're simply full of mysteries," Lucifer says. "You know I'll figure it out eventually. There isn't much in this world that remains secret from me for very long."

"I'm sure there isn't," I concede, "which is all the more reason for me to tell you nothing."

Lucifer smiles. "I like you," he tells me, "even if you are just a human."

Lucifer pushes away from the railing. "Until next time, Jessica."

He phases away, and I finally let myself breathe again.

CHAPTER FOUR

An hour later, Chandler and Isaiah come back to my house to let me know Mason has agreed to let us use his villa. Isaiah takes Chandler back to his apartment to pack some clothes while I do the same. I pack my overnight bag with two days' worth of clothing because I'm not sure how long we'll be staying at the villa, trying to make a connection with the third vessel. My heart beats with excitement, filled with hope that Mason will come to see me while I'm there.

The last time I was at the villa, Mason and I shared a closeness that propelled us to finally admit we had feelings for one another. I can still remember Mason holding my hand everywhere we went in his home, and how he let me touch the scar on his face as I told him how perfect he was in my eyes. I desperately want a chance to finish the conversation we were having back then, before Malcolm and Malik's sudden appearance ruined the moment. If Mason could just see himself through my eyes, I feel sure he would finally be able to understand how truly special he is, at least to me.

When Isaiah and Chandler return, they tell me what they learned from Lilly.

"She says it belonged to some archangel named Chamuel," Chandler tells me.

S.J. West

"Chamuel was able to bring peace to almost any situation," Isaiah tells me. "It makes sense, considering Chandler's power to evoke emotions."

"Then it's most likely Chandler has his archangel's crown?" I ask.

Isaiah nods. "Yes, that's what Mason concluded as well."

"Mason?" I ask. "Was he at Lilly's?"

"Yes."

I feel like banging my head against the wall. Why didn't I insist that I go with Chandler? It would have been the perfect excuse to see Mason again. But I couldn't do that to Lilly. I couldn't be that selfish when she was still trying to deal with the fact that I'm the vessel for her father's soul. No matter how much I would have loved the opportunity to see Mason again, I knew such a selfish act wouldn't have been right.

I call Mama Lynn to let her know I will be gone for a few days. She tells me to be careful, like she always does, and Isaiah phases us to Mason's villa.

We find ourselves standing in the living room. The fire is lit, and a tray of cheeses, meats, fruits and sliced bread sits on the large wooden table separating the couch and fireplace, like someone prepared the area for our arrival.

"Is Mason here?" I ask, knowing who that someone had to have been.

"No," Isaiah says regretfully. "In fact, he asked me to let him know when you decide to leave. I don't believe he plans to come here while you're using the house."

My heart sinks with disappointment, but I suppose I should have expected Mason's refusal to be under the same roof as me.

I feel Chandler grab my hand.

"Come on," he urges, his face lit up like a kid's, "let's go explore."

With Chandler by my side, I discover a multitude of things about Mason's personal sanctuary. Unlike the last two times I was here, I actually venture outside the villa, and discover that the grounds contain a formal garden, swimming pool, tennis court, olive grove, and child's playground. I have to assume the playground is for Jonathan and Angela's children, but wonder if Mason ever envisions having more children of his own one day.

The thought of Mason holding a child he doesn't have to worry about being cursed makes me ache to find a way to make the vision come true for him. The pain he suffered having to watch Jonathan's transformation into a werewolf every night broke him in more ways than one.

When did kids even become more than a fleeting thought for me? The question brings me up short. Having a child of my own has never been very high on my list of priorities. The thought of having one with Mason seems so natural for some reason, like it's what's supposed to happen. I try to shake the image from my mind, but a vision of Mason holding our child in his arms lingers.

When we go back inside the house, Chandler and I discover a billiard room, gym, and entertainment room loaded with one of the new holographic TVs, and a music center, which instantly intrigues Chandler.

Before he becomes too consumed by it, I drag him back up to the living room so we can do what we came here to do, connect with the third vessel.

"Can we eat first?" Chandler whines. "We haven't eaten since lunch, and that was, like, three hours ago."

"You are such a baby," I complain. "Fine. Dig in."

Chandler and I eat from the tray I know Mason left for us. I'm not sure when he found the time to prepare his home for our arrival, but I'm thankful for his thoughtfulness.

After we eat, Chandler sits back on the couch, all slouched over, and lets out a loud burp.

I shake my head at him. "Say 'excuse me'," I tell him.

"Excuse me," he says, a Cheshire grin on his face, the poster child of complete satisfaction.

"If only your adoring fans could see you now," I say.

"They would still love me, like you still love me."

"I don't have much choice," I say. "I'm connected to you forever. They're not."

"Is it so bad that you're stuck with me until death do us part?"

I find his choice of words a strange way to put it, but I say, "No. I don't mind being connected to you for that long. I'm getting kind of used to having you around."

Chandler sits up and holds his hand out to me. "Come on. Let's try to find the next vessel. I'm curious to know if we'll have the same kind of connection with them too."

I take Chandler's offered hand as we sit beside one another on the couch.

"When I had my vision of you," I tell him, "all I did was listen to the sound of the wood popping in the fireplace. Let's try to concentrate on that and see what happens."

We both close our eyes and remain quiet, allowing the sounds of the fire to surround us. I'm not sure how long we sit there, but eventually Chandler says, "This isn't working either, is it?"

I open my eyes and look over at him.

"No, it's not. I just don't understand why it isn't. It's supposed to be easier with two of us, but it seems like it's harder. Though, I might know someone who can help us."

In my head, I call to Michael.

He instantly appears, standing in front of the fireplace.

He smiles at me. "I'm glad you called to me."

"Can you help us? I thought you said it would be easier when there are two of us trying."

"Uh, Jess, who are you talking to?" Chandler asks, looking between the fireplace and me.

"Michael. I can see him now when I'm awake."

"Wicked," Chandler says, smiling. "Can he help us?"

"Don't know yet, you keep talking," I complain. "He can't talk over you."

Chandler puts a hand to his lips, and makes a motion like he's locking them with a key.

I look back at Michael.

"What are we doing wrong?"

"It's not so much that you're doing anything wrong," he says hesitantly, "but you're the one who is blocking the connection."

"Me?" I ask in surprise. "How?"

"When you connected with Chandler, it was right after you and Mason first began to share your feelings for one another. You were open to allowing someone else in. Now, you're closed off again."

"How do I open myself up again?"

"I'm not sure, but I still believe Mason is the key to your success."

"But he won't see me."

"But he did see you. He came to the funeral. He wants to be with you, but he still feels that would be selfishly placing you in danger."

"Have you any idea how I can prove to him that he's wrong about that?"

"No; I wish I did."

Out of the corner of my eye, I see Chandler hold up his hand, like he's in school, asking for permission to speak.

"Go ahead," I tell him, slightly amused.

"What's he saying? Can he help us?"

"He thinks I'm the reason we can't connect. My emotional state because of Mason is blocking the connection."

"So, how do we fix that?"

I sigh heavily. "I have no idea."

Michael fades away, apparently no longer having any more useful information to impart.

Chandler and I finally decide to give up for the rest of the day and just have some much-needed fun together. We go back into the entertainment room. While flipping through the available movies on Mason's holographic TV, I notice three new additions: all three of the original *Star Wars* movies. I know they're new because they're displayed in blue instead of purple, indicating they haven't been played yet. I smile wanly because I know Mason placed them on there for me. He probably thought I would find comfort watching them, just as I did when I was sick.

As the evening draws late, Chandler and I retire to our separate rooms, which are right beside one another.

"Ok, I know this is going to sound like I'm a complete weirdo," Chandler says to me, looking somewhat shy about what he's about to say next. "But would you stay in my room with me until I fall asleep?"

"Why?" I ask, drawing out the word, because this seems like a very peculiar request.

"Because I don't like sleeping in new places," he confesses. "I always make my agent stay in my room until I go to sleep when we're in a new city. It's just that first night. I can't relax enough to fall asleep without knowing someone else is with me."

"You're such a baby," I tease. "Let me get in my pajamas, and I'll be right there."

Relief floods Chandler's eyes and he smiles shyly. "Thanks, Jess; you're the best."

I go to my room and slip into my pink flannel pajamas. When I enter Chandler's room, he's already in bed without a shirt on, up on his elbows, waiting for me.

"You have pants on under those covers, right?" I ask.

Chandler smiles. "Nope; can't sleep with clothes on either."

I pull a small chair over to his bedside, and he lays his head down on his pillow.

"Now, you can't leave until I'm asleep," he says. I hear the worry in his voice that I might not heed his rule, and decide not to pick on him about it.

"I won't leave," I say. "I promise."

I turn off the lamp on his nightstand, casting the room in complete darkness.

It doesn't take more than thirty minutes before I hear Chandler's soft snoring. As quietly as I can, I pad over to the door and leave the room, making sure I close the door behind me so softly not even a mouse can hear it.

When I turn to go to my own room, I feel like my world has come completely unglued. Standing at the end of the long hallway is Mason, watching me.

I feel my heart tighten in my chest at the sight of him.

"Don't go," I beg, knowing that if I don't say something, he might phase away before I have a chance to speak with him.

"I just came to get something," he tells me, even though I don't see anything in his hands. "I thought the two of you were asleep."

I see his eyes drift to Chandler's door and back to me.

"Chandler can't go to sleep in a new place without someone being with him," I tell Mason, wanting to make sure he understands the reason I'm coming out of Chandler's room so late at night.

"It's really none of my business," Mason says, his voice devoid of emotion.

I take a tentative step forward. Mason doesn't move.

"Thank you for coming to the funeral," I tell him, continuing to slowly make my way to him up the hallway, feeling a desperate need to close the distance between us, not only physically, but emotionally too.

"I wanted to make sure you were all right," he says, eyeing my progress towards him warily, but not telling me to stop. His gaze lingers on my face, caressing me. I can feel his longing to reach out to me, but he holds himself back.

"I wasn't sure I would see you again, after last time," I say, remembering how Mason had looked at me in my bedroom, like he was taking a mental picture of me to last him the rest of his life.

"I can't seem to make myself stay away from you," he confesses, looking slightly ashamed over his own weakness.

"I don't want you to stay away," I tell him. "Mason, please; I need you by my side."

"I can't. It's not safe for you."

"I'm safer with you than without you," I tell him, trying to make him see reason. "I can't think about anything but you, and it's making it impossible to connect with the third vessel. I need you in my life. I can't live without you in it."

"I'm sorry, Jess; I can't take the risk of something happening to you because of me. I'll try to stay away from you. In time, I know you'll forget about me. I'm sorry."

Mason phases before I have a chance to convince him how wrong he is.

I turn to go back to go to my room, fully intending to give myself permission to cry myself to sleep.

CHAPTER FIVE

The next morning I find Chandler in the kitchen, scrambling eggs and frying sausage links.

"Hungry?" he asks me when I sit down at the table.

"Not really," I say, laying my arms on the tabletop and burying my face in them.

"What's up, Jess?" he asks, concern in his voice.

Not even bothering to lift my head, I tell Chandler about seeing Mason the previous night, in the hallway.

I hear him switch off the stove and walk over to the table to sit down across from me.

"Listen," he says. "I want to try something."

I lift my head and look at him. My eyes still feel scratchy and puffy from crying myself to sleep the night before.

"Try what?" I say, sounding completely despondent, even to my own ears.

"Yesterday, when I went to see Lilly, I did something I'm not very proud of, but, for your sake, I had to know."

"Know what exactly?" I ask, sitting up straighter in my chair, my curiosity piqued.

"I had to know if Mason really loved you, or if he was just playing games with you." Chandler grimaces, like he's ashamed to say the rest to me. "I used my power on him."

"You what?" I almost scream. "What the hell were you thinking, Chandler? I'm surprised you're still alive!"

"I apologized," Chandler says, looking properly contrite for his invasion of Mason's privacy. "I might have apologized *after* I had what I needed, but I did say that I was sorry."

"What happened? Did it work?" I hate that I'm sort of glad Chandler did what he did, but I can't help it. A desperate, love-sick woman will take any evidence that the man she loves still loves her, even if that evidence was obtained in a totally unacceptable way.

"It wasn't much different from the time I used my power on those Watchers who were trying to kill us. The only difference was that I didn't just tap into his sorrow; I tapped into his love for you, too."

"What did you feel?" I ask, holding my breath, waiting for his answer.

Chandler holds out his hands to me. "Like I said, I want to try something. I want to see if I can channel his feelings, so you know firsthand how he feels about you. Maybe if you know, your mental block will disappear, and we can find the third vessel."

I'm hesitant to do as Chandler asks. What if Mason doesn't love me as much as I love him? What if I find out something I just don't want to know?

"I'm not sure it'll work," Chandler says, seeing my indecision, "but, if it does, at least you'll finally know."

Taking a leap of faith, I place my hands in Chandler's.

"Here goes nothing," he says, closing his eyes.

I feel a warmness emanate from our joined hands, and then it hits me like a bolt of lightning from the sky. My heart swells with so much love I'm not sure it's big enough to contain it all. Mixed with the love is a sense of fear, fear of losing it all. Guilt and sorrow seem to surround the love, constricting it to the point where it's suffocating my heart. Happy tears spring to my eyes, because I finally know, without any doubt, that Mason loves me.

Chandler lets go of my hands and looks at me. "You felt it, didn't you?"

I nod because I can't speak. I bury my face in my hands and let myself cry tears of relief. In my heart, I knew Mason loved me, but I never knew the depth of that love until now. How someone who feels that way about another person can force himself to stay away, takes more willpower than I can ever hope to have.

"Are you ok?" I hear Chandler ask me, sounding concerned that maybe he shouldn't have shared Mason's feelings with me.

I nod, wiping the tears from my eyes, and finally finding my voice, "Thank you. I needed to know."

Chandler smiles. "I know you did. Now, maybe you can concentrate. Otherwise, we're doomed," he says, drawing out the last word to sound ominous.

I laugh.

Feeling lighter of heart than I have since the night Mason left me, I dig into the breakfast Chandler made, and tell him I think we should go back upstairs to the living room to try to connect with the third vessel again.

The fire in the fireplace has long since burned itself out, but Chandler makes quick work of building it back up.

"And how does a rock star know how to build a fire?" I ask.

"Boy Scouts," he answers.

"Of course you were a Boy Scout," I say, shaking my head. "I should have known."

Chandler and I sit on the couch again and turn to face one another. We hold hands and concentrate on connecting with the third vessel.

Since Michael said my ability to open up enough to connect with the next vessel is directly related to my feelings for Mason, I ask Chandler to channel Mason's love into me once again, hoping it's enough to completely break my mental block.

Just as I feel my heart swell with his love for me, I see a vision of a woman dressed in an off-the-shoulder white sweater and black Capri pants, dancing barefoot, around a room filled with all types of fabrics. She has short black hair cut into a stylish bob, with thick curls that bounce happily above her shoulders as she dances. I see her pick up a long piece of gauzy white fabric and twirl around with it in her hands, to music that has a happy beat. When she turns around, I can't see her face because the fabric is obscuring it, but I do see a cursive black 'A' appliqué stitched on the upper right corner of her sweater. The vision fades, and I open my eyes.

"Did you see her?" Chandler and I ask at the same time.

We laugh.

"Do you know who she is?" I ask him.

"I think I might," he says, completely amazed by the fact.

"Who is she?"

"I think that was JoJo Armand. She's a French fashion designer."

"How do you know a fashion designer?"

"I don't know her personally, but I've been to a couple of her fashion shows. My agent said it was good PR to go, so I did."

The name sounds familiar, and I remember why. Angela told me the dress Mason bought for me to wear to the masquerade ball was from the House of Armand.

"I need to call Isaiah," I say, standing up quickly to fetch my phone from my room.

It doesn't take long for Isaiah to come get us.

"Have you located her?" I ask Isaiah when he arrives.

"Yes. She's at her design studio in Paris. I sent Malcolm over there to speak with her on our behalf. Apparently, they're friends."

"That helps," I say. "At least she won't think we're a bunch of lunatics right off the bat."

Isaiah places his hands on our shoulders, and we find ourselves standing in the room we just saw in our vision. Rays of bright sunlight shine through the large windows making up all four walls of the loft we're in. It's a lot like being in a glass house that's ten stories in the air. The Eiffel Tower can be seen in the distance to our right, making me realize how surreal my life has become.

JoJo Armand is standing on the opposite side of the room from us, her hands on her hips, nodding at something Malcolm is saying to her. Almost as soon as we phase into her workspace, her eyes are drawn to us. Just from the vision we had of her, I know JoJo is someone who has a natural effervescence, but, when she looks at us, it seems to multiply tenfold.

"Bonte' divine!" She says, running over to us, her curls bouncing around her shoulders. JoJo looks to be in her mid-thirties, but her love of life makes her look almost like a teenager. Her joyous smile is infectious, and we instantly know we've found our third archangel.

She squeals in delight as she hugs me and then Chandler.

"Jess and Chandler?" she asks, a French accent tingeing her words.

"Yes," I answer. "We've been looking for you."

"*Oui, oui*, Malcolm told me that. He said I would have to wait for you to come to explain what is going on."

JoJo takes our hands and practically drags us over to a sitting area in her studio. The furniture is modern and doesn't look very comfortable, since there are no backs to any of the chairs, just thick padding covered in white leather placed on top of steel frames.

Once we're sitting on either side of JoJo, she says, *"S'il vous plait*, tell me what is happening. Why do I feel like I have finally been reunited with two of my very best friends?"

Much the same way I did with Chandler when I first met him, we explain what we know to JoJo. She seems to take it all in stride, without asking too many questions.

"Is there anything you want to ask us?" I say after we've explained the situation to her.

"Do you both have your crowns and talismans?" she asks.

"We have our crowns," Chandler answers, "but I haven't found my talisman yet."

"I have always wanted a crown," JoJo says, a wistful look on her face. "It's just like when I was a little girl and wanted to be a real princess. Now, I am a princess of Heaven, *c'est vrai?*"

"Yes," Chandler answers, obviously knowing a little more French than I do, "a very powerful princess."

JoJo smiles brightly. "So, what should we do now?"

"We should probably attempt to find the next vessel," I say, "but there's no guarantee it'll work the first time. It took Chandler and me a while to finally be able to find you, and we were only able to locate you so quickly because Chandler's been to some of your fashion shows and was able to recognize you instantly."

"Ah, do you like my clothes?" JoJo asks Chandler. "Did you buy for a lady friend?"

"A few lady friends, actually," Chandler admits with a cocky grin. "And, yes, I do like your designs. They always show off a lady's figure to its best."

"*Merci*," JoJo says, and bows her head at the compliment.

"I actually have one of your dresses," I admit.

"*Lequel*?" JoJo asks, but I have no clue what she just said. I must look confused because she then says, "Which?"

I describe the dress to her.

JoJo nods excitedly. "*Oui, oui*, I remember that dress. I wondered who ended up wearing it. It is one of my favorites. Your lover has very good taste."

I feel my eyebrows draw together with her use of the word 'lover'.

"Not a lover?" she asks, shaking her head.

"Not yet," Chandler answers with a sigh. "We're working on it."

I feel my cheeks burn.

"Maybe I can help with that," I hear Malcolm say.

I look over at Malcolm, who is still standing on the far side of the room with Isaiah.

"Oh, yeah?" Chandler says to him. "What are you thinking?"

"I say we ambush Mason," Malcolm replies. "Dress Jess up, prepare a romantic setting, and throw him into it."

"Doesn't sound like much of a plan," Chandler says, completely unconvinced it will be enough to work, "but guess it's worth a try."

"Excuse me," I say. "Don't I have to agree to do that first?"

"Do you want Mason back or not?" Malcolm asks.

"Yes, but..."

"No, there're no buts," Malcolm replies. "The only way to make Mason see reason is to force it on him. I thought you would be willing to try anything."

"Well, I am, but..."

"Ok, then," Malcolm smiles, but it makes him instantly look like he's up to no good. "Leave the details to me."

"Dress up?" JoJo asks. "I will handle the dressing up. How much time do I have?"

"I say the sooner the better," Malcolm says. "Give me until tonight to get things ready."

"Ok, now that we're through planning Mason's ambush," I say, "maybe we should try to concentrate on finding the fourth vessel." I look over at Isaiah. "Could you take us back to Mason's villa? It seems to work there the best, at least for me."

Once we're back in the living room at the villa, Chandler, JoJo, and I stand together, facing one another, and make a circle, holding onto each other's hands.

"What do I do?" JoJo asks, barely able to control her excitement.

"I concentrate on the noises from the fire," I look over at Chandler. "Did that work for you?"

He nods. "Yeah, just try to block out everything else except that."

JoJo nods, causing her curls to bounce.

We all close our eyes and concentrate. After a few minutes, I open my eyes.

"Not working for me," I say, feeling confident it's not my emotional baggage that is causing the problem this time.

Chandler and JoJo open their eyes. JoJo shakes her head, indicating she didn't see anything either.

"Nope," Chandler confirms. "Nada."

"Maybe you just need more time together," Isaiah suggests. "Jess, you and Chandler spent time alone together before it worked. Perhaps the two of you simply need to spend time with JoJo before you try again."

"Come back to my studio," JoJo urges us. "I will make you a dress for your date with your future lover."

"Do you think you could stop calling him my lover?" I ask as delicately as I can.

I don't want to offend JoJo's choice of words, maybe it's a language barrier problem, but I can't say she isn't making me feel extremely uncomfortable with that particular term.

"We haven't even kissed yet, much less become lovers."

"Désolé, I forget you Americans are so…umm, what's the word… provincial. But, you want to become lovers, *oui?"*

I bite my lower lip and glance from Chandler to Isaiah, not exactly comfortable having this conversation in front of them.

"Dire non plus," JoJo says, squeezing my hand. "I will make your dress, and we will see what happens. If he tears it off of your body, do not worry. I will make you another."

Chandler smirks, and Isaiah just looks extremely uncomfortable with the turn of the conversation. I'm pretty sure my face is so red I look like a tomato.

"Don't suppose you could make it so I can become invisible whenever I want?" I ask, wishing I had such a magical piece of clothing at that very moment.

JoJo just laughs. I almost tell her that I'm completely serious, but hate to drown her enthusiasm with my sarcasm.

When we make it back to JoJo's studio, she ends up asking me questions about Mason, like his favorite color, his hobbies, etc., etc. I suddenly realize I don't know most of the answers, and can only guess at them. It's strange that I know more about Chandler in that regard than the man I'm in love with. I make it a priority to learn everything I can about Mason as soon as he'll let me.

JoJo calls in a team of seamstresses to help her with my dress. She decides to make it out of lavender silk. The dress ends up being far classier than I thought she was planning to make at first. With all the talk of clothes being ripped off, I assumed it would be something rather skimpy. But the dress ends up being something you would wear to a fancy party, where long dresses with billowy material are expected.

The gown she creates is simple and classic. With its sleeveless bodice and ruched top, it shows off my shoulders, and certainly lifts my breasts to new heights. The waist is encircled with a sown-in belt made of dazzling crystals, and the skirt is long and free-flowing. When I walk around the room in it, I feel the extra material attached to the back float in the air, as though I have a permanent wind machine blowing on me.

JoJo calls in her personal stylist who applies my makeup and curls my hair, letting the strands cascade over my shoulders. It's similar to the style I wore to the masquerade ball. I begin to wonder if everyone in the world, except me, has a personal stylist.

Once I'm primped for my proposed ambush of Mason, I stand in front of JoJo's large, gold-framed mirror, which is almost as tall as the glass walls in the room, and stare at myself. I have to admit, I really do clean up pretty nicely when I have a team of stylists and designers to help out.

Chandler puts his hands on my bare shoulders and starts to massage them for me. It's only then I realize how tense I am.

"Don't look so worried," he tells me. "You know it doesn't matter what you wear, right? He loves you."

I look at him in the mirror.

"It only matters what you say," he reminds me.

"And that's supposed to make me feel less nervous?" I laugh.

"No, but don't get caught up with how you look. You're gorgeous even in your Watcher uniform. All Mason is going to care about is what you say to him. Don't leave anything unsaid, Jess. Lay all your cards on the table. If he doesn't pick them up, then at least you'll know you did everything you could to make him see reason. I just want to see you happy. I don't like seeing you so sad. You know I can feel it, right?"

I hadn't even thought about that.

"I forgot," I say. "Can you turn it off, or do you always know what other people are feeling when you touch them?"

Chandler smiles. "No, I can turn it off, but I like knowing how you feel. I like feeling the love you have for me. It makes me feel…loved," he says with a shrug, not having a better way to put it.

"*Vous êtes belle*," JoJo says, coming to stand beside me. A twinkle of pride lights her eyes as she looks at me in her dress.

I have a feeling she called me beautiful, so I don't ask for a translation.

"Well, if that doesn't grab his attention, I'm not sure what else will."

Directly behind me is Malcolm. I turn to face him.

"Are things ready?" I ask, raising a delicate eyebrow at him. "Whatever it is you have planned."

"Yes, the stage is set. Are you ready to go get your man?"

I nod. "Yes."

"Good luck," Chandler says, giving me an encouraging smile.

"*Bonne chance*," JoJo says, kissing me on both cheeks, and I know she's wishing me luck too.

Malcolm holds out his hand to me, and I accept it.

In an instant, we're standing in Mason's living room in his Colorado home. A multitude of white candles is lit around the room, creating a soft glow. Floral arrangements are practically on every surface, making the room look like a florist shop. A blazing fire is burning in the corner fireplace, and there is a scattering of red rose petals leading from where I stand, into the hallway, stretching as far as I can see from my position.

"It's a trail," Malcolm says, seeing my eyes follow the stream of petals out of the room. "It leads from the elevator to you. I wanted to make sure he couldn't miss you."

"Why are you doing this?" I ask Malcolm, turning to him. It seems like such an uncharacteristic thing for him to do for me.

"Consider it my apology for treating you so harshly in the beginning," he replies, looking a bit chagrined, "and Mason is a good friend. I don't like seeing him in so much pain."

"Do you have any idea what I can say to make him change his mind about leaving me?"

"The only good advice I can give you is to let him see how you feel about him. Don't hide anything. He's going to play the stubborn card, but don't let him get away with it."

I nod, having already decided on that. "I won't."

Malcolm looks me up and down in carnal appreciation. "And if he doesn't take advantage of what you're wearing, I'm always available."

I feel my mouth gape open at Malcolm's obvious insinuation.

He simply laughs before phasing away, leaving me alone to wait for Mason.

I look down at my dress to make sure everything is in its proper place. When I look back up, I see a man standing in front of me, surrounded by a black aura, who is definitely not Mason.

"Hello," Asmodeus says, before grabbing my arms and phasing me.

CHAPTER SIX

Asmodeus phases me so many times I begin to feel like my body is turning into jelly, much like the time Mason phased me over and over. But this feeling is a hundred times worse. Asmodeus doesn't seem to care he's hurting me and continues to phase us until he finally reaches his destination. Once there, he lets go of my now-bruised arms, and I fall to the grassy ground in a heap of silk.

When I finally regain a little bit of my strength, I force myself to look at my surroundings. We're in a field I recognize. It's the same non-descript field Mason and I went to when we tried to follow Lucifer and Asmodeus from the Watcher apartment complex. I'm filled with a small ray of hope that Mason might actually find me here, but realize that the chances of that happening are slim to none.

"Did you have some of the rebellion angels help you cover your trail from Mason's house?" I ask.

Asmodeus smiles. "Pretty smart for a monkey. Yes, so don't expect to be rescued. Not even Lucifer knows where we are."

"What do you want with me?"

"I want to kill you."

I close my eyes, wishing I had the strength to call on my sword, but knowing I would lose it to Asmodeus even if I did have it. I simply wasn't physically strong enough in my current condition to wield its power anyway.

"Why?"

"Because you're making Lucifer weak," Asmodeus says scathingly. "I've never seen him care one whit about a human's well-being before you."

"Why is that so bad?"

"Because it's causing him to lose focus as to what we need to do."

"Which is?" I ask, hoping Asmodeus' hatred of me and over-confidence will make him say things he shouldn't.

Asmodeus kneels in front of me on one knee and practically spits in my face. "You won't live long enough to find out."

"What are you waiting for?" I ask. "Kill me."

"I can't kill you directly because I was ordered not to harm you," Asmodeus replies, filled with regret. "But Lucifer didn't give that order to another one of my brothers."

"So we're waiting on him?"

"Yes. He will be here soon."

"Is he another prince of Hell?"

Asmodeus grins. "We thought you might have figured it out by now; but, I take it from your earlier question, you still don't know what we're up to."

"We'll figure it out and stop you."

Asmodeus laughs harshly. "Good luck with that after you're dead."

Another man phases in, and I have to assume he's my executioner. He's taller than Asmodeus by a few inches, with short red hair and a craggy face, wearing a grey flight jacket and black jeans. Just like Asmodeus and Lucifer, he has a black aura surrounding him.

He looks down at me in complete disgust.

"Mammon," Asmodeus greets the new arrival, "please dispose of this puny human for me."

"You're sure Lucifer doesn't know of this plan?" Mammon asks, eyeing me like a roach he's about to step on.

"Do you think I would be so stupid? Of course he doesn't know. Now, kill her so we can be done with it and force him back to the way he should be."

Without even giving it a second thought, Mammon strides up to me and grabs me by the throat, easily lifting me up in the air. I feel his fingers close on my windpipe, making it impossible for me to breathe. I try to pull his hand away from my neck, but can't find the strength to even grasp his arm. I suddenly wish I were invisible.

I feel myself fall to the ground.

"Where the hell did she go?" I hear Mammon scream. "I just had her!"

I place a shaky hand on my throat, trying to draw in a breath, but find it impossible. My throat feels completely closed.

"I don't know," Asmodeus says, coming to stand by Mammon. "There isn't a phase trail, so she doesn't have the power to phase."

"She couldn't have just vanished into thin air," Mammon argues.

"And, yet, she did," Asmodeus says, not mad, just intrigued by my disappearance. "Let's go. Lucifer's probably already wondering where we are, and I don't want to raise his suspicions."

Mammon and Asmodeus phase away while I still attempt to take a breath. Just before I feel like I'm about to pass out, I'm able to draw a small amount of air into my lungs. I close my eyes and use my last breath to call the one person I hope can hear me.

"Zeruel."

I fall back onto the ground.

Just before I completely lose consciousness, I hear, "I've got you, Jessi."

I hear agitated voices. Two men are having an intense argument, but my mind is far too muddled and my body too tired to make an effort to understand what they're saying. I desperately try to claw my way out of the black abyss I'm in, but I don't even seem to have enough strength to open my eyes. Giving up, I let sleep overtake me, drowning me in its wake.

I feel a pair of strong arms enfold me. I don't know if it's a dream or reality, but I smell Mason's particular woody scent, mixed with a touch of cinnamon.

"Don't leave me," I beg.

"I'll never leave you," I hear Mason say, and hope I'm not dreaming.

"Jessi."

I hear my father's voice and open my eyes.

I'm in my bedroom, covered up to the neck by my comforter.

"You came," I say, feeling tears of happiness that my dad heard me call to him.

He smiles down at me. "Of course I came. I told you I would if you asked me to."

I struggle to sit up but still feel weak. My dad puts his hands under my arms and lifts me, as if I don't weigh anything at all. He props me against the pillows at my back. I look around the room and feel my heart sink with bitter disappointment.

Mason is nowhere to be seen. I must have just been dreaming that he was holding me and promising he would never leave me.

"What's wrong?" my dad asks.

I shake my head, not having the strength to tell him why I'm crying.

"Are you looking for Mason?"

I gasp, wondering how he knows.

"I just thought…" I close my eyes, allowing myself to relive that small moment of joy I felt in the dream when I thought he was with me, holding me in his arms, promising never to leave me again.

"Jessi, look at me."

I open my eyes and look at my father through the veil of my tears.

"Mason was here. He just left to go get some of his things because we weren't sure how much longer you would be asleep."

"He was here?" I ask, needing to know it wasn't just a dream or a hallucination.

My dad smiles at me. "Yes, he was here. You didn't dream it. That's what you're thinking, right? That it was a dream?"

I nod. "But why; what made him come?"

"When he saw the phase trail in his living room, he knew you had been taken. From what I heard, he had every Watcher in the world helping him try to track you down. When you called for me, I found you and brought you here. He almost attacked me when he saw me in your house," my dad chuckles. "I had to explain to him who I was, and, thankfully, he believed me. After I healed you, he refused to leave your side. I finally told him to crawl into bed with you to hold you, hoping that would heal the shock your mind was in. That, more than anything, I think, helped you the most."

Directly behind my father, I see Mason phase into my bedroom. He's wearing a grey sweater, much like the black one he wore the first night I met him. His eyes find mine, and I see the relief he feels from seeing me fully awake.

"Hey," I say, feeling shy all of a sudden.

He smiles, and my heart lights up like a firecracker on the Fourth of July.

"Hey," he says back.

My dad stands up. "I think you two have a lot to talk about. I'll be in the living room if you need me."

When my father walks out of the room, Mason sets his black leather overnight bag on the floor.

He looks back at me, unsure what to do next. I extend my arm towards him, beckoning him closer. He quickly closes the distance between us, grabbing my hand and bringing it to his lips to place a gentle kiss on top of it. Sitting down beside me on the bed, he holds my hand, like it's the most precious thing in the world to him at that moment.

"Did you mean it?" I ask him.

"Mean what?" he asks, looking confused.

"You said you would never leave me," I remind him, as even in my delirium I can remember his words clearly. "Did you mean it?"

"Yes," he says. "I'll never leave you again." He looks down at our joined hands. "I never should have left you the first time. Maybe if I hadn't…"

"Don't drive yourself crazy with maybes," I tell him, placing my free hand under his stubble-covered chin to force him to meet my eyes. "The important thing is that you're here now. And, I hate to be the one to inform you, but I never intend to let you leave me again. Is that understood?"

A lopsided grin graces his face. "Yes, that's understood. It's not something you ever have to worry about anyway; you're pretty much stuck with me now."

I smile, realizing it's the first true, happy smile I've had since before the night Mason left me.

"Good. Now that we have that settled, tell me how long I've been asleep."

"A week."

I sigh. "Why do I keep losing so much time sleeping?"

"Jess, what happened? Who took you?"

"Asmodeus. And someone named Mammon showed up to actually kill me. He's another prince of Hell, right?"

Mason nods. "Yes. They were gone by the time your father reached you. How did you escape? Your father said you were almost dead by the time he got there."

I shake my head. "I don't know. One minute Mammon was squeezing my windpipe, and then it was like I became invisible to him and fell through his fingers. They couldn't see me, so they phased. I used what little air I had left to call for my dad, because I knew he could heal me."

"JoJo Armand made the dress you were wearing, right?"

I nod.

"Maybe that's why her crown began to send out the homing signal that night. We weren't sure what triggered it to activate."

"Has she got it?"

"Yes, Chandler went with her to get it. It wasn't far. It was hidden inside an old chest of clothes that belonged to her grandmother, at her parents' house."

"Have they found their talismans yet?"

"No, but I'm pretty sure I know where Chandler's is and, now, with this new information about JoJo, I have an idea which one might be hers. I assume you'll want to be with them when they get their talismans."

I nod. "Yes, I would like to be with them. When can we go?"

"You need to rest a little more," Mason tells me, and I can see from the expression on his face that I won't be able to convince him otherwise. "They almost killed you, Jess. Not just the choking, but the phasing. Your dad was able to heal most of the physical damage, but the trauma to your brain almost put you into a coma. So, rest is the first thing you need to focus on, and I plan to make sure you get it."

"You've gotten awfully bossy," I tease, liking the bossiness very much, but not daring to admit it. You only boss when you care. I should know. I've done it enough.

"Where you're concerned? Yes, I will be very bossy. I can't lose you," he says, a catch in his voice, letting me know how much almost losing me affected him.

I pull him towards me, trying to use my physical presence as a reminder that I'm all right. "You're not losing me. I'm like bad luggage. You'll never be able to get rid of me."

I hear Mason chuckle, and it's the sweetest sound on Earth.

Mason decides my first visitors should be Mama Lynn and Faison.

"You should know I told them everything," Mason tells me.

Shocked is too mild a word to describe how I react to this statement.

"Everything? Why?" I ask.

"Because they needed to know what was going on. They love you. They deserved the truth, especially when we weren't sure you would live."

I see the pain in Mason's eyes, because he truly did believe I might have died from my injuries.

"Thank you," I tell him, feeling a great weight lift from my shoulders that I didn't even know was there. Keeping so many secrets from my family had been a burden on my heart. Now that they knew the truth, I had to wonder how they would react to me.

When Mama Lynn and Faison walk into my bedroom, they immediately envelop me in a group hug. It's then I know nothing has changed. They still love me.

"You had us so worried, Jess," Mama Lynn says, her hands cupping my face. She shakes her head at me. "Don't do that again. I don't think my old heart can take it."

"It wasn't on purpose," I assure her. I look at both of them. "So, Mason said he told you everything. How are you dealing with knowing what's really going on?"

"Well, I wish you had told me Lucian was the devil," Faison huffs as she sits cross-legged on my bed beside me. "Good grief; it's no wonder you didn't want me talking to him."

"You're still our Jess," Mama Lynn says to me, knowing what I'm really asking. "Maybe now you know why I made you go to church so much when you were younger. I told you there was a God."

"Are you seriously going to use the 'I told you so' line on me?"

"Well, it fits, I think," she says rather smugly. "You didn't believe me, but now you know I was right."

"Yes, He exists but that doesn't mean I have to instantly like Him," I say, not wanting to discuss my rather turbulent feelings about God with a devout Southern Baptist. "Anyway, I'm just glad you guys know the truth. I hated keeping everything hidden from you two."

"So," Faison says in a low voice, "how are things going with your own personal angel since you woke up?"

"You know he wouldn't let us come in here, but for just a little while each day," Mama Lynn tells me, an obvious sore point with her.

"And Chandler and JoJo were only allowed to come in here for a few minutes. He was very protective of you."

I smile, liking the idea of an overprotective Mason.

"Things have been great so far," I tell them, "but he still wants me to rest before I get back to work."

"I think that's a good idea," Mama Lynn agrees. "You've been through a lot, and Lord knows you have a lot on your plate at the moment. Don't rush yourself."

"Let Mason pamper you," Faison advises me. "Enjoy it while it lasts."

"But I have a lot to do," I tell them. "We still have four more vessels to locate."

"Just trust in the Lord," Mama Lynn says, patting one of my hands. "He won't let Lucifer win."

"Why do you have so much faith in Him?" I ask.

"Because He's always led me down the right path. I found you and Faison didn't I? Who do you think let that happen?"

"Did Mason tell you about my biological mother?" I ask her.

"Yes. I don't remember meeting her, but I'm sure glad she picked me. I couldn't imagine my life without you in it. I don't even want to think about the possibility."

"Have you met my father?" I ask Mama Lynn.

"Oh, yes, he's so nice. We were told everything about that, too. Odd that the father you grew up with isn't your biological father," she shrugs, "but you don't have to be related by blood to be a parent."

A fact she knows all too well.

"So, back to Mason," Faison says, not wanting to let her original subject go so easily. "What do you think about a double wedding? I'm sure John Austin won't mind."

I stare at Faison, considering the real possibility that she has completely lost her mind.

"What?" Faison asks innocently. "I think it's a good idea; plus, I already talked to JoJo about designing our dresses."

"You did what?" I practically scream.

Mason instantly appears in the doorway.

"It might be time to let Jess rest some before she sees her next set of visitors," Mason says, coming up with a good excuse to get my family out of the room before I have a coronary.

"Think about it," Faison says, raising up on her knees and giving me a peck on the cheek, before getting off my bed and following Mama Lynn out of the room.

I stare after them, wondering how exactly Faison's mind comes up with some of her outrageous ideas.

"What happened?" Mason asks me, coming to stand beside my bed. "I heard you yell."

"I don't want to tell you, so please don't ask," I say, knowing if I relate Faison's idea to Mason it would simply be too embarrassing, for both of us.

"Ok," Mason says, drawing the word out, like he's not quite sure why I won't tell him what happened. "Maybe you should get some rest before Chandler and JoJo come over later."

"Is my dad still here?" I ask.

"Yes; do you want to see him?"

I nod. Mason leaves the room, and my dad comes in with a smile on his face. I can tell he's pleased I asked for him.

"What's up, Buttercup?"

I giggle. "I haven't heard that in fifty forevers," I tell him.

"What? No one else calls you 'Buttercup'? Color me shocked."

"What's put you in such a good mood?" I ask.

"Well, I get to spend time with my daughter. Why wouldn't I be in a good mood?"

"I'm sorry if I made you feel like I didn't think of you as my real father the other night. You're my dad. You will always be my dad."

He leans in and gives me a chaste kiss on the lips. "I know, Jessi."

He's silent for a moment, and I see a contemplative look on his face.

"What are you thinking about?" I ask.

"Mason."

"What about him?"

"I like him. I think he'll treat you right. You know, he asked me for permission to court you."

"Court me?"

"It's a bit old-fashioned to ask a father's permission to date his daughter, but I kind of liked it. Shows me he really cares about treating you right. And I know he's not just interested in funny business," my dad says, wiggling his eyebrows up and down. "You only court someone you intend to marry one day."

I involuntarily swallow hard at this news, suddenly feeling overwhelmed.

My dad's eyebrows lower as he sees my reaction. "Does that scare you? Because, if it does, I can tell him to back off, you know."

"No," I'm quick to say, "please don't do that. I just never saw myself ever getting married before now."

"Why not?"

"I've just never thought too far ahead into my future."

"Well, you love him, right?"

I nod. "He's the only man I will ever love."

My dad smiles. "Then what's there to think about, Buttercup? Grab onto happiness while you can. And you have my blessing if you want to marry him."

"Between you and Faison, I feel like marriage to Mason is a done deal."

One side of my father's mouth quirks up into a half smile. "Yeah, that Faison is a piece of work, isn't she? You know, she and JoJo have already designed your wedding dress."

I bury my face in my hands. "Please tell me Mason didn't hear them talking about it."

"Well, I could tell you that, but it wouldn't be the truth," my dad chuckles.

I just shake my head in dismay. I feel my dad pull my hands down from my face.

"Hey," he says, "he didn't seem to mind it. He actually looked amused by the whole thing."

Reluctantly, I smile.

"He loves you," my dad tells me. "Just enjoy the courtship phase of the relationship. I have a feeling he'll make it special for you."

"Thanks, Daddy."

My dad smiles. "You're welcome, Buttercup."

"How long can you stay with me?" I ask.

My dad sighs. "Yeah, about that; I need to be heading back. Souls to make and all," he tries to joke. I can tell he doesn't really want to go, and that's all I need to know.

"It's ok," I tell him. "I know you'll come when I need you."

"Anytime, anywhere," he confirms.

I give him a hug, fully knowing my dad is truly back in my life.

CHAPTER SEVEN

I take a long nap after my dad leaves. When I wake up late in the afternoon, I find Mason lying in bed with me, reading a book. When he sees me stir, he snaps the book shut and lays it on the nightstand on his side of the bed. Turning on his side to face me, he smiles, causing my heart to ache just at the mere sight of how handsome a small stretching of the lips makes him.

"Hey," he says. "Did you have a good nap?"

I nod.

"Are you hungry?"

I nod again.

"Can you speak?" he teases good-naturedly.

I nod but don't say anything, causing him to laugh; a sound I love.

"And what would you like to eat for lunch?" he asks, knowing I can't nod my way out of his question.

"Honestly?" I say, raising up on an elbow and resting my head against my hand. "I could go for a grilled cheese sandwich, tomato soup, and a cold glass of milk."

"Then that's what you'll have," he says, leaning in and kissing the tip of my nose before standing up. He pulls his cell phone out of his pants pocket and quickly finds the number he's looking for.

"Isaiah, come to Jess' house." And he ends the call.

"Does everyone do what you tell them?" I ask, wondering why he's always so brusque with others sometimes.

"Everyone but you," Mason says with a smile, "but I think we established that fact the first night we met."

I smile at the reminder. "Yes, I guess we did."

There's a knock on the door, and Mason phases to answer it. I hear him and Isaiah speak before he phases back into my room.

"Isaiah will stay with you until I return with your food."

"Ok," I say reluctantly, wishing I had just told him to make whatever might be in my kitchen. I really don't want him to leave. I feel so much better when he's close.

"I won't be gone long," he promises, obviously seeing my reluctance about him leaving. "And after you eat, I'll get Isaiah to bring Chandler and JoJo over to see you. They've been hounding me all day to let them come over."

"I want to see them too," I say, letting him know the feeling isn't one-sided.

"After you eat," Mason promises as Isaiah walks into my room. Mason winks at me. "Be right back."

After he phases, I look over at Isaiah.

"Glad to see you're feeling better," my one-time mentor tells me, coming to stand by my bedside. "You gave us all quite a scare. I don't think I've ever seen Mason so frantic before."

"Really?" I ask. I know this statement coming from Isaiah is saying a lot, considering how long he's known Mason.

"He called in every Watcher in the world when you disappeared. It didn't matter what we were doing. He ordered us to his house immediately to search all the branching phase trails for you. I'm just glad your father got to you in time."

"Me too," I admit. "I didn't think I would make it."

"You almost didn't, from what your father told us. If he had been a minute later, you would be dead. Mason thought he had lost you."

"Well, I'm fine now, but Mason seems bound and determined to keep me in this bed until he thinks I'm completely well."

"Give him some time, Jess. You gave him a good scare. He needs time to recover, just as much as you do."

I hadn't thought about it like that.

"Ok, Isaiah. I won't push him to let me go back to work."

"Thank you."

Fifteen minutes later, I hear the rattling of dishes in my kitchen and know Mason is back. He walks into my bedroom with one of my folding trays in his hands, laden with the requested bowl of tomato soup, grilled cheese sandwich, and glass of milk.

"That was quick," I comment as I sit up straighter while Mason sets the tray across my lap.

"Knew of a good bistro that would have what you wanted," he tells me. Once I'm settled, he turns to Isaiah. "Why don't you bring Chandler and JoJo over in about thirty minutes?"

"Thank God," Isaiah says, lifting his eyes to the heavens. "They've been driving me insane about coming here to see Jess."

"Yes, they've been rather insistent," Mason admits with a wry grin. "Thirty minutes."

Isaiah phases, and I begin to eat.

"Can I ask you something?" I say between spoonsful of soup.

"You can ask me anything," Mason replies.

"You and Isaiah are the most punctual people I know. Like, I know when you told him thirty minutes, he'll be back here in exactly thirty minutes, to the second. How do you guys do that?"

"All Watchers have an internal clock of sorts. That's why we're never late or early. It's almost a compulsory need to always be on time."

"I wish Faison had something like that inside her," I say. "She's almost always late for things. It drives me nuts."

Mason smiles. "Our need to be exactly on time can be a little annoying, to tell you the truth. I wish I could force myself to be late or even early to something, but I can't seem to."

"Hmm, a challenge," I say, considering the various delightfully inappropriate ways I can make Mason late to something. I smile.

"Maybe I can find a way to make you late the next time you have to be somewhere."

Mason looks intrigued. "And how would you accomplish such a feat?"

I shake my head. "Can't tell you that; then you would be expecting it. You'll just have to wait and see."

Mason smiles. "I look forward to your attempts. I'll make sure to let you know the next time I have to be somewhere."

"Please do," I say. "Can I ask you something else?"

"Yes?"

"Are you going to let me out of this bed anytime soon? I'm already getting bored just laying here and sleeping."

"Hmm, let me think about it. I would rather you rested, but I can see how you would get bored. I'll see what I can do."

Mason is cleaning up my dirty dishes when Isaiah appears in my bedroom, with Chandler and JoJo on either side of him. They immediately envelop me in a group hug, much like Mama Lynn and Faison did.

JoJo begins to spout so much French at me I can't decipher a word of it. I look to Chandler for help.

"She's just glad to see you," Chandler says, finding our bouncy little French counterpart amusing.

JoJo huffs and says, "I was so worried about you, *mon amie*. You had us sick to death with worry. We thought we had lost you."

"I'm fine now," I tell them. "Please, don't worry anymore."

"Your guard dogs have been a bit irritating," Chandler grumbles. "They wouldn't let us come when you first woke up. I want you to know we tried."

"I know," I tell him, cupping the left side of Chandler's face with my hand, immediately soothing his ire. "Mason is just overprotective at the moment. I don't think he's going to let me go back to work for a couple more days either."

"That's fine," Chandler says. "You do need your rest, but he seems to forget you need us too."

"And how are things between the two of you?" JoJo asks. "You and Mason."

"He promised he wouldn't leave me again," I tell them, "and I believe him."

"At least he figured out how stupid it was to leave you the first time," Chandler says. "Too bad it took you almost dying to show him what an idiot he was being."

"Don't be mad at him," I say to Chandler, knowing he only has my best interests at heart. "He's been through a lot in his life. He just thought he was doing the right thing to keep me safe. Now he knows I have enemies of my own, and that I'm safer with him than without him."

"And I intend to keep you safe."

I look up and see Mason leaning against the doorframe to my room, his gaze steady on me. "They'll have to kill me to get to you."

"I think I have a way to stop them from trying to kill me," I say.

"And how do you plan to work that small miracle?" Chandler asks.

"Tell Lucifer what they did. If anyone can stop the other princes, or anyone else under his command, from trying to kill me, it's him. Even Asmodeus didn't try directly, because Lucifer ordered him not to harm me when we were in Antarctica. He had to call in Mammon to do the dirty work for him."

"It should work," Mason agrees. "None of them will go against a direct order from Lucifer. They know the consequences of disobedience."

"I'll just have to wait until Lucifer comes to have one of his little chats with me," I say. "Until then, we'll just have to keep an eye out."

I look at JoJo. "So, I heard you found your crown."

"*Oui, oui!*" she says excitedly. "Lilly says it belonged to her father, Michael."

"You have Michael's crown?"

"*Oui,*" JoJo says, her eyes downcast. "Poor, sweet Lilly seemed a bit upset when she found out. It was only afterwards that I learned Michael is her father. If I had known, I would have better understood her reaction."

"She's been through a lot," I explain. "I'm still waiting for her to come see me to speak with Michael directly."

"What do you mean by directly?" Mason asks.

"I can call on Michael when I'm awake now," I tell him. "Didn't I tell you that?"

"No," Mason says, his eyebrows drawn together, "you didn't. Have you tried to contact him since you woke up?"

"No."

"You might want to try," Mason suggests, "just to make sure you can still call him when you need to. I'm not sure what damage might have been done to your brain after Asmodeus phased you all those times."

I nod, suddenly becoming frightened I won't be able to connect with Michael anymore.

As soon as I call to him, he appears in my room, still wearing the faded blue jeans and white t-shirt with black angel wings I dressed him up in the first time we met.

"Glad to see you're better," he tells me.

I smile. "Glad to see you didn't disappear on me."

"I assume you see him," Mason says, his eyes wandering to the empty spot where only I can see Michael standing.

"Yes, he's here," I tell Mason. I look back at Michael. "I just wanted to make sure I could still contact you."

"Our connection can't be broken," Michael assures me. "I'm a part of you until we defeat Lucifer."

"Will I lose you after that?"

"If that's what you want to happen. I will always be a part of you, Jessica. Once we've accomplished our mission, I can stay hidden within you, like I have for most of your life. I don't want to burden you with my presence."

I shrug. "I'm kinda used to you now. I don't think I'll want you to stay in the background anymore."

Michael smiles, pleased. "I'll let you get back to your friends. They're probably a little jealous they can't talk to their archangels like you can."

"Ok."

Michael smiles at me and fades away.

"*Bonté divine*," JoJo says. "I wish I could speak to my angel too."

"You will," I reassure her. "It won't be long now. We'll start looking for your talismans soon." I look over at Mason. "At least, as soon as Mason thinks I'm well enough to go with you."

"Two days," Mason promises. "I would just feel better knowing you're fully recovered first." Mason's eyes travel to Chandler. "Chandler's talisman may be tricky to get, if my guess is right about where it is. I want you fully well before we try."

"You know where it is?" Chandler says, turning to face Mason, obviously hearing this news for the first time.

"I have a theory," Mason hedges, not committing completely.

Chandler turns back to me. "Ok, two days; then we go get my toy." He smiles like a kid at Christmas.

"And mine?" JoJo asks Mason. "Do you know where it is?"

"I'm pretty sure I do," Mason says, seeming more confident about the whereabouts of JoJo's talisman. "But Joshua is still doing some research on the people who should have it. He feels confident he can find them soon."

"So, we sit and wait," JoJo says, completely despondent.

Chandler looks at Mason. "Could you give us a moment alone with Jess?"

Mason looks uncomfortable with the requests. "I don't like leaving her unprotected."

"Just a couple of minutes," Chandler promises.

Mason hesitates but finally nods and leaves the room.

Chandler turns back to me. "Take this."

He hands me a bracelet made of a strand of red silk, a rolled piece of black leather, and a thick silver chain with a silver angel charm dangling from the middle.

"We made it for you while we were waiting around this afternoon," Chandler tells me, placing it around my right wrist and fastening it.

"Thank you," I say, "it's beautiful."

JoJo leans into me and whispers, "It will tell you things."

I feel my face scrunch up in confusion.

"It's a talking bracelet?" I ask, feeling stupid for asking such a question.

Chandler smiles indulgently. "No, but it will tell you what people are feeling, and if you are in any danger. Once we learned what JoJo's power was this morning, we figured out how to transfer some of our powers to something you can wear. She made the bracelet to warn you of danger, and I placed my own special whammy on it so you can know how whoever you're touching feels about you. I thought it might come in handy, in case Mr. Moody tries to hide his feelings from you again."

Now I understand why they asked Mason to leave.

"It doesn't feel right to use that type of power on Mason," I say. "It would be like invading his private thoughts."

"It'll only work if you make it work," Chandler says. "The warning of danger part is passive; it's always on. If you want to know how people feel about you, you have to ask it to tell you."

"Like, say it out loud?"

"No, just think it."

I remembered back to the night Asmodeus attacked me. I could remember thinking I wanted to be invisible, and suddenly I was. The bracelet must work on the same principal.

"I still don't understand how you made the dress so I could disappear when I needed to," I say to JoJo.

"I have thought about that," she says. "Do you remember asking me that day if I could make you something that would make you invisible?"

I nod, because I do remember that small wish.

"When I was draping the dress, I remember thinking about your odd request, and how funny it would be to create such an outfit. I believe that is when my gift ...umm...came on?"

"It makes sense," I say. I look down at the bracelet they gave me. "Thank you for the gift. I won't abuse its power."

Mason walks back into the room with Isaiah by his side, and I know exactly two minutes have already gone by.

"I think Jess should get some rest," he says to my friends, gently telling them that it's time for them to leave.

Chandler leans in and kisses me on the forehead, while JoJo kisses me on the cheek.

"See you later, when we're allowed," Chandler grumbles, not even trying to hide his irritation from being kept from me.

"*Au revoir, ma cherie.*"

My friends go to stand with Isaiah, and he phases them back to wherever it is they're staying.

Mason comes to stand by my bedside as I sink back down underneath my comforter.

"Why don't you take a nap?" he suggests.

"All right," I say, not having the strength to argue, just falling into a dreamless sleep.

CHAPTER EIGHT

When I wake up from my nap, I notice that it's mostly dark in the room, with only my nightstand lamp providing light. I flop over onto my back and look beside me, hoping to see Mason on the other side of the bed reading his book. Mason is nowhere to be seen, but his pillow is facing me lengthwise, with a white note card perched on top of it. It's the same exact card stock as the one he left me Christmas morning. My name is written on the front in a curly calligraphy font with red ink. A single red rose lies beside the note.

I pick up the card and the rose. The note on the inside reads:

You are cordially invited to have dinner with Mr. Mason Collier at his villa. If you accept the invitation, please ring the bell on your nightstand.

I look over at my nightstand and, sure enough, there is a bell made of cut crystal sitting there.

I lift the bell and ring it twice, not quite sure what the action is supposed to set into motion.

Almost instantly, Faison, Mama Lynn, and JoJo walk into the room.

"I thought you would never wake up!" Faison says in exasperation. "It's almost seven o'clock. We've gotta work fast."

"Work fast?" I ask.

Faison, never one to be shy about things, throws my comforter off my body and practically drags me out of bed. I falter somewhat and almost fall, but JoJo catches me.

"*Oh zut!*" JoJo exclaims, bearing most of my weight with her tiny frame.

Before my petite French friend topples over, I'm able to make my legs wake up enough to stand on my own two feet.

JoJo turns on Faison hotly, showing her fiery Parisian temper. "*Pas plus*! She is in a fragile condition. Be more careful!"

Faison face blanches, looking as white as a ghost. "I'm so sorry, Jess. I wasn't thinking."

I put an arm around Faison's shoulders. "It's ok. You didn't mean it. Just help me out a little, ok?"

I am gently whisked into my bathroom, where Mama Lynn prepares a bubble bath in my marble tub for me. I'm allowed to soak in it for a little while, just to bring feeling back into my legs, before I'm advised it's time to get out and get ready.

As JoJo styles my hair into a neat, plaited bun at the back of my head, Faison dabs on a little makeup to give my pale face a bit more color. Mama Lynn goes into my closet and pulls out a dress I've never seen before. She walks over to JoJo and hands it to her.

"Ah," JoJo says, taking the dress, "*merci beaucoup*."

JoJo looks at it with a critical eye while I feel myself gaping at how short the dress's skirt is.

"Am I supposed to wear that?" I ask, completely sure there must be more to it than what I'm seeing. Leggings, perhaps? Or a trench coat?

"*Oui*," JoJo confirms, holding the dress up to her body so I can see it completely.

"Do I get to wear something over it? Or under it?"

JoJo looks confused, and then laughs like she thinks I'm joking with her. "*Non*, this is it, *cherie*. There is no more."

"We figured if that doesn't get you kissed, or who knows what else tonight, nothing will," Faison says.

I feel like burying my face in my hands, but know Faison will kill me if I smudge my makeup.

I look at the dress and know I can't possibly make it look as alluring as it does on the hanger. It looks like something Number Six on the old *Battlestar Galactica* show would wear, and I know I don't have a voluptuous figure like that.

The dress is made out of a black material that looks like a mixture of rayon and spandex. The top has a strappy front and back with a very deep neckline dropping low into the area between the breasts. The material at the top of the dress is ribbed with solid seams, and an hourglass shape is constructed down to the fluted skirt, which seems to fall on JoJo just above her knees. Since I'm a couple of inches taller than her, I can only imagine it will fall to mid-thigh on me.

"I don't think I have the legs to carry off something like that," I confess, eyeing the dress warily.

"Sure you do," Faison says, full of confidence. "You've just never shown them off before, is all. Trust me, Mason will love it. What man wouldn't?"

"So, your plan is to throw me half-naked at him, and see what happens?" I ask, completely flabbergasted.

"You are too old to have never kissed a man, *cherie*. This dress," JoJo says shaking the dress on its hanger, "will insure that happens tonight."

I see Mama Lynn nodding her head in full agreement.

I resign myself to the fact they won't let me wear something else, and slip the dress on. When I look at my reflection in the full-length mirror, I have to agree with them. If this dress doesn't get me kissed, nothing short of the hand of God pushing Mason into me will.

JoJo opens her purse and pulls out her cell phone to call someone.

"She is ready," I hear her say.

Isaiah instantly appears in my room.

I watch as his eyes take in my new attire.

"Wow, that's some dress, Jess."

Isaiah's comment propels me into action. I walk into my closet and pull out a black wool coat that goes past my knees. I almost never wear the coat, because it's too heavy. After buttoning it up to my neck, feeling safely cocooned inside its warmth, I walk back into my bedroom and hold my hand out to Isaiah.

"Good luck!" Faison says.

Thankfully, Isaiah phases me quickly before anyone decides to give me a pep talk, and I find myself standing inside the dining room in Mason's villa.

Mason stands across from me on the other side of the dining table, dressed in a finely-tailored black suit, white shirt and black tie, looking classically handsome.

"Enjoy your meal," Isaiah says, before quickly phasing away to give us privacy.

I have a hard time taking my eyes off Mason. I don't really have to look at the dining room, because I remember what it looks like from self-guided tour Chandler and I took of Mason's home.

It's a medium-sized room, with a circular table in the middle meant to seat eight people in taupe-colored-fabric-covered chairs. The table itself is draped with a low-hanging lacey white cloth. On the ceiling are exposed dark oak beams, and I know three tall arched windows, which look out onto the formal Italian garden, are directly behind me.

Now sitting in the middle of the table is an arrangement of pale peach and white roses. Two candle globes sit on either side of the flowers, and provide the only illumination in the room.

Mason walks over to me. "Here, let me take your coat."

I wrap the fingers of one of my hands around the lapels of the coat at the neck.

"I'd rather keep it on for now, if you don't mind."

"Are you cold?" Mason asks, full of concern. "I can turn the heat up to make it warmer in here."

"I would rather just keep the coat on," I say, hoping he doesn't ask for a more detailed explanation of why I'm being so insistent.

"Ok," he says uncertainly. "Well, are you hungry?"

"Yes," I say, "very."

Mason walks over to one of the two places set with silverware and crystal water goblets. He pulls out one of the chairs for me, and I sit down, finding myself smiling at his show of respect.

"I'll be right back," he says before phasing.

Mason reappears almost instantly with two small plates in his hands. On each plate are two small silver skewers with slices of melon, ham, and mozzarella cheese.

"I thought since you're in Italy," Mason says, setting one of the plates down in front of me, "you might like an Italian-style dinner."

"Thank you," I tell him, not wasting any time, and digging into the appetizer with gusto.

I feel, more than see, Mason staring at me while I eat, and end up looking over at him. He looks amused.

"What?" I ask, wondering if I have something on my face. I pick up the linen napkin from the table to dab my lips just in case.

"Nothing," he says with a shake of his head. "I just remember a time when you didn't want me to look at you while you ate. You don't seem to mind it now."

"You've pretty much seen me at my worst," I say with a slight shrug. "If seeing me sick or crying my eyes out hasn't scared you away by now, nothing will."

Mason smiles, cocking his head to the side. "Why would you think watching you eat would scare me away in the first place? I think it's cute the way you completely devour your food."

I almost choke on the piece of ham in my mouth.

"Well, if you didn't cook such delicious food, I wouldn't eat it so quickly," I say, thinking this is a completely logical defense.

"Oh, I'm not complaining. If a girl has a healthy appetite for food, it usually means she has a healthy appetite for other things too."

The light of amusement and secret promises in Mason's eyes makes me look away. I may not be very experienced in dealing with men, but I know a come-on line when I hear one.

"So what's the main course?" I ask, deciding to completely ignore Mason's double entendre.

Mason stands. "Be right back."

I take a deep breath, waiting for his return. When he reappears, he's holding two plates. Each plate holds two slices of rack of lamb over various herbs, roasted tomatoes, and risotto.

Since Mason didn't have time to eat his appetizer while he was making his gentle insinuations about my appetite, he ends up not having much time to talk during the main course, which gives me ample opportunity to enjoy the tender lamb he cooked to perfection.

"Is there dessert?" I ask after finishing my entrée.

Mason smiles, phases, and returns immediately with a white bowl filled with two scoops of what looks to me like sherbet.

"Mango gelato," he informs me.

The bowl only has one spoon.

He picks up the spoon and scoops up some of the gelato.

"Here, try some," he says, positioning the spoon in front of my face.

I part my lips and let him slide the spoon in and out of my mouth.

I nod. "It's good," I say, wondering if he just wanted me to taste it before he brought me a bowl of my own to eat from.

I watch as he scoops some more out of the bowl and eats some himself. It's only then I realize he intends for us to share the dessert with the same spoon. The act seems rather intimate, and I find myself feeling slightly flustered. My body feels like it's on fire, and I desperately want to get out of my coat to cool off.

"Are you all right?" Mason asks, setting the bowl on the table. "You look hot. Why don't you take the coat off?"

"I can't," I say, shaking my head determinedly.

"Why not?" he asks, confused by my refusal.

"Because I'm completely mortified by what I let them dress me in," I admit.

A slow smile spreads Mason's lips.

"It can't be that bad," he says, obviously thinking I'm over-exaggerating.

"Yes, it can."

"JoJo wouldn't dress you in something she didn't think looked good on you."

"Yes, she did."

Mason stands and holds his hand out to me. "Do you trust my judgment?"

I nod.

"Then let me see the dress, Jess. I won't lie to you. If I think it's hideous, you can put your coat back on."

I place my hand into his outstretched one, and let him pull me up out of my chair. He begins to undo the buttons of my coat for me, and slowly turns me around to pull it off my shoulders. When I turn back around to look at him, he's staring at me, eyes filled with a burning need. I instantly snatch my coat out of his hands and slip it back on.

"Jess," he says, his voice hoarse, "why are you hiding yourself from me?"

"Because I know what she did," I say, feeling my temper flare. "JoJo made this dress to make sure you would feel the way you do now."

How could I have been so stupid not to have thought about that before? JoJo wanted to insure Mason would have no will of his own and want to do nothing more than kiss me. The dress had to be the reason Mason was looking at me the way he was, full of lust and longing.

"Jess, it's not the dress that makes me feel this way," Mason says. "It's you."

"No, it has to be the dress making you look at me like you want to eat me," I say, completely confident I'm right.

Mason places his hands on my shoulders and slides them down my arms until he's holding my hands in his.

"What makes you think I would need her power to influence how much I want you?"

I look down at our hands and shake my head.

"I don't know," I say in a small voice.

Mason lets go of one of my hands to gently place his index finger underneath my chin to make me look up into his eyes.

"I want you to listen to me very carefully," he says, dead serious. "Even when you were sick and dressed in those god-awful Santa Claus pajamas, I wanted you. It's not the dress. It's you, Jess. How can you not see how desirable you are?"

"Lack of self-esteem?" I try to joke, finding my attempt not a joke, but something I realize is actually true.

"Come with me," Mason says. "I want to show you something."

Before I know it, Mason has phased us to one of the terraces overlooking a neighboring vineyard in the distance. It's dark outside, the only light coming from the full moon in the sky casting a silvery glow on the world below it.

"It's beautiful," I say of the view.

"No, you're the only beauty here, Jess."

Mason brings the hand he still holds to his lips and gently brushes them against my knuckles, making me gasp. The warm feel of his breath against my skin sends pleasant shivers, like tiny bolts of lightning, dancing across every nerve ending in my body. I feel his lips stretch into a pleased smile against my fingers. He seems pleased by my instant reaction to him.

"You are the most beautiful woman I know," he tells me, placing his free hand on my lower back before taking a step closer to me until our bodies are only inches apart. He rests his forehead against mine, and the tips of our noses touch. I take a deep breath because I can't seem to get enough of the way he smells.

"I've imagined us standing here like this a thousand times since we first met," he confesses, making my heart melt into a puddle of bliss.

He lifts his head from mine and plants a small kiss on the tip of my nose. I close my eyes and feel him trail small, tender kisses across my left cheekbone and down the side of my neck to my shoulder. All I can hear is my own ragged breathing. When he begins his assault back up my neck, he makes a maddening detour to a spot just behind my ear that I never even knew existed. My sharp intake of breath makes him smile against my neck.

Unable to take his torturous kisses anymore, I pull away and take two steps back.

Mason watches my retreat with a puzzled frown.

"You're driving me crazy," I tell him, trying to catch my breath.

"That was the general idea," he says, with a roguish grin, completely pleased with his accomplishment.

"I don't want crazy," I tell him, shaking my head slowly. "I want you to kiss me. I want you to be my first real kiss, Mason. And when we kiss, please, don't hold anything back, because I want the moment scorched into my memory. When I'm eighty-years-old, I want to be able to look back on this moment and remember it so clearly I can feel your lips against mine. I want you to kiss me like it might be the one and only kiss we ever get to share."

Mason bridges the distance between us before I can take another shuddering breath. Cupping my face between his hands, he looks into to my eyes and says, "I love you."

His lips descend on mine, finally given permission to release the floodgates of his pent-up passion, forever branding the feel of his lips against mine into my memory. He crushes his body against me, enveloping me in his arms, and lighting every one of my senses on fire. I feel his tongue slip between my lips and can't prevent a moan from escaping my throat at the pleasure that small part of him coaxes from my soul. I wrap my arms around his neck, desperately needing him closer, deepening the kiss and matching the movements of his tongue with my own.

I'm not sure how long we stand there, drinking each other in, but, finally, I feel like I need to breathe, and reluctantly pull away. My lips feel bruised from our kissing, but I wouldn't want them to feel any other way. It's proof of Mason's desire for me, and, if I could live feeling this way, for the rest of my life, I would die happy.

Mason continues to hold me close, and I'm glad to discover I'm not the only one having difficulty breathing.

"My God, that was a kiss," he says in amazement, making me smile.

"Yes," I whole-heartedly agree, "it certainly was, Mr. Collier."

"I've never been kissed like that, ever," he declares sincerely.

I pull back and see the earnest expression on Mason's face.

"Have you been kissed a lot?" I ask, remembering what Angela told me about Mason's other women. I would be lying if I said I didn't feel some jealousy towards those faceless women. I'm selfish. I admit that freely.

"Enough to know a kiss like that only happens once in a lifetime," he says to me.

"Just once?" I ask, leaning into him, brushing my lips lightly against his but not kissing him. "Can we try for twice?"

I press my lips against his tentatively, darting the tip of my tongue against his lips and eliciting a groan originating from deep inside his chest. Before I know it, he has his hands on my back and phases us to the living room. A fire blazes in the hearth. Between kissing Mason and the fire, I feel as though I might spontaneously combust if I keep my coat on for much longer.

Reluctantly, I pull away.

"I'm getting hot," I explain, undoing the buttons of my coat quickly and letting it fall to the floor behind me.

Mason's eyes rake my body with undisguised want.

"Hot doesn't come close to describing how you look in that dress," he says, his voice hoarse, not bothering to hide his desire for me.

Suddenly, I don't feel self-conscience at all about what I'm wearing; not if it makes Mason look at me like I'm all he'll ever want in life.

"Can I let your hair down?" he asks unexpectedly.

I nod, not quite understanding why he wants to do such a thing, and turn my back to him so he can pull the myriad of bobby pins from the bun JoJo styled my hair into.

I hear Mason curse a few times, trying to dig the pins out.

"Could I make a request?" he asks, finally pulling out the last of the pins, and running his fingers through my hair to undo the braid.

"You can ask me for anything," I say, remembering that word could hold a plethora of meanings in this situation.

"Please don't do that to your hair again," he begs. "I like it down around your shoulders."

I turn to face him. "I can do that for you, if you do something for me."

Mason pulls me in closer to him, and I drape my arms over his shoulders.

"And what can I do for you?" he asks.

"Kiss me."

Mason smiles, and, before I know it, he's pulling me down on top of him as he lies back on the couch. My hair makes a natural curtain, hiding us from the world as we kiss again. This time it's a slow kiss, each of us testing the other's limits and likes.

I begin to feel Mason's phone press into my belly, and instinctively swat it to the side with the back of my hand so it's not poking me. I have a fleeting thought that the phone seems larger than I remember.

Mason gasps, like I've hurt him.

I pull away from him and look at his face. He has his eyes closed and his jaw clenched.

"Did I hurt you when I moved your phone?" I ask, worried by the expression he's wearing.

"That wasn't my phone, Jess," he says, slowly taking a deep breath.

It doesn't take me long to figure out what it was I actually moved. Now I understand why it seemed larger than his phone should have been.

"Oh," I say quietly, pulling away from Mason to sit on the other end of the couch.

I have no idea what to do in this situation. I feel flushed because I've just touched a very personal spot on Mason, completely by accident. I look over at him and see him lying there with his eyes closed, pinching the bridge of his nose with the thumb and index finger of one hand.

"Did I hurt you?" I ask again, not really knowing if what I did actually did hurt him.

"No," he finally says, opening his eyes and sitting up. "You didn't hurt me; the complete opposite, in fact."

I feel my heart race at the implication of his statement, but can't seem to make myself look up at him and meet his gaze. I feel him staring at me, but don't know how to handle the situation we find ourselves in. What does he expect to happen next? I feel sure he's been in similar situations before, and the natural progression of things would lead us to the bedroom. But I know in my heart I'm not ready for that yet.

I see Mason's hand lying between us, palm up.

"I think it's time I took you back home," he says gently.

I look up at him. "You want me to leave?"

He shakes his head. "No, I don't want you to leave. But I should get you back home before it gets much later. You still need your rest."

"Are you making me leave because I won't..." I can't even say the words 'make love to you' out loud, so I say instead, "because I'm not like the other women you've brought here?"

Mason moves in closer to me, trapping me with his gaze.

"Now, you listen to me very carefully," he says in a voice with a hard edge. "Other than Jonathan's wife, you are the only woman I have ever brought to this house."

"But Angela told me...she told me about the other women you've been with."

Mason's jaw clenches. "She shouldn't have said anything about that. It's none of her business. I never brought any of those women into my home, Jess. They meant nothing to me. You mean everything to me."

"Then why are you making me leave?"

Mason sighs heavily. "Because I want you so badly right now, I'm not sure I would be able to control myself. I don't want you to leave. I want to take you to my bed and show you how much I love you. But you're not ready for that. I know that. I can see it in the way you're looking at me right now. And I couldn't live with myself if your first time was rushed. You deserve more, and I want to be the one who gives you a beautiful experience. When we finally do make love for the first time, I want it to be just like our first kiss, scorched into both our memories forever. So, please, don't even think for one second that I want you to leave; but I need to take you home now, for both our sakes."

I place my hand in his and say, "Ok," rendered almost completely speechless by his explanation, and feeling like the most loved and desired woman in the world, a feeling I've never experienced before.

Mason phases us to my living room. Isaiah is sitting on my couch, texting something on his phone.

"I'll be back in an hour," Mason tells Isaiah.

Isaiah nods in understanding.

Mason looks back at me and gives me a chaste kiss on the lips.

"I'll be back, but you should go on to bed and get some rest."

I nod like an obedient child. "Ok."

Mason kisses me one more time and phases.

I stand there, staring at where he stood only seconds before, finding it hard to move from my spot.

"Are you all right, Jess?" Isaiah asks.

I look at Isaiah and feel myself start to smile.

"I'm perfect," I tell him, feeling completely and utterly happy.

I go into my bedroom and change into my favorite pink flannel pajamas. When I lay down in my bed, my mind is going ninety to nothing, reliving my evening with Mason over and over again. I hug the pillow on Mason's side of the bed, watching the minutes slowly creep by on the digital clock on my nightstand. I know if I can just stay up a little while longer I can see Mason again.

Sometime around the half hour mark, I end up falling asleep. When I wake up, I see that it's two in the morning. I hop out of bed, rubbing the sleep from my eyes, and walk into the living room. Mason is sitting on the couch, reading a book.

"I tried to stay up until you got back," I tell him, crawling onto the couch beside him.

Mason puts his book down and draws me in closer to him, cradling me in his arms and letting me rest my head on his chest.

"Well, I'm glad you didn't," he says, caressing the side of my face tenderly. "You need your sleep. You're still not completely healed yet."

The warmth of his body and my own tiredness make me feel drowsy.

"Why did you have to leave before?" I ask.

"I needed to do some things," Mason says vaguely.

"Like what?" I ask, trying to stifle a yawn.

"Like take a cold shower before I came back here to be with you all night."

I know the reason for the cold shower, and smile.

"Then come lay with me in my bed," I say. "My chastity should be safe for the rest of the evening."

Mason chuckles. I like the feeling his laughter invokes within my soul, all happiness, sunshine, and butterflies.

Mason lifts me easily as he stands and walks into my bedroom. Gently, he lays me down on my side of the bed and tucks me underneath the comforter. I hear him take his shoes off before he crawls in on the other side and pulls me into his arms.

He plants a gentle kiss on my forehead before saying, "Sweet dreams, Jess."

I smile, because I know that's exactly what I'll have.

CHAPTER NINE

I wake up the next morning cocooned in warmth. Mason's arms are around me and one of his legs is draped over mine. I snuggle my head against his chest and sigh contentedly, certain life can't get any better than this.

I hear the creak of a rocking chair in motion on the front porch. I close my eyes and mentally say a few choice words, because I know who is waiting for me outside. Not wanting to disturb Mason's slumber, I slowly extricate myself from his hold to get out of bed. I grab my purple fox-trimmed coat from the closet and slip on a pair of slippers before stepping out my front door.

"Good morning," Lucifer says to me, bringing the rocking chair to a standstill.

"Morning," I say, stifling a yawn with the back of my hand.

I lean my back against the porch railing in front of him. He's dressed rather sharply in a black tuxedo, covered up mostly by a black wool coat.

"I haven't felt you lately," Lucifer says to me, "so I decided to come and check to make sure you're still alive."

"I've been healing."

"Healing from what?"

"From Asmodeus and Mammon trying to kill me."

The brewing storm that enters Lucifer's eyes reminds me of a tornado I saw once when I was a child. A dark swirl of anger encompasses his face, and I half expect the ground beneath my feet to begin trembling from his wrath.

"They did *what*?" he asks menacingly, tempering his anger as much as he can in my presence.

I go on to tell Lucifer what happened the night of the attack, glossing over how I was able to escape, of course.

Even though his anger isn't directed towards me, I can feel the heat of Lucifer's rage like a blazing fire against my skin. I'm just thankful I won't be on the receiving end of his full fury.

"You will not be attacked again," he promises me. "I would have thought Mammon had more sense than Asmodeus, but I guess I was wrong. They will pay for what they did to you, I can promise you that."

"Why do you keep them around?" I ask. "They obviously don't seem to trust your judgment, because of your insistence on keeping me safe. Are they really that important to your plan?"

Lucifer sighs, "As soon as I'm through with them, I'll send them back where they belong. Until that time, I need their power to find the others."

"What are you planning?" I ask, desperately hoping he'll tell me, or at least give me one small clue to know what we're up against.

Lucifer stands and walks the short distance to me. He raises his hand to gently run the knuckle of his index finger across my cheek. I instantly wonder what he's thinking and feeling.

The bracelet around my wrist becomes warm. Before I even realize it, I know exactly how Lucifer feels about me.

He feels torn between his need to accomplish some great task and his desire to keep me protected. I know he desperately wants me to know him better, to fully understand him. Confusion seems to be the predominate emotion he feels when he looks at me, like he can't quite understand why I mean anything to him. I'm just a human, after all; why should he care whether I live or die? He knows I'm more than just a mere human, just not more of what. He doesn't feel love for me, not exactly. His curiosity about me makes him yearn to be around me, and I know he'll use any excuse from now on to come see me more often.

"I need to leave now," he says, dropping his hand back to his side.

The front door opens, and Mason steps out.

Lucifer looks at Mason's disheveled appearance, all wrinkled clothes and haphazard hair. It's painfully obvious Mason's just gotten out of bed.

Lucifer's eyes narrow in on Mason. "Hello, Mason."

"Lucifer," Mason replies, saying Lucifer's name like it's a cuss word.

"I hope you're treating Jess with the respect she deserves, and not just using her like the other women I've seen you with."

"I love her," Mason says, making sure Lucifer knows how he feels about me.

"I suspected as much," Lucifer replies. He turns back to look at me. "I can't say I approve of your choice in men, but I suppose you could have done worse. At least I know he's not one to say those words lightly, like human men are wont to do. I assume you love him as well?"

I nod. "Yes. I love him."

"No accounting for taste, I suppose," he says, like he's disappointed in me. "I'm leaving now. You have nothing to worry about as far as your physical safety is concerned. The princes and the Watchers under my command will not be bothering you again; you have my word on that. After I get through with Asmodeus and Mammon, they won't even *think* your name, much less try to hatch a plan to harm you."

Lucifer looks over at Mason. "And if *you* hurt her, well, you know what I can do to you."

"I'm fully aware," Mason says, crossing his arms over his chest, staring hard at Lucifer.

"Then I will leave the two of you for now." Lucifer looks back at me. "But I will be back."

Lucifer phases and Mason walks up to me, wrapping his arms around me.

"What were you thinking, coming out here alone to talk to him?" he questions. "Why didn't you wake me up?"

I encircle his waist with my arms and lay my head on his chest.

"I didn't want you to worry. Plus, you looked so comfortable in bed I didn't want to wake you. You know I needed to talk to him anyway, to tell him what happened."

"At least we don't have to worry about you being abducted again," Mason says, kissing the top of my head.

"At least," I agree.

"Hey, you two!"

I lift my head from Mason's chest and see John Austin walking up the steps to my porch, with a white cardboard box in his hands. Even from where I'm standing, I can smell the heavenly aroma of Beau's cinnamon rolls.

"Hey, John Austin, is it Wednesday already?" I ask, knowing the answer, but feeling a need to ask it anyway.

"Got proof in the box that it is," John Austin smiles at us. "Mama Lynn asked me to go fetch the two of you some rolls this morning. She said you guys would probably be hungry after last night."

The amused twinkle in John Austin's eyes tells me he suspects Mason and I might be hungry from some suspected physical exertion from the night before.

I reach for the box and murmur a low, "Thanks," suddenly feeling like a tainted woman, when I am anything but.

"Well," John Austin says, "I'll let the two of you enjoy your breakfast. See you later."

After John Austin leaves, I feel like burying my head inside the box in my hands. I look up at Mason and notice he's wearing an amused grin.

"Why are you smiling?" I ask.

Mason looks down at me. "Because, apparently, your family thinks I'm completely irresistible to you. They already think I've had my way with you, and, if Faison has her way, we'll be married before I even get to ask the question."

I slowly open the lid to the box in front of my face to hide from Mason's laughing eyes. I feel the lid being pushed down gently and have no other recourse but to look up at Mason, who still looks amused by my family's actions.

"You know I don't mind," he says gently. "I'm glad they think we belong together."

My heart dissolves into a puddle of happiness at the earnest expression on Mason's face. I know he means what he says, but I still can't believe someone like him can love someone like me the way he professes to. I'm just a nobody from a small rural town, who fell into a life filled with more wonder than I ever thought could exist.

"How can you look so irresistible when you've just rolled out of bed?" I ask, marveling at the beauty of the man standing in front of me. "It's not fair, you know; I'm sure I look a hot mess."

Mason smiles, and I instantly see his want for me spark in the depths of his eyes.

"How long will it take to make you understand how incredibly gorgeous and sexy you are? Even in pink flannel pajamas, all I can think about is making love to you."

I feel my body begin to tingle, from the tiny hair follicles on my head to the very tips of my toes. I want nothing more than for the man standing in front of me to take me in his arms and show me what making love is supposed to feel like.

But a small part of my psyche sends up a red hot flare, signaling that the time isn't right yet. I should simply enjoy these small moments with Mason because I have no idea what will happen if we try to make love.

How will I react? Will it dredge up memories from my past that will taint what's meant to be a sharing of our minds, bodies, and souls; or will I run away from him, not having the courage to fight against the demons from my past which are sure to rear their ugly heads?

Mason seems to sense my internal struggle because the flames of lust in his eyes suddenly become contained.

He smiles at me, making my body relax because I know the discussion is over for now.

"Come on," he says, taking the box of rolls out of my hands, "let's go inside and eat."

While we're sitting at the kitchen table, I remember to ask Mason about some things Lucifer mentioned.

"What is it that Lucifer can do to you?" I ask. "He's always threatening that he can hurt you, but neither of you have said how exactly."

"He could kill me if he wanted to," Mason says.

I stop eating. I place the roll back on my plate, and give Mason my full attention.

"What do you mean, he could kill you?"

"It's basically the same power you have, Jess. When you killed the changeling that first night we met, and what you and Chandler did to Baruch, that's the power of an archangel. He could turn me into a pile of ash with one touch."

"Why hasn't he then? If he considers you a threat, why hasn't he just killed you off?"

"Then where would the fun be for him? He likes to taunt people, me especially, I think."

I decide to switch the topic away from death, because Lucifer killing Mason is not something I want to even consider as a possibility.

"Lucifer also told me that the princes of Hell all had their own specialty. What did he mean by that?"

"You've heard of the seven deadly sins, right?"

"Yes."

"Each of the princes is in charge of one."

"What are Asmodeus and Mammon in charge of?"

"Asmodeus' specialty is lust and Mammon's is greed. They're each capable of evoking those emotions in humans."

There is a knock at the door.

Mason goes to answer it and comes back with someone I wasn't expecting to see… Malcolm.

"Glad to see you're feeling better," Malcolm tells me.

He's dressed in a white shirt open at the front, and a pair of white twill pants and tan sandals.

"What brings you here, Malcolm?" Mason asks in his usual brusque way when speaking to others.

It makes me realize how different Mason is when it's just the two of us. When he's with me, he's much more relaxed. He's able to joke, tease, and laugh with me. With others, he's curt, short-spoken even. It's just another example of how much our relationship has grown since the night we met.

"Lilly wanted to know if Jess is well enough to speak with her today."

I stare at Malcolm, suddenly becoming nervous.

"I'll speak with her," I hear myself say, but the words aren't mine.

I was actually thinking about asking for a few more days before I had to face her, but, apparently, Michael had other ideas. It's the first time he's used me in such a way, and I find that I don't like it. Not one bit.

"Good," Malcolm says. "Will an hour give you enough time to get ready?"

I nod because I feel like, if I open my mouth, Michael will say we're ready now, and I really don't want to meet with Lilly in my pink flannel pajamas.

"Then, I'll be back."

Mason comes over to me and kneels by my chair. "What just happened? You didn't sound like yourself when you said you would speak with Lilly."

I marvel at Mason's ability to know me well enough to tell I hadn't been in control in that moment.

"Michael spoke through me," I say, not trying to hide how frightened that moment made me feel. "He said he wouldn't try to control me, but he just did."

"Talk to him," Mason urges. "I'm sure it was only because of Lilly. He's her father. He's probably wanted to speak with her for a long time now. I don't think he meant to scare you. Michael was never one to do that to people. Lucifer used fear to control, but not Michael; he was always the voice of reason and understanding. Let him explain."

I nod. "Ok."

I walk into my bedroom and sit on the side of my bed before I call to Michael. He instantly appears.

"I'm so sorry," he immediately says, coming to kneel on one knee before me. "Please, Jess. It wasn't something I planned to do. It just happened. I couldn't let the opportunity pass by, and I knew you wanted to wait. Please forgive me for using you like that."

"I didn't know you could do that," I say in almost a whisper. "It scared me."

"I know," Michael hangs his head in shame. "It was stupid and rash. I will never do it again. I promise you."

Now I feel bad. The way Michael looks tells me just how sorry he is for using me for his own purposes. I reach out, wanting to bring him comfort, but only find air when I try to touch his shoulder. I know what it's like to want to speak with your father, and pity Lilly because she's never even met Michael. At least I got to spend the first seven years of my life with my dad. This will be her first time having any sort of communication with her father, and it will end up being filtered through me. That, more than anything else, helps me decide what my next course of action should be.

"I want you to use my body to talk to Lilly," I tell Michael.

His head snaps up at my suggestion. "I couldn't do that to you. It would be like violating your body, and I just promised I wouldn't do that again."

"I know," I say, taking a deep breath, "but Lilly needs to hear what you have to say. I know what it's like to want your father close. She'll want to hear how much you love her. She's not going to want to hear it through a third party. She needs to know how much you care for her, Michael. Trust me; it's important."

"You would do that for us?" Michael questions earnestly. "You would give us that time?"

Before I chicken out, I say, "Yes."

Michael smiles sadly and closes his eyes. Twin tears stream down his face.

"Thank you," he says. "Thank you, Jess."

I quickly get ready and wait for Malcolm to come get me.

"Do you want me to go with you?" Mason asks.

I've already told him the agreement I've made with Michael. I know he's scared about what I'm going to do. He worries Michael won't be able to relinquish control over me once he takes it. I can't say the thought hasn't crossed my mind, but something deep within my soul tells me everything will be all right.

"Please, don't worry," I say, drawing him into my arms and kissing him lightly on the lips. "I'll be fine. Michael doesn't want to control me. This wasn't even his idea."

Mason sighs heavily. "I know, but what if he can't find a way to give control back to you?"

"That won't happen," I say confidently. I think it's my confidence more than anything that wipes the worry from Mason's face.

Without warning, Mason is crushing me to him, completely possessing my lips with his in a mind-blowing kiss. When he finally pulls away, we're both physically shaking from the experience.

"I'm not complaining," I say, swallowing air, "but where did that come from?"

"I wanted you to have something to remember while Michael has control of you. I intend to finish that kiss when you get back."

I smile. "Well, there's no way in hell that I'm not coming back now."

Mason chuckles, and I know everything will work out just fine.

CHAPTER TEN

Exactly one hour after he left, Malcolm reappears in my kitchen. I sigh because I know he has free rein of my house now.

"Ready?" he asks, holding out his hand to me.

I stand up and feel Mason grab my hand before I'm able to walk over to Malcolm.

"Come back to me," Mason says.

I hear the worry in his voice, and see in his eyes his trepidation about what I'm about to do.

"I won't be long," I promise, squeezing his hand reassuringly.

I walk up to Malcolm, and he places his hand on my shoulder.

A warm ocean breeze flutters my hair against my neck. I find myself facing a glass wall, with seamless sliding glass doors open to the outside. Palm trees, a blue ocean, and black sand make up the outer surroundings of the glass, steel, and cement home I'm standing in.

"I'll leave the two of you alone," Malcolm says, looking at someone behind me before he phases.

I turn around to find Lilly standing on the other side of the room by the opposite glass wall. She's wearing a white eyelet sundress.

"Thank you for coming," she says.

I see uncertainty in her eyes, and instantly wish I could erase it.

"Lilly," I say, taking one step forward, "your father and I decided it would be best for you to speak with him directly, instead of me telling you what he wants you to know."

Lilly looks confused. "What do you mean by 'speak directly'?"

"I'm going to let him control my body and talk to you."

Lilly gasps, obviously not expecting this turn of events. "He can do that to you? Why would you let him?"

"Because, if I were in your shoes, I would want to talk to my dad without having another person basically just relaying messages back and forth. He loves you so much, Lilly. He deserves a chance to tell you himself, to be with you and feel you."

I see Lilly's eyes glaze over with unshed tears at what's about to happen.

"Thank you," she says with a nod, signaling she's ready to meet her father.

I close my eyes and call to Michael.

The sensation is weird, to say the least. When he takes control of my body, I can still feel everything, but it's like the sensations aren't immediate. It's almost like there's a time delay between him moving me and my feeling it.

"Hello, Lilly," I hear myself say, realizing Michael is addressing his daughter for the very first time.

Lilly holds a hand up to her mouth, desperately trying to suppress a cry but unable to do so. I watch as tears spill freely from her eyes, and her shoulders begin to shake as she stares through me to see her father.

Michael walks over to his child and takes her in his arms. I can feel how happy it makes him to finally be able to touch and comfort her. Lilly cries on Michael's shoulder, drenching the long-sleeve blouse I'm wearing, with her tears. Michael holds her to him, never wanting to let her go.

Once Lilly's tears are spent, she lifts her head.

"I can see you," she says. "I can see you in her eyes. How is that possible?"

"Because you are my daughter; Lilly, I want you to know that I have loved you since the day you were conceived. I'm thankful to Jess for letting me say that to you in person, and to tell you how proud I am of everything you've been able to accomplish in your life. And I don't mean just your win over Lucifer either. I'm proud of the way you let yourself find love and fight for it. I'm proud of the children you've had, and what a wonderful mother you are to them. A father couldn't be prouder than I am of you and what you've been able to accomplish, even with all the obstacles placed in your way. You have so much strength, so much power, yet you don't take advantage of it. You only do what you have to. What father wouldn't be proud of a daughter like you?"

"I've wanted to talk to you so many times during my life," Lilly says. "And now that you're here, I can't think of anything to say."

"I want you to know," Michael says, "that leaving you and your mother was one of the hardest things I've ever been asked to do. Please tell me you understand why I had to do it."

Lilly nods. "I know. God explained it to me. You had to leave because, if you didn't, I wouldn't have been able to end up where I needed to be. I won't lie and say I liked it, but I understand. I don't blame you, and I don't blame Him. Please, don't feel any guilt over what you had to do. I wouldn't change a thing about my life because, if I did, I might not have Brand or my children. If I didn't have them, my life wouldn't be worth living."

"I don't want to impose on Jess for too long," Michael says, "but I'm thankful to her for giving me the opportunity to hold you and talk to you. Know that you can speak with me at any time through her. She is a true friend to me, and she can be one to you too."

Lilly nods. "I know; I felt that the first time we met."

Michael brings Lilly back into his arms for one last embrace, and kisses her on the forehead.

"I love you," he says.

"I love you too, Daddy," Lilly replies.

When Michael gives me back control over my body, I immediately stretch to chase away the cobweb feeling in my extremities.

"Thank you, Jess," Lilly tells me, giving me a heartfelt hug.

"Anytime," I tell her.

When she pulls away from me, she takes my hand, and we sit down together on a white L-shaped sofa in the room.

"Malcolm's kept me informed on your progress since the attack," she tells me. "How are you feeling?"

"I'm still a little tired, but other than that I feel fine. I actually feel the best I have in a long time."

A knowing smile spreads Lilly's lips. "This wouldn't be due to a certain angel, would it?"

I laugh nervously. "Most definitely."

Lilly's smile falters. "You know, after Baruch attacked you, Mason came to see me that night."

"After he left me?"

Lilly nods. "Yes. I've never seen him so upset before. He was inconsolable. I told him he was being an idiot, but Watchers are notorious for self-sacrifice; Mason most of all. He felt it was the best way to keep you safe. It took you almost dying at the hands of Asmodeus and Mammon for him to see how much safer you actually are with him around."

"Lucifer says I don't have to worry about any of them anymore," I tell Lilly.

"Has he figured out why he's drawn to you yet?"

"No, but I take it from the way you just said that you think it's because of Michael too."

Lilly nods. "It makes sense. They were best friends. Michael was the one who had to bring Lucifer to Earth for his exile. I don't think either one of them fully realizes how much they still mean to one another. Even though my father's soul has melded with yours, Lucifer can still feel his presence within you."

"What do you think Lucifer will do when he finds out what I am?"

Lilly shrugs. "I have no way of knowing. My dealings with Lucifer were far different from the ones you're experiencing. We were enemies from the get-go, but, with you, he feels a growing friendship, a need to keep you out of harm's way. It's a side of him I've never seen. I wasn't even aware he could feel anything but greed and hatred."

"Do you think I'm meant to change him in some way?"

Lilly's eyebrows lift in surprise. "I never thought about that possibility," she says. "God hasn't mentioned it to me, but who knows what He has planned?"

"I know this will sound completely insane," I say, "but Lucifer isn't all bad."

Lilly looks shocked that I think this.

"I'm not saying he isn't evil," I qualify, "but there's a part of him that's actually noble. He might not have a lot of standards, but protecting his friends seems to at least be one of them. I don't think he would ever intentionally hurt me."

"So, what is your theory on what his reaction will be when he learns you and my father share a soul?"

"Honestly? I think he'll just be relieved to know why he likes me. The mystery will finally be solved. I don't think he'll hurt me when he finds out. He cares too much for Michael."

Lilly sighs. "You might be right. I guess we'll know soon enough; it's only a matter of time before he figures it out."

I see Malcolm phase into the room with Brand by his side.

Lilly locks eyes with her husband almost immediately and I feel the connection the two of them share with one another, like a wave of energy hitting me in the chest.

"I was worried," he says, explaining his sudden appearance. And I know he wasn't worried I might do something to harm Lilly, just worried how she would handle speaking with her father for the first time.

Lilly stands and walks over to him. Brand brings her into his arms and holds her tightly. I instantly see her relax against him, as if he's the only home she needs.

"There was never anything to worry about," Lilly tells Brand. "It was better than I could have hoped for."

Malcolm walks over to me.

"Ready to go?" he asks, obviously wanting to give Brand and Lilly some time alone to speak about what happened.

I stand and nod.

Malcolm instantly phases us to my front porch.

I look at him. "Why didn't you phase us inside the house?"

Malcolm grins. "I figured you didn't want me doing that. I won't do it unless you ask me to. I owe you that much."

"Why do you feel like you owe me anything?"

"If I hadn't taken you to Mason's house that night…"

"Wait," I say, holding up a hand to make sure he doesn't say anything until I'm finished. "Don't go blaming yourself for that. Besides, everything worked out in the end. Things happen for a reason, and, honestly, if it hadn't happened, I probably wouldn't have Mason back in my life. I'll chance a near-death experience for him."

Malcolm grins. "So, I heard about the date last night."

My eyes narrow on him. "Who told you about that?"

"Isaiah."

I shake my head. "I didn't realize he was the gossiping type."

Malcolm shrugs. "Like I've told you before, we've all been worried about Mason for years. We like seeing him happy for probably the first time in his life. Don't begrudge us sharing in your happiness. It's been a long time coming."

"It's just…kinda weird, all of you rooting for us. Freaks me out a little bit. I feel like everything we do is being judged by all of you."

Malcolm shakes his head. "Not judged, just observed from afar."

"What about you?" I ask.

Malcolm looks confused. "What *about* me?"

"I don't understand how you can be around Lilly and Brand so much. Even I can feel the love they share for one another when I'm around them, and I barely know them. How can you stand to be around them when you're in love with Lilly?"

Malcolm goes completely still and silent. It's unnerving. Finally he says, "I love her enough to only want to see her happy."

"But don't you deserve to find happiness with someone who can love you back?"

"My happiness stems from Lilly and her family's happiness. Besides, I'm not sure there *is* a person for me."

"Maybe she just hasn't been born yet," I suggest.

"Perhaps," Malcolm reluctantly agrees.

"Speaking of loving someone, Joshua wants to take Caylin to Chandler's concert in Denver on Valentine's Day."

"Yes, I've been made aware of that," Malcolm's eyes darken. "She's too young to be dating, in my opinion."

"Joshua's a good kid," I say in my young friend's defense. Anyone who is thoughtful enough to give me a Yoda Christmas ornament is ok in my book. "Are you going to give them a hard time if they go out together?"

"No, but I will be watching… from a distance. They won't know I'm there."

I sigh. "Well, I guess that's better than having you sit between them and glaring at Joshua the whole evening."

"I don't completely disapprove of the boy," Malcolm grumbles, "but he's young, with far too many rampaging hormones running around to be let loose on Caylin. She's too innocent to have to deal with a teenage boy in his prime."

I don't tell Malcolm, but I feel sure Caylin can handle herself around Joshua. She certainly knew how to turn Malcolm into mush with just one doe-eyed look. Joshua didn't have a chance.

When Malcolm leaves, I find Mason in my kitchen, preparing lunch, and he's not alone. Inwardly, I sigh, because I was really looking forward to finishing a certain kiss I was promised.

Chandler and JoJo are sitting at the kitchen table, playing a game of cribbage. They both look up and move from their seats to come give me a hug. Their close presence brings peace to my soul.

"So, Mr. Moody has been Mr. Happy since he came to get us," Chandler whispers to me. "I guess things turned out all right last night?"

"*Oui, oui*," JoJo whispers excitedly. "Tell us what happened."

I feel myself blush, at a loss for words.

"I take it from the red on your cheeks you guys finally kissed," Chandler says knowingly.

I nod, and JoJo makes small jumps up and down as she giggles her happiness.

"And just what are you three whispering about?" Mason asks, bringing two plates of food to the table before walking over to us.

Chandler and JoJo step away, allowing Mason free access to me. He puts his arms around me, and I lay my head on his chest. I suddenly realize we're in the same position in which I left Lilly and Brand. I'm home.

Mason pulls away to look down at me. "How did it go?"

"It went well. She seemed happy when I left."

"Good. Now, are you hungry?"

I nod and Mason takes my hand to lead me to the table.

We all sit and enjoy the simple lunch of penne pasta and grilled chicken, sprinkled with a touch of parmesan cheese.

"So, no one has told me what I missed during the time I was recovering," I say. "Besides JoJo finding her crown, anything else happen that I should know about?"

I see JoJo put her fork down on the table, Chandler pushes a piece of chicken around on his plate, and Mason's looking anywhere but at me.

"Ok, what happened?" I ask, knowing they are purposely keeping something important from me.

"Nothing that any of us could control," Mason finally says, looking me straight in the eye. "The Tear opened up twice while you were sleeping."

"Twice?" I ask, completely sure he's mistaken.

"Yes," Mason answers.

"Then why are we wasting time?" I ask, agitated. "We need to be looking for JoJo and Chandler's talismans, not just sitting around. Plus, we have to find the other archangels. The more time we waste, the more lives get ruined."

"You needed the rest," Chandler tries to argue before I cut him off.

"I'm fine!" I storm, not understanding how they can just sit around when the world needs saving. "After lunch, we get back to work. Is that understood?"

"But, Jess…" Chandler tries to say, but I give him 'the look'. Everyone has 'the look', but usually you don't bring it out except on special occasions. It's the look that warns people you are not someone to be trifled with. You had better do what the person giving you the look says, or there will be trouble. And I feel confident they don't want to deal with trouble from me.

"But nothing," I grit out. "Back to work. That's it. Now eat."

JoJo and Chandler become completely dedicated to finishing their lunch in record time. When I look over at Mason, I see an amused expression on his face.

"What?" I ask, irritated that no one thought it important enough to tell me the Tear opened twice while I was unconscious.

"I'm just amazed by you," he says, smiling.

Damn that smile. Even when I'm mad, it makes me just want to reach over the table and kiss him into tomorrow.

"Stop smiling at me," I tell him as sternly as I can, fighting back a small smile of my own.

This only makes Mason's smile grow wider. "If I don't, will I get in trouble?"

From the twinkle in his eyes, I can only imagine he would enjoy any discipline I might dish out.

I feel JoJo and Chandler watching us, and instantly redirect my attention to them.

"Eat," I order them both.

Without question, but with smiles of their own, they continue eating.

I look back at Mason, and he's still smiling at me.

"Stop," I mouth silently, shaking my head, trying to concentrate on eating the lunch on my plate. But he continues to stare at me, all the while, smiling from ear to ear.

Unable to bear it anymore, I drop my fork noisily onto my plate, grab the hand Mason has on the table, and drag him into the living room, pushing him up against the wall with one hand and keeping him there.

"Are you going to punish me now?" Mason whispers suggestively so the other two can't hear.

"Stop smiling at me," I order him. "I can't think straight when you do that."

Mason takes the hand I have on his chest and uses it to bring me into his arms.

"Is that all I have to do? Smile at you to bring out this feisty little vixen I see?"

I narrow my eyes at him, trying my best to look completely unmoved, but I feel myself failing miserably at staying mad at him.

"Oh, the hell with it," I say, wrapping my arms around his neck and bringing his lips down to mine, finally continuing the kiss Mason started before I left to meet with Lilly.

I'm not sure how long we stand there kissing, but I finally hear someone clear their throat beside us.

I instantly pull away and see Chandler staring at us, like a kid who's just caught his parents doing something they shouldn't in front of their child.

"Sorry," I say to him, "but he was asking for it."

"Can I ask for it again?" Mason asks cheekily.

"Normally, I wouldn't have interrupted," Chandler says, "but Isaiah is here, and he says he has something important to tell us."

Chandler turns and walks back into the kitchen, looking desperate to get away.

I look at Mason and point my index finger at him sternly. "No more smiling."

And, of course, he smiles.

"But it worked out so well the first time. If you want me to stop, you really need to come up with a better punishment. Otherwise, I'll just wear a permanent smile on my face until the end of time."

I roll my eyes at him and walk into the kitchen.

"You are completely incorrigible," I say over my shoulder.

"Yes," I hear Mason say, rather proudly. "Yes, I am."

Isaiah is sitting at the kitchen table with a half-empty cup of coffee in his hands. It makes me wonder just how long Mason and I were making out in the living room.

"Isaiah," Mason says, reverting back to Watcher commander mode, "what do you have to tell us?"

Isaiah stands. "I came to tell you that Joshua and Nick have completed the tasks you assigned them."

"Both?" Mason asks, surprised to hear this news.

"Yes," Isaiah says, his eyes darting towards me and back to Mason, "both."

"What tasks?" I ask, sensing that at least one thing Joshua and Nick did concerns me directly.

"Why don't we all go to headquarters together?" Masons suggests, but I can tell he's purposely avoiding my question. He looks at Chandler and JoJo. "I think it's time you two met the other people on our team."

Isaiah and Mason phase us all to headquarters. Joshua is in his normal spot in front of the holographic display console, and Nick is sitting beside him, studying some papers with a lot of numbers on them.

"Jess!" I hear an excited voice say behind me, and see Angela jogging over to give me a hug. "We were so worried about you."

"I'm fine now," I reassure her.

Angela pulls away but keeps her hands on my upper arms. "Jonathan told me to give you his love when I saw you again. He was so worried for you after the attack."

I see Angela's eyes glance in Mason's direction, and know instantly that Jonathan had been worried about what would happen to his father if I died.

"I'm feeling a lot better," I tell her, hoping she reports back to Jonathan, to relieve Mason's son of any lingering worry for my welfare and, thus, the mental well-being of his father.

I can still vividly remember the dank little cavern in the mountains where Mason said he and Jonathan lived for the first one hundred years of Jonathan's life. I can fully understand why he's frightened for his dad's sanity.

Joshua and Nick come to stand with us, and we make introductions all around. JoJo takes an instant liking to Joshua, but not so much Nick. I actually start to feel sorry for Nick. Of anyone, he seems to be the odd man out of the group now.

Angela flushes slightly when she's introduced to Chandler.

I see Chandler give her his mega-watt superstar smile and warn him, "She's married…to Mason's son."

Chandler's mouth twists in disappointment. "Why does it seem like all the good ones are already taken?"

Now that the pleasantries are over, Mason gets down to business.

Mason turns to Joshua. "I hear you found Joseph's descendants."

"Yeah," Joshua confirms, going back to sit down at the control panel.

With a few taps on the panel's surface, Joshua pulls up a video of a group of people in the midst of preparing an outdoor feast, on what looks like a patio area on the backside of a house made of stone. I assume it's somewhere in the Middle East because of the way the people are dressed, plus it seems to already be nighttime there.

"Joseph, who?" I ask, coming to stand beside Mason.

Almost absently, Mason takes one of my hands into his as we watch the people on the holographic display.

"Do you remember the story of Jacob giving his son Joseph a coat made of different colored material?" Mason asks me.

"Yeah, his brothers got jealous and sold him to a slave trader. Then he became one of the most powerful men in Egypt, second only to the pharaoh."

"We think we've found Joseph's descendants."

"Ok," I say, trying to see where this is all going.

"I think JoJo's talisman may be the coat," Mason says to us.

"*Pourquoi donc?*" JoJo asks Mason.

"Because your powers seem to imbue clothing with special properties; especially protective ones, it seems," Mason tells her. "Joseph's coat held the power to make the wearer invincible. It was only because Joseph's brothers took the coat from him that he wasn't able to defend himself when they sold him."

"So his descendants have the coat? Where are they exactly?"

"They claim to have it," Joshua answers. "They live in the West Bank city of Nablus, in Israel. Joseph's descendants moved there after they escaped Egypt. Back in the old days, it was known as Shechem."

"They told me," says Isaiah, "that JoJo will have to come get the coat herself. They want to meet her before they just hand it over. We could take it from them by force, of course, but I don't think that's wise."

"*Non,*" JoJo says, shaking her head, causing her curls to bounce. "I will be happy to meet with them first. It is the least I can do for their help."

"Why don't the three of you go with Isaiah to retrieve the coat?" Mason suggests. "I need to discuss something with Nick anyway."

"Discuss what?" I ask, knowing this something probably involves me in some way.

"Let me check it out first," Mason says. "I'll tell you when you get back. I promise."

I sigh out of frustration, but fully intend to hold him to his promise when I get back.

I stand up on my toes and kiss him lightly on the lips. "When I get back," I warn.

Mason smiles and squeezes the hand he still holds. "When you get back."

Isaiah phases us to the backyard we just saw on the holographic display at headquarters.

The smell of sweet, spicy food fills the air. There must be at least forty people milling around, carrying plates of food and speaking to one another in a language I don't understand. None of them seems to realize we just phased in, and I know Isaiah must have not signaled our arrival with the customary popping sound of a Watcher's phasing. A rotund man with thinning hair, dressed in plain blue slacks and matching vest over a long-sleeve white shirt, walks up to us.

"Isaiah, my friend, so good to see you again," the man says, shaking Isaiah's hand with both of his, vigorously.

"Thank you, Ezra." Isaiah introduces Chandler and me to Ezra. When he comes to JoJo, he says, "And this is JoJo Armand. She is the one we've come to get the coat for."

Ezra's eyes light up with excitement. He shakes JoJo's hand so vigorously I see JoJo holding back a grimace behind her smile.

"*Bonjour*," she says to Ezra, trying to keep her smile on through the shaking.

"We are all so excited to meet you and see what happens," Ezra says, placing an arm around JoJo's shoulders. "Come, let me introduce you to the rest of my family."

Chandler and I stand off to the side, letting JoJo enjoy the spotlight of her celebrity among Ezra's family. They all seem excited to meet our friend, and JoJo graciously accepts their hospitality.

Finally, we are asked to sit down and enjoy the feast Ezra's family has prepared. Luckily, I'm still hungry, since I didn't get to finish my lunch, thanks to a certain angel who refused to stop smiling at me.

"What are you thinking about?" Chandler asks me.

I look at him, sitting across the table from me. "Mason."

Chandler rolls his eyes. "Should have known. What about Mason?"

I shake my head. "Nothing much. Just his smile; I don't know why it has such an effect on me."

"Because you're in love," Chandler shrugs, as if it's the most obvious thing in the world.

"I couldn't…." I stop, wondering if I should be having this conversation with Chandler. Normally, I would have this type of talk with Faison, but she isn't exactly available, and I have to talk about it with someone. "I couldn't go beyond just kissing last night," I confess.

Chandler studies me hard for a moment before asking, "He didn't try to make you go beyond that, did he?"

I shake my head vigorously. "No, in fact he's the one who insisted I go back home before things got to the point where neither of us could stop."

Chandler visibly relaxes. "So, couldn't, or wouldn't, go past kissing?"

"Couldn't."

"Why?"

I bite my bottom lip, contemplating how to answer.

"What if he touches me in certain spots, and I don't like it? What if I end up pulling away from him?"

"I assume this has to do with that business with your uncle."

I nod. "What if it brings back too many bad memories, and I never find a way to wipe those images from my mind?"

Chandler sighs, understanding my predicament. "I can't imagine the hell you went through with your uncle, Jess. But I do know one thing; unlike your uncle, Mason actually loves you. Hell, even if I just like a girl, I make sure to take things slow with her. The way Mason looks at you tells me he would take things extra slow. I don't think you have anything to worry about. You're not going to experience things the same way, because it will be with someone you love and someone you want to touch you. The two situations are complete opposites from one another."

"I don't want to hurt him," I say. "I don't want to flinch away from his touch, and I'm scared that's what I'll do without even meaning to."

"Well, you seemed pretty stuck to him this afternoon," Chandler says, raising a dubious eyebrow at me. "I wasn't sure you guys were ever going to hear me."

"We heard you."

"Yeah, the fourth time I cleared my throat, you did."

"Fourth?"

Chandler nods and I bury my face in my hands, completely mortified. I begin to laugh at the absurd picture in my head of Chandler trying to interrupt my and Mason's make-out session. Chandler soon joins me in my laughter.

"I'm sorry," I say, wiping tears from my eyes. "I didn't realize you had tried so many times."

"I felt like a peeping Tom," Chandler confesses. "You guys were so into each other, I wasn't sure you would ever come up for air. But you know what? For someone who just had her first kiss last night, you were doing some major damage to that man's mouth."

I sober up. "Do you think I was hurting him?"

"Oh, my God," Chandler hangs his head, as if he can't believe I just asked that question. "No, I was giving you a compliment, stupid. It means you were kissing him in a pretty majorly wicked way. I don't think I've ever had anyone be that into me."

"You will," I tell him, hoping Chandler finds love like I have. I feel confident he will.

After everyone is through eating, Ezra brings out a medium-sized wooden box from the house and sets it in front of JoJo. The box is ornately carved, and you can tell whoever made it took a lot of time to work the wood into something special enough to carry what is essentially a holy relic.

JoJo stands up from the table she is sitting at and looks to Ezra for permission to get what we came for.

"Please," Ezra says, sweeping his arm over the box, indicating that JoJo should be the one to open it.

JoJo looks over at Chandler and me, uncertainty and trepidation in her eyes. I give her an encouraging nod, and she smiles nervously back at me. Even from where I'm sitting, I can see her hands shake slightly as she gently lifts the lid of the box and peers inside.

JoJo, suddenly confused, looks back up at me for help.

Chandler and I go over to her and peer inside the box ourselves.

The coat has lost its color from years of storage. Seams are coming apart, and it appears to be disintegrating from age.

"What should I do with it?" JoJo asks me.

The material looks too fragile to take out of the box.

"Touch it," I suggest. "See what happens."

JoJo flexes the fingers of her right hand and runs the tips of them gingerly across the delicate fabric.

Almost instantly, the coat comes to life. Right before our eyes, it transforms into a beautiful multi-colored silk robe, with intricate embroidery stitched around the edges. Everyone, including me, gasps as we witness its magical transformation.

JoJo reaches inside the box and pulls out the coat. The coat seems to have every color in the rainbow. JoJo looks to me again for guidance.

"Put it on," I encourage.

JoJo slips the coat on and a warm glow, like the sun setting on the horizon, envelops her.

"Try to hit her," I tell Isaiah.

Isaiah looks at me like I've completely lost my mind.

"Don't do it hard, though," I warn. "You might hurt yourself."

Isaiah shakes his head, but does as I ask, and tries to hit JoJo on the arm. His fist bounces off her, and Isaiah is immediately sent flying through the air until his back hits a tree in the yard, stopping his flight.

Chandler whistles. "Glad you didn't ask me to do that."

"I wasn't sure what it would do to the person trying to hurt JoJo," I say with a shrug. "Figured Isaiah could take the most damage."

"Thanks a lot, Jess," Isaiah says, coming back to stand with us, but rubbing his back like it still stings from being slammed against the trunk of a tree.

"I owe you a day at a good spa," I tell him by way of reparation.

JoJo giggles like a kid and starts to dance around, much like the time Chandler and I saw her in our vision.

She holds her hands out to us.

"Dance with me," she begs, shaking her hands at us, urging us to join in on her fun.

I shake my head, but place my hand in hers just the same. So does Chandler.

Before I know it we're spinning around in a circle, like we're playing Ring around the Rosie. JoJo's effervescent giggling is contagious, and we all find ourselves laughing like children, finding a carefree moment in our otherwise-chaotic lives.

CHAPTER ELEVEN

When Isaiah phases us back to headquarters, Mason is nowhere to be seen.

"Where's Mason?" I ask Nick, who is there to greet us.

"He had an errand to run," Nick says hesitantly.

I instantly know something is up.

"What kind of errand?" I ask, crossing my arms in front of me and taking a you- better-answer-me-or-else stance.

"You'll have to ask him when he comes back," Nick answers, taking a cautious step back away from me. "I promised I would let him explain."

Nick continues his retreat, heading back over to Joshua who is still sitting at the control panel.

JoJo turns to Isaiah, "Could you take me back home, *s'il vous plait*? I would like to get my crown and talk to my archangel now."

"Mason told me to take you to his villa when you were ready to meet your archangel," Isaiah tells her. "We're going to use it as a safe haven for all of you."

"You should go with her," I tell Chandler, "just to make sure she's comfortable."

Chandler nods.

I turn to JoJo. "You will probably sleep for a couple of days," I tell her.

"*Oui, oui*, I was warned."

I kiss her on the cheek. "Good luck with your angel. I'll see you soon."

JoJo smiles, and Isaiah phases her and Chandler to Mason's villa.

I feel a presence behind me, and turn. Joshua is standing there, shuffling his feet nervously, obviously wanting to talk to me about something.

"I wanted to apologize to you in person," he says to me.

"Apologize for what?" I ask, having no clue what he's talking about.

"Asmodeus; he tricked me into letting him come into the house the day you were abducted."

This is the first I've heard of this. I wondered how Asmodeus could have phased into Mason's home, but didn't really have too much time to think about it because of everything that happened afterwards.

"How did he trick you?" I ask.

"I was helping Malcolm set the room up for you. We arranged for a local florist to deliver the flowers. Asmodeus killed the delivery guy, and took his place to gain access to the house. I should have been more careful. I didn't even pay attention to the guy when he came in, Jess. I sort of wondered why he kept putting the arrangements on his shoulder to bring them in, but didn't even think he was using them as camouflage to cover his face. I was busy texting Caylin, and just didn't pay enough attention to what was going on. I'm sorry. I was a complete idiot."

"Listen, don't blame yourself for what happened," I tell him. "I certainly don't blame you."

"Well, it taught me an important lesson," he says. "Not only were you kidnapped and almost killed, but now we have to move everything."

"Move everything?"

"We can't stay here," I hear Mason say behind me. "This house has been compromised."

I turn to face Mason, and feel my heart light on fire at just the mere sight of him. He's wearing his grey wool coat. He smiles at me, which just adds to the ache I feel to touch him.

"Where have you been?" I ask him.

"Calabasas, California."

"Never heard of it," I admit. "What's so important there?"

Mason walks up to me and takes my hand.

"Let's go somewhere else and talk about it."

Mason phases to the living room in his villa. He lets go of my hand and takes his coat off, tossing it on one of the smaller couches. I sit down on the main couch, because I feel like I probably shouldn't be standing to hear whatever it is he's about to tell me.

Mason sits down beside me.

"I found someone for you," he says, hesitant to give me this information.

"My mother?" I ask breathlessly.

Mason shakes his head. "No; we still haven't been able to locate her yet."

Now I'm completely baffled. I felt sure his big news would concern my mother. My biological father was dead. So, who did that leave?

"Then who did you find that I would want to see?" I ask.

"Nick found your grandfather; your father's father."

My mind reels at this news. "How did you even know where to look?"

"While you were recovering, Zeruel and I had a lot of time to talk," Mason tells me. "He told me what he knew about your father's past because he felt it was important that you get to know your human family."

"So, I have a grandfather?" I ask. It never even crossed my mind to attempt to find my father's side of the family.

"Yes. And he lives in Calabasas, California. Apparently, he's the one who set up your trust fund, not your parents."

"So he's rich?"

"Yes, he's quite well off. He used to be an attorney for some people in Hollywood. He made a lot of money, some of it from work and some of it from wise investments. He set up the trust fund because he wanted to make sure you were provided for."

"Why didn't the government find him when my parents disappeared?"

"Your biological father's name wasn't on your birth certificate. Your mother just made up a name because she didn't want your grandfather to have any legal rights to you. When Zeruel came to help your mother and be a father to you, your grandfather didn't have a clue where they took you. After years of trying to track you down, he finally found you. By that time, you were almost eighteen, and he felt like he would be imposing in your life if he suddenly showed up then."

"That's why I got my trust fund when I turned eighteen?"

Mason nods. "He still wanted to provide for you, but made the lawyer tell you the money was something your parents set up, not him."

I swallow hard, trying to digest what Mason has just told me.

"When you went to see him," I say, "did he say whether or not he wants to meet me in person?"

"He's wanted to meet you for a very long time." Mason takes my hand in his. "The only question is if you want to meet him."

It was a good question, one I had to think about, for about a second.

"Of course I want to meet him," I say, tears springing to my eyes at the thought of actually getting to meet a blood relative. After all these years, I was being given a chance to meet someone I shared a genetic background with, a heritage. Why wouldn't I want to meet my grandfather?

"Ok, I'll set up a time when you can go see him. How about tomorrow night?"

I nod vigorously and throw my arms around Mason's neck. "Thank you," I say, tightening my hold on him.

"You're welcome," he wraps his arms around me, and I hear him breathe deeply while his face is buried against my neck.

"Are you smelling my hair?" I ask, trying to think when I last washed it.

Mason chuckles. "Yes," he admits, sounding like I caught him doing something he maybe shouldn't.

"That's ok," I reassure him, taking a whiff of my own against his neck. "I like the way you smell, too."

"What do I smell like to you?"

"It's kind of woody, with a hint of cinnamon."

"Must be the soap I buy from Malik and Tara's company."

"I love it," I say, allowing myself the pleasure of drenching my sense of smell with him.

Mason pulls away from me. "I love you."

I smile. "I love you, too."

I see his eyes drop to my lips before he leans into me.

"I also love the way you taste," he says, gently pressing his lips against mine in a chaste kiss.

"You're quite delicious yourself," I reply, leaning in to deepen the kiss, but Mason pulls away.

I know I look confused, because I am confused.

"What's wrong?" I ask.

"We need to talk about something before we go any further."

"Ok," I say, suddenly concerned this conversation might be going in a direction I won't like.

"While you were getting JoJo's talisman, we were watching the satellite feed back at headquarters."

I still feel like I'm in the dark. "And?"

"Why can you talk to Chandler so easily about things, and not me?"

I see the hurt on Mason's face, and instantly know he overheard my discussion with Chandler about why making love might be difficult for me.

"How much of our conversation did you hear?" I ask.

"I had Joshua switch the audio off when Chandler asked if you couldn't or wouldn't go past just kissing. It didn't feel right to listen in on what was meant to be a private conversation between the two of you."

I sit back on the couch. I should have known they would be watching us back at headquarters, and I make a mental note to myself to be more cautious about what I say from now on when I'm within range of the Watcher spy satellites.

"It's not that I can talk to Chandler more easily than I can you. He's become a sounding board for me about you. I appreciate his advice on certain things, that's all."

"Would you tell me what your answer was to his question?"

I look at Mason, and see that he's listening intently for my next words.

"I want to go past just kissing," I say. "I want you so badly my body aches, to the point where it's unbearable. But I can't make love with you yet. Even though every tiny cell in my body wants nothing more, I'm just not mentally there yet."

"It would be nothing like what you experienced before," Mason says softly. "That much I can promise you."

"But can you promise me I wouldn't flinch away or even try to run away from you when you touch me? I can't make that type of promise to you. I don't want to hurt you like that. I don't want you to think I don't want you, when I do."

"Then, we'll take it slow," Mason says. "We can try to push the boundaries when it feels right, and see where it leads us. If I touch you in a way that makes you feel uncomfortable, just tell me to stop. That's all you have to say, Jess. Say stop, and I will. And you won't hurt my feelings if you flinch, because I know how hard it is for you. I know what you've been through. There's nothing in this world you could do that would really hurt me, except leave me."

"Well, there's no way in hell I'm ever leaving you," I profess, which garners a pleased and relieved smile from Mason.

"You and that smile," I say, roughly pushing Mason back onto the couch with both my hands, and lying on top of him. "It's always getting you into trouble, Mr. Collier."

Mason's smile widens. "I like being in trouble with you; leads to interesting punishments."

"Hmm," I say primly, tracing the edge of Mason's jaw with my index finger, running it slowly down the center of his neck until I reach the small bit of chest revealed by the V-opening of his white button-down shirt. "I can see you're going to be a handful, Mr. Collier."

"Maybe even two," Mason says, taunting me with his maddening, cheeky grin and mischievous eyes.

I reach up and begin to trace the outline of his lips with my finger.

"Insubordination will only get you one thing," I murmur, feeling Mason's warm, quick breaths against the tip of my finger, telling me he's almost to his breaking point.

"And what's that?" he asks, almost as a groan.

I move closer until our eyes are level with one another.

"Submission by kissing," I say, pressing my lips lightly against his.

"I can live with that," he replies as I continue to barely touch his lips with mine.

With a groan built out of frustration, Mason grabs me by the upper arms and deftly positions me under him, instead of on top. He plunges his hands into my hair on either side of my head, and plunders my mouth with his tongue in a kiss that literally takes my breath away. Mason moves his body down onto mine, and I know the hardness I feel against my thigh isn't his phone this time. The realization that I can arouse him in such a short amount of time makes me feel powerful and desired. I feel him wedge the leg he has near the inside of the couch in such a way that lifts the proof of his arousal so it isn't resting against my leg anymore.

I break the kiss.

"What are you doing?" I ask, taking the opportunity to catch my breath.

With blazing heat in his eyes, he leans down to continue the kiss while saying, "Kissing you."

I bring my hands up to his face to stop him.

"No, I mean with your leg," I say.

"I didn't want to make you uncomfortable," he says hesitantly. "It's not exactly a part of my body I can control, Jess."

"It wasn't making me uncomfortable," I tell him. I grin. "Especially now that I know it isn't a phone."

The heat of desire in Mason's eyes intensifies, and his lips descend against mine like he's laying claim to me, possessing me. I feel him slowly lower his body back down on top of mine, and I smile against his lips at the feel of him against me. I run my fingers through the hair at the back of his head, content to keep him there forever. After a while, I feel him gently begin to move his hips against mine. The feel of him makes my body ache to accept what he has to offer, but the warning signal blaring inside my head over- rules everything else.

"Stop."

Mason pulls away immediately. He gets off me and kneels beside the couch.

"I'm sorry," he says, breathing heavily.

I shake my head. "Please don't be." I reach out and cup the side of his face with my hand. "You didn't do anything wrong."

"I should have had better control."

"I'm glad you lose control when you're with me," I tell him. "It makes me feel like the most desirable woman in the world when you do."

Mason takes the hand I have on his face and brings it to his lips to kiss the palm.

"You are undoubtedly the most desirable woman I have ever met," he proclaims, making me smile.

He kisses the inside of my hand one more time before standing up and pulling me to my feet.

"But, I need to take you home now," he says. "I need a few minutes without you around."

I nod, understanding that his request isn't meant to hurt me but protect me.

Mason phases me to my house and gives me a tender kiss.

"I'll be back soon."

After Mason phases, I sit down heavily on my couch. My phone buzzes, and I fish it out of my front pants pocket. It's Faison.

"Hey, you back home yet?" she asks me.

"Your timing couldn't be more perfect. I just got back. What's up?"

"I found some pictures of bridesmaid dresses that I like, but can't figure out which one I like best. Can Mama Lynn and I come over? I want your opinion, since you'll have to wear it."

"Sure. Come on over. I'm alone."

"Why isn't Mason there with you?"

"He had to tend to something," I say, hoping I sound vague enough for Faison to not delve any further into the subject.

"Attend to what?" she asks, and I can tell she's suspicious.

"Had to take a shower I think."

Faison is quiet for a few seconds before saying, "Be right over."

I end the call and brace myself for the interrogator I feel sure is walking to my doorstep.

CHAPTER TWELVE

Surprisingly, Faison doesn't try to interrogate me right away. She waits a good five minutes before setting in.

"So, a shower… in the middle of the day, huh?"

I look at her and Mama Lynn, knowing they've already discussed why Mason would need a shower before it was even dark outside.

"It's not the middle of the day; it's almost suppertime," I say, avoiding direct eye-contact with either one of them as I stare at a crack in the table.

"Hmm," Faison says knowingly, not easily thrown off the scent now that she smells blood. "Sounds like someone might have taken my advice, and is working her way onto the naughty list this year."

I stare at Faison, not believing she just said that to me.

"Any help here?" I beseech Mama Lynn.

Mama Lynn smiles. "Jess, you know we just like seeing you happy, and being with Mason makes you happy. Everyone around the two of you can see that."

"We aren't disgustingly lovey-dovey, like Faison and John Austin, are we?"

"I take offense at that question," Faison says, but with a smile because she knows I'm right.

"Not quite that bad," Mama Lynn concedes, "but it's there, plain as day. Now, have you talked about getting married yet?"

I rest my forehead on the table. Dear Lord, did I really want to meet my blood kin? Would my grandfather torture me as much as Faison and Mama Lynn about my personal life? If my grandfather is a nosey body too, I feel sure I won't survive my family. As it is, I know Mama Lynn and Faison won't stop bugging me until Mason and I are married, with two children. That might not even be enough. I'm not completely sure.

I raise my head and stare at their expectant faces.

"No, we have not talked about marriage. We just really started dating. I don't think we're at a point where we need to talk about marrying each other yet."

"Why not?" they ask in unison.

"Because I'm not ready yet!" I say, and immediately regret yelling at them. "I'm sorry. I didn't mean to yell, but you guys have got to stop harping on the marriage thing. It is not happening anytime soon."

Faison sighs, "And here I was hoping we could have a double ceremony."

She pouts, which brings out a reluctant smile on my part because she looks like a petulant child.

"Listen, you'll be the first person I tell if and when Mason and I decide to tie the knot."

"Tie what knot?"

I look up, and see Mason standing against the entryway between the kitchen and living room. His hair still looks wet from his shower.

"A boat knot," I say, refusing to give him the satisfaction of answering a question I feel sure he already knows the answer to.

"I have a boat," he tells me, grinning slyly. "A yacht, actually."

"Ooh, could we go out in it one day?" Faison says, thankfully filled with a new purpose.

"Sure, name the day," Mason tells her.

"I'll get back to you on that," she promises.

"I'm going to go read my book while you ladies talk," Mason tells me, a slow, suggestive smile spreading his lips. "Let me know if you need any knots tied. I'm pretty dexterous with my fingers."

I stare after him as he leaves, completely flabbergasted that he made a sexual innuendo in front of my family. Or had my mind just so completely become obsessed with sex that I was taking everything he said as meaning something naughty? When I look back at Faison and Mama Lynn, I know he did just do what I thought.

Faison starts to giggle. Mama Lynn just lifts one of her eyebrows at me.

"Show me the dresses," I tell Faison, desperately needing something to take my mind off the devastatingly-handsome man waiting for me in my living room.

I spend a good thirty minutes with Faison and Mama Lynn, discussing dresses. We finally all agree on one, and they gather their things to leave.

"Can you and Mason come over for dinner tomorrow night?" Mama Lynn asks.

"No," I say hesitantly, not sure if I want to tell Mama Lynn the reason, but I don't want to keep her in the dark either. "I'm actually supposed to meet my grandfather tomorrow night."

Mama Lynn stops stacking the magazines in front of her, and looks up at me.

"Your grandfather?"

"Mason found my biological father's father. I'm supposed to go to his house and meet him."

"Oh," Mama Lynn takes a deep breath, "I see."

Worry creases Mama Lynn's brow as she finishes stacking the magazines. "Well, I guess that will be good for you. You'll finally get to see where you come from."

"Yeah," I agree, but don't elaborate on how excited I am about the meeting. I don't want to give the impression that I feel like my life thus far has been lacking in any way.

"I love you," I tell her.

Mama Lynn smiles wanly. "Oh, I know that, Jess; I just didn't realize you had any family out there."

"Me neither," I admit, "but, apparently, I have a grandfather."

"Well, maybe we can all get together one day," Mama Lynn suggests. "I would like to meet him too."

I smile. "Let me make sure I like him first, then we can decide if we want him in our family or not."

Mama Lynn smiles too. "Ok, Jess."

After they leave, I flop onto the couch by Mason, and he puts his book on the coffee table.

"Everything all right?"

"Yes."

"Do you need to talk about it?"

"No."

"Would you like to continue what we were doing at the villa?"

I look over at him and notice his hair is still slightly damp. It makes me smile.

"How many cold showers can you take a day?"

He brings me into his arms. "As many as necessary."

"You'll turn into a prune," I argue weakly.

"It'll be worth it."

Before Mason can kiss me, I see Isaiah and Chandler phase in behind the couch. I instantly get to my feet, not wanting the two of them to think all Mason and I do is make out.

"How's JoJo?" I ask them, straightening out my shirt.

"She's sleeping," Chandler answers, "which made me think of something."

"What?"

"If we're going to go get my talisman tomorrow, I'm going to be asleep for at least two days, right?"

"More than likely; that's what happened to me."

"Then I need your help hiding what's happening."

"What do you mean?"

"I have fans, some of them rabid. If I disappear off the face of the planet for two whole days, they're going to start asking questions."

Mason stands and turns to face Chandler. "What's your plan?"

"Well, the tabloids already think I have a thing going on with Jess. I was thinking she and I could go out to a public place tonight, and hop on a private plane to make it look like we're going somewhere secluded for some alone time. That way no one, including my agent, will wonder where I am. If I just disappear, there will be questions."

Mason sighs and looks at me. "He's right; there would be too many questions. It might look suspicious."

"Ok, so we go eat and pretend to get on a plane," I say with a shrug. "Sounds easy enough."

"Cool," Chandler smiles a smile I'm sure would melt the heart of many a teenage girl. "Let me call Deon so she can spruce you up a little."

"Seriously?" I ask, becoming completely exasperated. "Why does everyone think I need help getting ready for things? You guys make me feel like I need to hire a permanent stylist or something, because I obviously can't dress myself, put on makeup or fix my hair!"

The men in the room become deathly silent and still at my tirade. With a huff, I turn on my heels, leaving them in my wake.

"I will get myself ready," I inform Chandler. "No need to call your makeover squad."

I go to my bedroom and slam the door.

Mason quickly appears, standing by my bed.

"What?" I snap at him.

"I hate to admit it, but you completely turned me on back there."

I cross my arms, not in the mood to satisfy the need I see in his eyes.

And then he smiles at me, and my ire disintegrates into a pile of dust, against my better judgment.

"I just get tired of being treated like I can't make myself presentable. It's a little insulting."

Mason walks over to me and takes me in his arms. "You would look beautiful even if you were completely naked, without makeup and your hair freshly washed." Mason sighs. "Please promise me I'll be able to see you like that one day, because the picture I have in my mind just isn't enough."

I roll my eyes at him and drape my arms over his shoulders.

"Hopelessly incorrigible," I say before kissing him.

Once Mason finally leaves my room, I go take a shower and get myself ready for my pretend date with Chandler. I put my hair in hot rollers, but wear it down like I promised Mason I would from now on. The soft curls bounce when I move, and it makes me wonder how JoJo is fairing with her archangel.

I decide to dress in comfortable clothing because I'm getting tired of looking so dolled up all the time. Surely, for a simple supper, I don't have to look like a movie star who just stepped off a Hollywood set.

I decide to wear a sleeveless, off-white, cowl-neck sweater dress with ribbed detailing around the waist and hem. I also pick out a herringbone moto jacket with an asymmetrical zippered front, over-sized notched collar, zippered front pockets, and small adjustable belt around the waist. I grab a pair of gray suede slouchy calf boots with wrap-around self-tie straps. Around my neck, I loosely tie a peach and lavender scarf.

When I look at myself in the full-length mirror, I think I look like the epitome of a rock star's girlfriend. Who needs a stylist?

I spray a little perfume on my neck and wrists and walk out of my bedroom to find my 'date'.

When I step into the living room, the men are standing around talking. Mason is the one who sees me first. His appreciative smile tells me I must have done a better than average job of getting myself ready for my faux date with Chandler.

Chandler turns around and whistles a soft catcall. "Looking wicked cool, Jess; I sure am a lucky man."

"Just remember whose girlfriend she actually is," Mason warns Chandler, in a tone that is all at once commanding and menacing.

"Yeah, yeah," Chandler says off-handedly, "you've made that perfectly clear a few times already."

I walk up to Mason and put one arm around his waist as I stand beside him.

"So, where are you taking me for supper?" I ask Chandler, attempting to break the tension that has built between the two men.

"I thought we would go to Nobu. Should be a lot of paparazzi outside it; always is. It's a popular place with the A-list crowd in New York."

I turn my attention to Mason who continues to scowl at Chandler, as if just his glare will insure that my impudent little rock star friend will behave tonight.

"Hey," I say, squeezing Mason around his waist to gain his attention.

Almost reluctantly, Mason slides his eyes from Chandler to look at me. I can feel how tense his body is.

"Will you be here when I get back?" I ask.

"Yes," Mason slides his eyes back to Chandler. "I'll be here waiting for your safe return."

"You know where Nobu is, right?" Chandler asks Isaiah, obviously ready to get out from under Mason's intense scrutiny.

"Yes," Isaiah answers.

Mason kisses me lightly on the lips.

"Come back to me," he whispers.

I smile, a little confused by his statement.

"Always," I reassure him.

Isaiah places his hand on Chandler's shoulders and mine. Just before we phase, I wink at Mason. He smiles, and I know he'll be all right until I make it back home.

CHAPTER THIRTEEN

Chandler and I are seated almost immediately when we reach the restaurant. The architecture inside makes you feel like you've stepped into a modernistic take of a Japanese countryside. We are seated in a private corner behind a line of birch tree trunks with strips of wood planks attached to their tops, meant to mimic tree limbs as they reach up towards the ceiling. Our chairs scrape against the dark wood floors as we sit down next to a wall made of river stones.

"Do you eat here a lot?" I ask Chandler, noticing a few celebrities from movies and TV shows scattered around the room, enjoying their meals.

"Every once in a while," Chandler says, unaffected by the room full of celebrities as he considers the menu. "Especially when my agent thinks I need to be in the public eye a little more."

I look at the menu, having a hard time deciding what to eat. I finally settle on a bowl of miso soup and the Colorado lamb chops with balsamic teriyaki. Chandler decides to get the tenderloin of beef with pepper sauce.

While we wait for our meal, I study the crowd around us and feel myself go into Watcher-agent mode, looking for any troublemakers. I see a few tearers scattered around the restaurant, but none of them seem to present a threat of any sort.

I feel Chandler staring at me and look over at him.

"What?" I ask, wondering why he's looking at me so intently.

"How are you so sure Mason is the one for you?" he finally asks me.

"Should we really be talking about this here?" I ask out of the side of my mouth, glancing quickly around us for anyone listening.

"No one's going to overhear us," Chandler assures me. "How do you know?"

"Because he makes me feel special, like I'm not as screwed up as I think I am. It's hard to explain." I pause for a minute to gather my thoughts. "My heart feels on fire every time we're together. He's a part of my soul now. I can't live without him. I wouldn't know how to, nor do I even want to anymore."

Chandler lifts his eyebrows as he contemplates what I've said. "How do you know there isn't someone else who could make you feel the same way?"

"That would be impossible."

"But you don't know for sure, do you? You'd have to open yourself up to someone else to find out."

"I have no desire to try."

Chandler shifts in his seat and puts his elbows on the table to lean towards me. "I don't think you'll know for sure Mason's the only man for you unless you do. He's the only man you've kissed, so how do you know it's as special as you think it is? You have nothing to compare it to."

"I don't need a comparison," I say, becoming irritated. "What's up with you tonight? Why are you questioning me so hard about Mason?"

Chandler shrugs nonchalantly and sits back in his chair.

"I just think you owe it to yourself to make sure he's the one for you. He's your first real boyfriend, Jess. I don't think you've had enough experience to know for sure he's the one you're supposed to be with."

Our food comes, providing a good excuse to cut the conversation short.

I eat silently, not bothering to attempt to make small talk while we eat. What is up with Chandler? He's usually so supportive of my relationship with Mason. His odd behavior makes me suspicious.

After supper, we make our way out of the restaurant. Chandler casually puts his arm around my shoulders before we go outside to be photographed by the paparazzi.

"Ready?" he asks me, his rock star smile at the ready.

"Ready as I'll ever be, I guess." I take a deep breath to prepare myself for what's about to happen.

As soon as we step outside, a multitude of camera flashes go off in my face. Instinctively, I try to shield my eyes with one of my hands. Chandler gently grabs my hand and pulls it down, because the whole point of us doing this is so the tabloids know we're together. Chandler stops to talk to one of the reporters asking him questions.

"So what are you guys planning to do next?" the woman asks.

"Taking my sweetie to a private island, to get her away from all this for a few days," Chandler says good-naturedly.

"Care to share where this island is?" the reporter asks. I can practically see her salivating over getting an exclusive from Chandler about our romantic getaway plans.

Chandler laughs, "You and I both know, if I did that it wouldn't be private anymore."

One of the many nameless photographers milling about shouts, "Give us the money shot, Chandler!"

Chandler looks down at me, as if he's contemplating the photographer's request. I have no idea what the money shot could be, but, by the look in Chandler's eyes, I have a feeling it's not something I'm going to like.

Before I know it, Chandler has his arms wrapped around me, and his mouth is covering mine. At first, I'm too shocked to react, but when I feel him attempt to push his tongue between my lips, I roughly push him away. I don't care that the photographers are snapping wildly at my reaction to the kiss, because all I can think about is getting into the limo that is waiting for us at the curb. Otherwise, the headline for tomorrow's paper will be *Chandler Cain Murdered by Watcher Agent Girlfriend.*

As I storm towards the limo, the chauffer instantly opens the door for me. I crawl inside it and see Isaiah sitting there, directly opposite the backseat to accompany us back to the airport.

"I need some time alone with him," I say to Isaiah, desperately trying to control my temper. "Can you meet us at the airport?"

Isaiah nods but doesn't seem pleased by my request. I feel sure he just witnessed what Chandler did, because of the storm brewing in his eyes.

"I'll meet you there," he promises and phases away.

Chandler gets into the limo and the chauffer closes the door behind him. Neither of us says a word. I don't even look his way. When I feel like we're a safe distance from the prying lenses of the paparazzi, I turn to Chandler, and slap him so hard against his right cheek the palm of my hand stings from the contact.

"Geez, Jess!" Chandler cries out, cradling his cheek.

I point my index finger at him and say, "Don't you dare say it was just a kiss. I thought you were my friend! You don't do something like that to your friends!"

I feel the hot sting of tears burn my eyes and do nothing to prevent them from falling. I want Chandler to know how much he's hurt me.

"You know what I went through as a child," I say through my tears, taking a deep breath. "How could you act like him, and force yourself on me like that?"

I watch as my words slice through Chandler's heart, causing more pain to surface in his eyes than my slap did.

"Oh, God, Jess," Chandler says, his eyes wide with the horror of what he's done. "I didn't even think about it like that. I'm so sorry."

He looks contrite, but I'm not sure it's enough to make me forgive him.

"Why?" I ask, begging for an answer.

Chandler's head falls back against the top of the seat, like he's suddenly lost all the energy from his body. He closes his eyes and shakes his head slowly from side to side.

"I had to know," he whispers.

"Had to know what?" I ask just as softly.

He lifts his head and looks at me. "Ever since we met, I've felt more connected to you than anybody I've ever met before in my life. I know we've been chalking up our instant closeness to the archangel thing, but part of me had to know if it was more than that, especially after we met JoJo. I just don't feel the same connection with her that I do with you. This is the closest I've ever felt to being in love with someone, Jess. I had to know if I had a chance to make you want me too."

I wipe the tears from my face. "Is that why you were asking me so many questions about Mason? Were you trying to plant doubt to see if you had a chance with me?"

Chandler nods. "I never meant to hurt you. I just did something stupid. When that photographer asked me to give him the money shot, I knew what he wanted. I used it as an excuse to kiss you. I needed to know what it felt like."

"And what did you feel?"

"Honestly?" Chandler says, looking completely abashed. "It felt like I was kissing my mom."

I stare at Chandler for a little while before asking, "And how often do you try to stick your tongue in your mother's mouth?"

My question makes Chandler shiver in disgust, and I can't help but laugh a little, relieving some of my tension.

"Never," he reassures me. "Don't take this the wrong way, but it was probably the worst kiss of my life. It felt so wrong on *so* many levels."

I take a steadying breath. "That's because it *was* wrong on so many levels, Chandler."

"I know. I was an idiot. Please say you can forgive me," he begs desperately. "If you can't, I'll just tell the driver to take me straight to the Brooklyn Bridge so I can jump off of it, because I can't live without your friendship, Jess. I need you. Now I know what I feel for you isn't romantic love, just friendship love. I just suck at telling the difference."

I sit back next to Chandler and take his hand in mine. "I'll forgive you this one time. But one chance is all you get with me, Chandler. Don't screw up again."

Chandler sandwiches my hand between his.

"I promise," he solemnly swears. "I won't act like such a stupid imbecile again. I can't lose your friendship. You and JoJo are the only real friends I feel like I have in this world."

"No," I say to him, "you have at least four more."

Isaiah is waiting for us at the airport, as promised. Chandler is the first to exit the limo, and receives a scathing look from Isaiah. If I know Isaiah at all, I feel sure he used his time away from us to inform Mason about what transpired outside of Nobu.

When I get out of the limo, I see more photographers on the tarmac, awaiting our arrival.

"Ok, I know I don't have the right to ask," Chandler says to me, "but could you please act like you're head-over-heels in love with me for the next few minutes? Just give them something to shoot. They need to think you've forgiven me for what happened back at Nobu, and that we're jetting off for a romantic getaway for a few days."

I lift an eyebrow at him. "No kissing."

He raises his right hand, like he's about to make an oath. "I swear, no kissing. But we should probably at least hold hands."

"Ok."

As we walk up to the private jet waiting for us, I see at least five photographers there, with cameras at the ready.

"How do you live like this?" I ask. "They're always following you around."

Chandler shrugs. "Comes with the price of fame. I enjoy having people hear my music too much to trade it all in because of a little lost privacy. Besides, if you're ashamed of what you do in public, maybe you shouldn't be doing it."

While the photographers are busy taking our picture, Isaiah quickly slips into the private jet unnoticed. Chandler and I hold hands, and he doesn't try to do anything else, even though one of the photographers does ask us to kiss for him.

"Already got in trouble for doing that in public once tonight," Chandler jokes to the man. "Don't get me in trouble a second time."

Chandler's attempt at damage control to cover up my reaction to his kiss seems to work. The photographers just laugh, and follow us until we're safely on board the plane.

As soon as we're in the air, Isaiah phases us back to my house.

The first thing I see is Mason's scowling face.

"Enjoy your evening?" he pointedly asks Chandler, his voice so low and menacing I suddenly fear for Chandler's life.

"Take Chandler home," I tell Isaiah, my request sounding more like an order.

Isaiah doesn't hesitate as he grabs Chandler's arm.

"Wait…" Chandler says, but doesn't have a chance to say any more before Isaiah phases him a safe distance away from Mason's wrath.

Mason's eyebrows lower, which just deepens his scowl and makes him look far too sexy in his jealousy. "You *do* realize I know where he lives."

"Yes, I know," I say, unbuckling the belt on my jacket. Mason's eyes follow the movement of my hands, "but you need to calm down before you talk to him again."

"I am calm," Mason says through clenched teeth, his eyes rising to meet mine. "Otherwise, I would owe you money to repair a hole in your wall."

I slowly undo the buttons on my jacket and watch Mason's eyes follow the movement of my hands again.

"He made a mistake," I say, letting the front of my jacket peek open while unwinding the scarf from around my neck. I lay the scarf on the back of the couch in front of me and begin to slowly remove my jacket.

Mason silently watches me, but I can see his anger quickly being replaced by something far less destructive. I walk over to him and wrap my arms around his waist, looking him straight in the eyes.

"You didn't say how you liked my outfit," I tell him.

He reaches up and slides his right hand around my neck until his fingers are in my hair.

"You look beautiful," he replies, his voice now hoarse with desire, not anger. "You always look beautiful, Jess. And I know what you're doing."

I don't even bother trying to pretend I'm at all innocent in my actions.

"Is it working?" I ask, lowering my eyelashes as coquettishly as I can.

Mason uses the hand at the nape of my neck to gently grab a fistful of my hair and tilt my head back, to make me look into his eyes.

"You know it is," he replies, his gaze sliding from my eyes to my lips, which are parted and desperately waiting for him to kiss me.

Abruptly, he lets me go and turns his back to me as he walks a few steps away.

"Was your reaction to the kiss genuine?" he asks, his back still to me. "Did you really not enjoy it?"

"It was awful for both of us," I tell him, not having to exaggerate. "He knows it was wrong to do."

Mason turns to face me. "Then why did he do it?"

"He needed to know if what he feels for me translated into romantic love. He knows now that it doesn't. We can never be more than good friends. I think he just had to prove it to himself. Trust me; he knew how upset I was with him for doing it. My hand still hurts a bit from making that point crystal clear."

This pulls a reluctant half-smile from Mason. He walks back over to me and lifts the hand I used to slap Chandler.

"This hand?" Mason asks, rubbing his thumb softly across the top of my fingers.

I nod, watching to see what he plans to do next.

Mason lifts the hand to his lips and plants a small kiss on the back of it. Not stopping there, he slowly begins to plant all-too-brief kisses up my arm, making me instantly thankful I wore a sleeveless dress. He doesn't stop his slow torture against my skin until he reaches my shoulder.

He gently sweeps my hair off my shoulder, to my back, and pulls down the side of the cowl neck of my sweater dress to expose my neck for further exploration. He continues the slow assault with his lips, causing my heart to race into my throat. I lean my head to the side slightly to give him complete access to my flesh. He works his way up to that newly-discovered sensitive spot I have right behind my ear, causing me to take in a sharp breath.

He travels from that spot and whispers in my ear, "I don't want any man but me to ever kiss you."

I nod in full agreement, but don't feel like I can voice my acquiescence because I'm having a hard enough time just trying to breathe during Mason's slow seduction.

"Only me, Jess," he says, before languidly making his way back down my neck.

"Mason, please," I finally manage to strangle out.

"Please what?" he asks against my neck, sounding content to continue his slow torture of my body.

"Please don't make me beg," I ask, even though the request ends up sounding like I'm begging him anyway.

Mason lifts his head and looks at me. The smoldering heat within the depths of his eyes lights every nerve in my body on fire.

"You never have to beg me to kiss you," he tells me, leaning in and planting a soft, much too brief kiss against my lips. "You have all the control here, Jess. Whatever you want, whatever you need of me, all you have to do is say it, and it's yours. I'm yours."

My heart feels like it's about to beat out of my chest. His words leave me breathless. I instantly decide I want to try whatever it takes to break through my mental barrier about making love to the man in front of me. I know there's no one in this world or any of the countless other worlds in the universe who can make me feel the way I do, standing in front of him now. Every inch of my body is crying out for his touch.

I take his hand and tug, silently telling him I want him to follow me.

I head towards my bedroom

Mason stops but keeps hold of my hand, forcing me to stop too.

"Jess?" he asks.

I look back at him. His real question is written plainly on his face.

"I can't make any promises," I tell him, wanting to be completely truthful, "but I want you. I don't want you just to be the only man I ever kiss. I want you to become the only man I ever make love to. And I can't have that unless we try. So, I say again, I can't make any promises. I don't know how far this will go tonight, but never have any doubt that I want you."

"I will stop whenever you need me to," Mason vows, and I have no doubt in my mind he'll do whatever I ask of him.

"Am I being selfish," I ask, "to just expect you stop whenever I say to?"

"No," he says firmly. "If anything, I'm the one being selfish, letting you take me to your bed when I'm almost positive you're not ready for this yet."

I shake my head. "Don't say that. Don't even think it. I'm the one in control, remember? And I want you in my bed, even if it's only for sleeping or reading a book or watching a movie. It feels empty without you in it now. I never thought I would feel that way, but you make me want things I never thought I would. I want you in my bed, Mason Collier. You're the only one I'll ever want lying beside me."

I tug on Mason's hand, and he doesn't resist this time.

Once we reach my bed, I turn to face Mason, not sure what to do next. Thankfully, I don't have to make the decision.

Mason sits on the side of the bed and slips off his shoes. I sit beside him and take my boots off as well. The act is simple, something you do every day, but, in this situation, the small act of taking off our shoes together holds open a door of endless possibilities.

Mason stands up, and I start to wonder if he's planning to leave. He turns on the lamp and walks toward the door to flip the switch that controls the ceiling light to turn it off. The dimmed lighting makes the moment feel softer, more intimate. When he walks back over to stand in front of me, I look up at him expectantly.

He leans into me, pressing his lips against mine, gently at first, and then becomes more demanding. Eventually, I lean back on the bed, weakened by his kisses, and he follows. He lies half on me and half on the bed, that way, I'm not supporting his full weight. His lips never lose contact with mine as his tongue continues to plunder my mouth, testing my limits.

I feel his right hand come to rest on my stomach. Never breaking the kiss, Mason's hand slowly slides down to my side and moves up until it's cupping the side of my breast. I feel myself tense slightly. Mason doesn't move his hand from its spot for a long time, seeming content to just kiss me and give me time to get used to the intimate contact.

Once I relax again, Mason's hand moves back down my side, to my hip, and stops there for a while, just holding me. After a few minutes, I feel his hand on my bare leg, just below where the dress cuts off at mid-thigh. He slides his hand up the outside of my thigh, underneath the dress, and back up to the side of my hip. It's only when he tries to move his hand toward my inner thigh that I feel an irrational panic set in, causing a deep, unwanted memory of another time someone touched me there to surface.

I break our kiss and say, "Stop."

Mason immediately withdraws his hand from underneath my dress, and wraps his arms around me to cradle me close to his body.

"I'm sorry," I say, feeling tears born of frustration and disappointment in myself burn my eyes.

"Shh," Mason says, holding me to him, attempting to lend me his strength. "Please don't cry. I die a little inside every time I see you cry."

This sweet declaration only makes me sob harder.

Mason holds me to him and gently starts to rock me. He begins to hum a tune I instantly recognize. The orchestra played the same song when Mason taught me how to dance. It brings back the memory of how gentle and patient Mason was with me that night. He allowed me to learn at my own pace. I realize he's doing the same thing now, by letting me adjust to the newness of our intimacy, not pushing me to do things I'm not ready for yet.

Once I'm able to pull myself together, I look at Mason, and only see concern in his eyes, not the disappointment I feared might be there.

"We'll get there," he promises, as if sensing I'm about to apologize to him again. "I'm in no rush, Jess. I've waited my entire life for you, and I'll wait for as long as you need me to. When we make love, I want it to be a memory you cherish forever, not one you look back on as a mistake, something you forced yourself to do for my benefit. You are the only person important in this equation. I'm just the lucky man who gets to help you find your way there."

I start to cry again.

"Jess, please don't cry," he begs, holding me to him. "I didn't say that to make you start crying again."

"I know. It's just…how can you be so perfect?" I practically whine.

I feel him chuckle at my question. "Only you think I'm perfect, so I won't complain about you seeing me that way."

I finally stop crying, and just lay there with Mason to catch my breath.

"Do you need to go take a cold shower?" I ask, realizing Mason may be having a hard time physically.

"No," he says, holding me closer, "your tears seem to have the same effect as a shower."

"Guess I'll just have to remember to burst into tears every time I tell you to stop."

Mason chuckles harder. "Please, don't do that on my account. I meant what I said. I die a little every time I see you cry. It hurts me to see you so sad."

We're silent for a while before I ask, "Stay with me tonight? I don't want you to go."

Mason kisses me softly on the lips. "Your wish is my command."

CHAPTER FOURTEEN

When I wake up the next morning, I hear the water in my bathroom turn off, and know Mason has just taken a shower. The idea of such an intimate sharing of space makes me smile. I'm happy he feels comfortable enough in my home to move around like it's his too.

I roll over and grab his pillow from the other side of the bed, hugging it to me. Inhaling deeply, I briefly wonder if the euphoria I feel from just breathing in Mason's scent is similar to how cats feel when they get a whiff of catnip. The idea of Mason being my catnip makes me giggle.

"What's so funny?"

I roll back over and see a half-naked Mason standing in the doorway of my bathroom, using one of my monogrammed white towels to dry his hair. He's shirtless and barefoot, only wearing a pair of black slacks. I feel my heart begin to race at the sight of him and sit straight up, continuing to hug the pillow to keep my world from reeling out of control. My breathing becomes shallow, and I have to remind myself to swallow before I start drooling all over his pillow. Clothed, Mason is irresistible but half-naked, his effect on me overpowers all of my senses, making it virtually impossible for me to even think straight, much less form a coherent sentence to answer his question.

He walks over to my side of the bed and sits down, still rubbing the towel against his wet hair to dry it, patiently waiting for my answer.

What the question was has totally escaped my mind, because all I can think about is him.

I let my eyes freely roam over his tightly-toned muscles and silky-smooth skin. Tentatively, I place an open palm on his chest, feeling the steady beat of his heart. He stops drying his hair and rests his hands on his lap, silently giving me permission to continue my exploration.

I swallow hard as I slowly sweep my hand down his taut chest to his well-defined abdominal muscles. I hear him take a sharp breath, and force my eyes to look up at his face. He's watching me with an intense gaze.

"Is this all right?" I ask, knowing he's allowing me free access to his body, even though I haven't been able to give him the same liberty with my own.

"I'm yours," he says, "mind, soul and body. You can do anything you want to me."

I smile and run my hand back up his torso.

"Are all angels this perfect?" I ask, marveling at his beauty.

"I'm not perfect, Jess."

I look back at his face and know he's still dwelling on his scar, something I've all but forgotten about.

I reach up and let the tips of my fingers trace the outline of the scar, wishing there was some way I could help heal his ancient wound.

"You're perfect to me," I tell him, and know my words might please him, but he'll never truly believe them until he's able to forgive himself.

I lift my hand from his face and hug his pillow tighter to me. As much as I would like to continue my exploration of Mason's body, I know now isn't the time. We have work to do, and if I don't stop now, I never will.

"Are we going to go get Chandler's talisman today?" I ask.

With the mention of Chandler, I see Mason's face darken. "Yes, we'll go get the boy his toy today."

Mason stands up swiftly, and I know he's still agitated over Chandler's antics from the night before.

"Could you find a way to not be mad at him," I ask, "for my sake?"

Mason walks over to a chair by the bay window and retrieves a dark gray button- down shirt lying across it. He slides his arms into the long sleeves, but doesn't button it up immediately. I find myself completely distracted by the sight of his body peeking out from the shirt opening, and realize I'm completely and hopelessly in love with the man scowling before me.

"In time," he replies, drawing me back from my appreciative ogling of his person.

"I'm sorry," I say. "Seeing you like that completely made me forget what we were talking about."

The scowl on Mason's face disappears to be replaced by a boyish grin, which completely scrambles any functioning brain cells I have left.

"In time," he continues in an amused voice instead of an angry one, "I will probably forgive Chandler for what he did. But don't begrudge me my disappointment in him. I need for him to know such behavior won't be tolerated, which is why I'm going to go have a talk with him while you get ready."

"Maybe I should go with you," I suggest, remembering Mason saying something the night before about holes in walls.

"No," Mason shakes his head resolutely, and I know there will be no argument I can make that will change his mind. "He and I need to have a talk, man to man. If what you told me last night is truly the way he feels about you, I'll know."

"Oh, yeah, I always forget you're a walking lie-detector," I say, remembering Mason telling me that was a gift of the Watchers who never drank human blood. "Then I have nothing to worry about." I shrug my shoulders, truly not feeling worried at all. "Maybe it's best if you hear it from him yourself; then you won't have any doubts."

Mason begins buttoning his shirt, and I sigh in disappointment. He obviously hears me, because his smile grows wider. I don't mind if he heard me. If it makes him smile like that, I don't care. I want him to know how much he affects me. I need him to know how much I desire him, because my body won't fully let me show him.

I rest my chin on top of the pillow and wonder how long it will take me to finally find release in his arms. My body feels like a wire pulled to its limit. The need I feel to finally consummate physically what my heart feels for Mason is almost overwhelming. It's the first time I feel like praying to a higher power to help me work through my issues quickly.

God's never played a key role in my life until recently. To be honest, I'm still having trouble believing in Him fully. To place my trust in Him to answer my prayer seems like a completely foreign concept.

Mason leans down and kisses my forehead.

"I won't be long," he promises. "I'll know pretty quickly how Chandler truly feels about you. If I think I can trust him around you, I'll bring him back with me."

"And if you think you can't?"

"Then you might not see him for a while."

I shrug.

"I'll see the two of you soon then," I say, full of confidence.

Mason phases, and I get up to take my own shower to get ready for the day ahead.

I'm sitting at the kitchen table, eating a bowl of Frosted Flakes, when Mason and Chandler finally appear.

Chandler is casually dressed in a white t-shirt with the words *Rolling Stone* stenciled on the front, faded gray jeans and matching jacket, and black and white Converse shoes. He's loosely holding his crown in his right hand.

"Should I change clothes?" I ask, guessing my thick cable-neck sweater might not be the best thing to wear where we're going.

"It would probably be a good idea," Mason answers, coming up to me and giving me a light peck on the lips. "A long sleeve shirt should do fine for where we have to go."

"And where is that exactly?" Chandler asks, taking a seat across from me at the table, resting his crown on its surface.

"The Cave of Treasures."

"Yeah, doesn't help me much," Chandler admits with a shake of his head. "Where is that?"

"Israel; on the west side of the Dead Sea, near a place called Ein Gedi."

"Oh, ok," Chandler says, obviously having heard of the place before. "I did a concert in Israel once. We went to a spa in Ein Gedi to relax afterwards. Cool place."

"I would suggest you bring your crown and sword today," Mason says to me.

"Why do I get the feeling you expect there to be trouble?"

"Because I do," he answers bluntly. "The cave was a burial place for a lot of people, but we're just interested in one occupant in particular."

"Who?" Chandler asks.

"A descendant of Cain. His name was Jubal."

"Why do you think my talisman would be where he's buried?"

"People often call Jubal the father of all musicians. He invented the very first instruments: the lyre and the pipe. It was said he could use music to move men's minds away from God. It's my guess your talisman is one of his instruments."

"But he sounds like a bad guy," Chandler says, somewhat offended. "I know what I did to Jess was wrong, but…"

Mason holds up his hand to stop Chandler. "It's not the instrument, but the man who uses it that determines how it affects other people. I'm not at all suggesting that you are anything like Jubal, but I believe his instruments do hold power, and are meant to serve a higher purpose now."

"What type of trouble do you expect to find in a tomb?" I ask.

"Some souls don't always pass on," Mason says. "The ghosts that haunt the cave might try to cause trouble. Your sword is the sword of righteousness. None of them will bother you if you're holding it."

"How do you know Jubal's tomb hasn't been ransacked after all this time?" Chandler asks. "It's been a few thousand years, right?"

"There was an archeological expedition back in the 1960s, but it wasn't at the true site of the Cave of Treasures. The location of the real cave is only known to a few angels and God. No one has disturbed it, because it's almost impossible to find, much less reach."

"What do you mean?" I ask.

"It's in a canyon on the side of a steep cliff. In the old days, there used to be a trail that went up to the cave, but, after years of erosion, the trail has vanished. Plus, after the Great Flood, the entrance was blocked by an accumulation of mud and stones. It's lain hidden for thousands of years."

I stand and walk over to the kitchen sink to wash my bowl out before I go to change out of my top. I feel a pair of strong arms encircle my waist, and I naturally lean back against Mason's chest.

"Need help changing out of your sweater?" he whispers in my ear, finding that sensitive spot behind my ear, and purposely driving me crazy with his lips as he kisses me there.

"We have company," I whisper.

"The boy is in the living room," Mason replies, nipping the bottom of my ear with his teeth, sending a pleasant shiver throughout my body.

"You keep that up, and we might never get out of this house, much less to this mysterious cave of yours."

I feel Mason smile against my neck as he trails kisses down to my clavicle, eliciting a sigh of pleasure from me. Suddenly, he steps away. I turn around to face him, wondering why he stopped so abruptly. I watch him as he adjusts his pants, and my eyes involuntarily spot the problem.

I smile, because I love the fact that just kissing me has such an effect on him.

"Do you need me to burst into tears?" I ask, having a hard time from keeping a pleased smile off my face.

Mason narrows his eyes at me, but I know he isn't mad at my teasing.

"Go change your shirt," he says in exasperation. "I'll be fine."

When I pass Mason, I give him a chaste kiss on the lips.

"I was going to say yes, by the way."

Mason lifts an inquiring eyebrow. "Yes to what?"

"About you helping me change out of my sweater, of course."

Mason raises both his eyebrows at me in surprise.

I smile sweetly at him before heading to my bedroom, alone.

I change into a peach V-neck long-sleeve shirt and grab my crown and sword from their spot on my dresser. It might seem odd to some people to keep them out in the open and not hidden away from prying eyes, but I see no reason why I can't keep them where I can reach them easily. Lucifer already knows I have them, and Mama Lynn and Faison know the complete truth about me now. In a way, the crown and sword bring me a strange sort of comfort, like my plasma pistol does, making me feel protected by their presence.

When I step back into the kitchen, Faison is there, practically drooling over a half-naked Chandler. He has his shirt off, and is leaned over the table, signing his name on the front of it with a black permanent marker. Faison looks up at me, her eyes as big as saucers at the sight of Chandler Cain standing shirtless in my kitchen.

"What are you doing?" I ask Chandler, setting my crown and sword on the table.

"Faison said you promised her a signed t-shirt from me," Chandler says with a shrug. He looks over at me and gives me a wink. "Thought I should make good on your promise."

I shake my head at him because he knows the effect he's having on my sister. I see Mason standing on the other side of the table, raising a dubious eyebrow in Chandler's direction.

After Chandler is finished, he hands the shirt to a grateful Faison.

"Thank you so much!" Faison says. Her eyes are lit up like it's Christmas morning and a half-naked Chandler Cain is her present. I have a feeling the picture of Chandler shirtless will forever be scorched into Faison's memory. She hugs the t-shirt to her and giggles.

"Did you come over here for a particular reason?" I ask Faison.

"Oh, yeah," she says, remembering there *was* an actual reason for her visit. "Mama Lynn wanted me to remind you about George's party tomorrow night."

A party I had completely forgotten about.

"Thanks for the reminder," I say, truly thankful.

"Who's George and what's the party for?" Chandler asks.

Faison explains. "George is a good friend of ours. Mama Lynn throws a party every year to celebrate the anniversary of him moving into our neighborhood."

"He's a tearer," I further explain to Chandler. "He's been like a part of our family since he came to Cypress Hollow. Geesh, I can't believe it's been ten years already. Make sure she knows I'll be there if I can. It's hard for me to plan too far ahead these days, but I'll make it a priority."

"Ok, Jess," Faison says, still hugging Chandler's t-shirt to her chest, like it's the Holy Grail. "Well, I better go. John Austin is waiting for me out in his truck to take me to work. I just wanted to stop by and remind you about the party." Faison looks at Chandler, and makes a great effort to keep her eyes focused on his face. "Nice to see you again, by the way," she tells him.

Chandler gives Faison his rock star smile. "The pleasure was mine, Faison."

I take hold of Faison's arm and steer her towards my front door before she salivates all over my tiled floor.

"Oh, my God, I can't believe he gave me the shirt right off his back!" Faison says excitedly. "I can't wait to tell the girls at the hospital."

I can't help but smile at Faison's child-like enthusiasm.

"Just remember," I remind her, "your true love is sitting out in that truck. Don't act all giddy about the t-shirt, and for Heaven's sake, don't tell him Chandler just took it off his back to give to you. I've had enough trouble with Chandler making indecent gestures lately."

"Oh, are you talking about that kiss?"

I look at Faison, slightly confused. "You already know about that?"

"It was all over the news this morning." Faison crosses her arms in front of her. "So what was the deal with that, anyway? You didn't look too happy, from what I saw."

"It was a mistake on Chandler's part, nothing more. We were just trying to provide him with a cover to be out of the public eye for a while. It wasn't something planned, at least not on my part."

Faison's eyes grow dark, and her earlier hero worship of Chandler is quickly turning to dislike.

"Did he force himself on you? I just figured it was for show, but if he hurt you, I swear to God, Jess…"

I smile, because I always love to see my little southern belle of a sister bring out her feisty, protective side.

"No, we talked about it. It was just a mistake. Trust me, he won't do it again unless he wants to be thrown through a wall by Mason."

This garners a reluctant smile from Faison. "I knew I liked Mason for a reason."

Turning serious, she asks. "How are things going with the two of you anyway?"

I smile. "Better than I could have hoped for." My smile falters, though.

"But?" Faison asks, not missing anything.

"I'm having a hard time…when we try to be intimate with one another."

It only takes Faison a second to understand my meaning, but when she does, she nods her head. "That's only to be expected, with what you've gone through. Don't you dare let him try to take things faster than you want, you hear me?"

"That's the thing. He's not pushing me at all. He's letting me set the pace of how far we go."

Faison smiles. "See, another reason I like him."

"I'm the one having trouble with it," I confess. "I want to share all of me with him so badly, but when he touches my body in certain places, it's like I have a mental block which turns into a physical block. It's getting aggravating."

"Look, you've been through a lot. Stop blaming yourself for not being able to go much further than kissing. You'll get there eventually. Plus, getting there is half the fun anyway. Don't rush things. Enjoy the newness of it all because things only happen the first time once."

I give Faison a hug, realizing her wisdom is far beyond her years. "Thanks."

"No problem."

Faison pulls back and looks at me. I can tell she's uncomfortable with what she's about to say.

"Uh, I don't know how the whole Watcher sex thing works," she whispers, "but you've got protection, right? I can always bring you guys some condoms from the Planned Parenthood department at the hospital."

I blush profusely with the reminder.

"Honestly, I didn't even think about that." Considering what Mason told me about the wives of the Watchers who became pregnant, I realize it's something I should make inquiries about. "Yeah, bring me some, just in case."

Better safe than sorry.

CHAPTER FIFTEEN

When I go back to the kitchen, Chandler has a white-and-black-striped T-shirt on underneath his jacket. There are also three new, black metal Maglite flashlights sitting on the table too.

"Quick trip back home?" I ask.

"Gotta love insta-travel," Chandler says with a grin. "Now, can we go get my talisman? I'm getting kinda jealous that you and JoJo have met your archangels, and I haven't been able to talk to mine yet."

I grab my sword and crown from the table.

"How is JoJo doing? Still asleep?" I ask Mason.

"Isaiah is with her, and, yes, she's still asleep."

"Man, I hate to not be there for her when she wakes up," Chandler says.

"I will be," I reassure him, "don't worry; I'll be there when you wake up too."

"We should all take a flashlight," Mason tells us. "Like I told you before, the cave is sealed from the outside. It'll be pitch black when we phase into it."

Not having any other place for it, I end up setting my crown on my head because I only have two hands. Seeing that I'm going to wear my crown, Chandler sits his on his head too.

"I really need to get a belt or something for this thing," I say, trying to hold the sword up in one hand, while holding the flashlight in my other.

"Maybe JoJo can make you something that's flame-retardant," Mason suggests. "A baldric would probably be the most comfortable sheath for you."

"What's a baldric?" Chandler asks.

"It's a sheath that allows you to wear the sword on your back. It would give Jess freer movement than having the sword on a belt around her hips."

"Yeah, but she would look wicked cool with a sword dangling from her hips."

Mason scowls.

"Why don't we go?" I suggest, not wanting to give Mason an excuse to keep Chandler, and his suggestions of how to make me look cool, away from me.

Mason tells us to turn our flashlights on before we phase. I'm glad he makes the suggestion because, as soon as we arrive, we're surrounded by nothing but stone and blackness. The cave smells musty and the air seems stale, like there are only minute cracks in the walls that let fresh air from the outside enter the space.

"Not exactly the Garden of Eden," Chandler complains.

"No," I agree, "not the Garden of Eden."

"This is where Adam and Eve were exiled after they were made to leave Eden," Mason informs us. "Come on; Jubal's resting place will be at the very back of the cave."

"Why the back?" I ask.

"Because, even in death, people feared he would use his powers to control their minds." Mason looks at the sword in my hand. "Can you make the sword show its flames whenever you want?"

"No," I say, lifting the sword in the air, "it's like it has a mind of its own."

"Just remember," Mason warns us, "there are disturbed souls in here. Try to stay out of their way. Some of them still don't realize they're dead."

"Uh, what happens if we can't stay out of their way?" Chandler asks.

"It won't be a pleasant experience. Especially for you," Mason says, full of ominous portent. "Since you're already sensitive to the emotions felt by others, I fear you might not be able to deal with the emotions felt by some of the souls. Many of them have been trapped here for a few thousand years, and are completely insane. Just be careful and don't let any of them touch you."

Mason leads the way deeper into the cave. Chandler stays close to my side, sweeping his flashlight into dark recesses, not wanting to take a chance that a ghost might be lurking in a corner or behind a rock. Mason's warning has struck a chord with my friend, making him extra cautious.

As we walk around a bend in the cave, we come to a complete stop.

There is a woman sitting in the middle of the cave floor, cradling a baby swathed in a blanket. She's rocking the child back and forth, singing to it in a language I don't recognize. As if sensing our presence, she looks up. Her eyes are missing, and the sockets look raw, like she intentionally clawed her own eyes out. She stands quickly and starts to yell at us, angrily. In that instant, I actually do fear for my own safety.

The sword in my hand comes to life. I feel it vibrate just before the blade bursts into flames.

Even with its sightless eyes, the ghost seems to stare at the now-flaming sword of righteousness, and flees, vanishing as she runs into one of the cave walls.

"Please, keep that on," Chandler says, exhaling deeply. "I seriously don't want to have to feel whatever that woman was feeling."

Chandler takes a step closer to me, and I instantly feel my protector mode switch on.

"I won't let anything harm you," I tell him.

I suddenly realize the role I am meant to play within the circle of archangels we are forming. Just as my father is a Guardian of souls, I am the guardian and leader of the archangels while they are on Earth. Without my father's strength, I might not be able to step into the role I'm meant to play for the others. I might not have the ability to channel feelings like Chandler, or make clothing that hold supernatural abilities like JoJo, but I'm just as important. The others will come to me when they need protection and guidance. I am their center.

As we head deeper into the cave, we end up passing many sad, pathetic souls along the way that are unable to find rest in death. Even without touching them, I can feel the depth of their sorrow, because it permeates the air with their hopelessness. Fortunately, the flaming sword in my hand seems to make most of them scatter before we get too close.

As we near the back of the cave, the figure of a little girl around the age of seven appears in our path. She is completely naked and shivering. Her hair and skin are damp, like she just stepped out of a bath. For some reason, I feel drawn to the child, and begin to walk towards her.

Mason grabs my arm just as I pass him. "Jess, what are you doing?"

"Trust me," I tell him.

Reluctantly, Mason releases my arm.

I hand him my flashlight. He takes it.

I walk over to the little girl and kneel before her. The flame of the sword illuminates her large brown eyes as she looks at me, but, unlike the other souls in the cave, she doesn't seem scared of the sword or me.

"I'm here to help you," I tell her.

She shivers, silently watching me.

"Are you lost?" I ask.

She nods her head, and I can hear the chatter of her teeth.

"Would you like to go home?"

She nods vigorously.

I lay my sword down beside me and hold my arms out to her, silently beckoning her to accept my embrace.

"Jess," Mason hisses, "what are you doing?"

I hear the worry in his voice, but know I have nothing to fear from the soul in front of me. She is simply lost, unable to find her way out of the maze of the cave. For whatever reason, her soul became trapped here when it was meant to go on. I know I can help her. I am my father's child.

Cautiously, the little girl walks closer to me. When she's so close I can feel her cold breath on my face, I wrap my arms around her wet body. She rests her damp head on my shoulder, finding comfort in my warmth.

Instantly, I know why she's been trapped inside this cave. It's like a movie playing in my mind. I see her drown in a river not far from where we stand. Her soul never fully understood she was dead, and she's been searching for her mother ever since.

"You're mother passed away a long time ago," I tell the little girl. "You won't be able to find her here. You need to pass on, too, if you truly want to be reunited with her again. Let go of this life. It's not the one you're meant to lead."

I feel her head nod against my shoulder. She lets out what sounds like a deep sigh, and, suddenly, I'm holding nothing but empty air.

I pick my sword up and stand.

"How did you know you could help her?" Mason asks as he and Chandler come to stand beside me.

"Her soul was innocent," I tell them. "Most of the souls in here aren't, but her soul was."

"How could you tell the difference?" Chandler asks.

I shrug. "I just knew. I don't know how exactly, but I have a feeling I might have inherited the ability from my dad."

"It's possible," Mason agrees. "It is a gift the Guardians have, to know the true nature of a soul."

Mason takes my free hand and holds both our flashlights in his other one.

"You worry me sometimes," he says, squeezing my hand.

I grin at him, knowing he was only worried about my safety.

"So, are we almost there?" Chandler asks.

I can tell he's anxious to find his talisman now that we are so close.

"Yes," Mason says. "Follow me."

At the end of the cave, we enter a large, cavernous space. The walls of the cavern hold a plethora of chiseled-out, body-length openings, and a scattering of bones can be seen lying within them. As we walk further into the room, I hear the strings of what sounds like a harp being played.

"Do you hear that?" Chandler asks, sweeping his flashlight in the direction of the music.

"Jubal," Mason calls out, his voice echoing against the walls, "show yourself!"

Almost instantly, a man appears at the far end of the cavern, sitting on top of a medium-sized stone. He's dressed in a brown, ratty-looking wool robe. His hair reminds me of Charlton Heston's hair when he played Moses in *The Ten Commandments*, except Jubal's hair is brown, and doesn't look like it's been washed for quite a while. He's holding what looks like a small harp in his right hand, propped up on a bent leg, strumming its strings, and producing the music we hear.

The song is a melancholy tune, and brings to mind the sad days I suffered through after my parents disappeared the night the Tear appeared in the sky. I can vividly remember being shuffled around to various social workers, who were overburdened with the number of children left abandoned that night. The stench of the state-run facilities, a mixture of bleach and Pine Sol, seems to permeate the air around me.

I look to Mason and see a sadness in his eyes that hasn't been there since the night he left me. Chandler seems to be the only one of us unaffected by Jubal's playing. My friend leaves my side and walks up to Jubal.

Apparently not used to such audacious behavior, Jubal stops playing, releasing Mason and me from our sad memories as he studies Chandler standing before him.

"Why are you not affected by my music?" Jubal asks Chandler, eyeing him as if he's a curiosity.

"I've had very little in my life to make me sad," Chandler tells him. "I guess you could say I've led a charmed life."

Jubal continues to play his harp, but the tune changes.

This time it reminds me of my talk with Lucifer, when he asked me if I wanted him to send Uncle Dan to the Void and cease the torture he was going through in Hell. An overpowering guilt wracks my body, because I know I should have asked Lucifer to spare Uncle Dan. Even though the son of a bitch deserved what he got, I couldn't imagine him suffering through an eternity of torment at the hands of Lucifer, or any of the minions under his command. My humanity should have overruled my quest for justice, leading me to ask for a reprieve for Uncle Dan. I didn't. An overpowering sense of guilt, and disappointment in myself, is brought out by Jubal's music.

When I look at Mason, I know exactly what guilt he is reliving. The scar on his face, made by God as a reminder of his failure to lead the Watchers down the right path, throbs bright red.

"Stop playing," I order Jubal, desperately wanting to stop the music's torturous effect on Mason.

Jubal doesn't stop. When he looks up at me, his eyes are filled with madness. It's then I know Jubal isn't in complete control of his actions. I get the feeling he couldn't stop playing, even if he wanted to.

I see Chandler jump to the side and look down at his feet. I look where Chandler is standing, and see a great serpent slithering on the cave floor around the stone Jubal is sitting on.

"He won't let me stop," Jubal says, eyeing the serpent with unadulterated hatred. "He came to me, you know," Jubal continues. "After I made the first of my instruments, he came and told me I could move the minds of men with just my playing; if only I had known then what I know now. He won't let me stop playing. He won't ever let me go."

Just as I'm about to take a step forward to strike the snake with my sword, the snake disappears, and reappears wrapped around Jubal's body like a corkscrew.

"Fight him," Chandler urges Jubal. "Make him leave you alone."

Jubal shakes his head, no fight left in him.

"He has won."

"Only if you let him," Chandler says. "Do something right for once. Help us."

Jubal looks up at Chandler. He stares at my friend for a long while, never ceasing his playing.

"How are you filled with so much hope?"

"Because hope gives you a reason to live. Help us and find hope in knowing you're doing something good for once; something he doesn't want you to do. Fight him, man."

Jubal places an open palm on the strings of the harp, signaling the end of his song.

"I will help you," Jubal says, looking at a pile of bones in one of the cut-out tombs to the wall on his right. "Go and get what you came for."

Jubal drops the harp, which disintegrates in the air like it was made of vapor. He wraps his hands just below the serpent's head, strangling it.

We watch in horror as the serpent's head grows large enough to swiftly swallow Jubal down to his waist. A cry of agony can be heard just before the scene disintegrates, just like the harp did, as if it was never there in the first place.

"Hurry; get your talisman," Mason tells Chandler.

As Chandler walks over to the tomb Jubal pointed out, I turn to Mason and still see the haunt of pain in his eyes. His scar pulsates with the feelings Jubal's music forced him to face again.

"Are you all right?" I ask him.

"I will be," he replies, "as soon as we get out of here."

I turn back to where Chandler is, and see him pull out something white that's about a foot long. The crown on his head begins to glow, and Chandler collapses onto the cave floor with a thud.

"Oh," Mason says, "I hope he didn't hurt himself."

I look at Mason and see a small grin on his face.

"You are so bad," I say, knowing he forgot to warn Chandler that he would instantly collapse if he was wearing the crown when he touched his talisman.

"Just think of it as getting even," Mason replies as we walk over to Chandler to make sure he's all right.

Mason lifts Chandler easily into his arms.

Even unconscious, Chandler holds tightly to his talisman. To me, it just looks like a piece of bone, with holes drilled into it.

"What is it?" I ask.

Mason studies it for a second and says, "It looks like a pipe made of ivory; hippopotamus ivory, most likely. Grab onto my arm," Mason instructs me, looking around the room warily. "Let's get out of here before Jubal loses his fight."

I grab hold of Mason's arm.

Mason quickly phases us to the room Chandler stayed in, when the two of us were at the villa. Isaiah is already in the room, because JoJo is sleeping in Chandler's bed.

"Everything went well?" Isaiah asks.

Mason lays Chandler down on the other side of the bed from JoJo.

"As well as could be expected," Mason answers. He pulls a folded blanket from the foot of the bed and covers Chandler with it. "Call either me or Jess if JoJo stirs earlier than expected."

Isaiah nods, understanding the order.

Mason reaches out his hand to me across the bed over my two friends. I place my hand in his, and we're instantly standing in my living room.

Mason pulls me to him and hugs me tightly.

I know he's still trying to overcome the effect of Jubal's haunting music. In all honesty, so am I. I hug him even tighter as we use one another to bring comfort to our ravaged souls.

CHAPTER SIXTEEN

After a while, I feel Mason's hold on me loosen, and I pull back to look at him.

"How are you?" he asks.

"I'm fine. How are you?"

Mason smiles. "I'm good. I'm always good when I'm with you."

I raise an eyebrow at him. "Just good? I can't say I feel very flattered if I just make you feel *good*."

Mason puts his hands on either side of my face.

"You make me feel like life is worth living," he tells me. "I feel good, happy, excited, loved. I feel everything when I'm with you. So, yes, I feel *good* when I'm around you, but that encompasses a lot more than just that one word, Jess."

"Hmm," I say, "I believe that deserves a kiss, Mr. Collier."

Mason smiles and leans down. "I was hoping you would say that."

We stand there, drinking in one another, until we're rudely interrupted by the buzzing of Mason's phone in his pants pocket.

"Are you just happy to be with me or is that really your phone this time?" I ask.

Mason smiles against my lips, not wanting to end what I had hoped to be a long, languid session of kissing one another.

"My phone," he replies irritably. "But I'm always happy to be with you."

Reluctantly, he pulls away and agitatedly grabs his phone and pulls it from his pocket.

"Yes?" he says to the poor person who chose such an inopportune moment to call. I watch as he closes his eyes, and I know he's frustrated about something. "Why do I have to have lunch with him?" Mason asks the caller. "When?" I see Mason's eyes travel to the grandfather clock I have in the living room, to check the time. "All right, I'll be there."

Mason ends the call and drops the phone back into his pocket.

"Who do you have to have lunch with?" I ask.

"The president," Mason grumbles. "I don't know why Nick makes me go see him to give him personal updates on the Tear situation."

"Maybe he's just scared, like the rest of the world, and needs you to comfort him and tell him everything will be all right."

"Nick could do it just as well."

"Have you met Nick?" I ask, thinking Mason has no clue how Nick rubs people the wrong way sometimes. "He doesn't exactly exude comfort. He's more like the interrogator, and you're the priest. Just go play nice with the president," I tell Mason. "I need to go to the grocery store anyway. I'm completely out of food here. Oh," I say, wrapping my arms around Mason's waist, "and on your way back, would you be sweet enough to drop by Paris and pick me up some of those chocolate croissants?"

Mason smiles. "I would be more than happy to do that for you."

"Bring back two boxes this time. I would like to take a box to my grandfather tonight when I see him."

"Are you ready for that?" Mason asks me.

I shrug. "I don't think if I had a year to prepare myself I would be ready to meet a stranger who shares a quarter of my chromosomes. I just hope we like each other. Otherwise, it'll be a short visit."

"Do you want me there with you, or do you want to meet with him alone first?"

"Alone," I say. "I don't want him to feel like he's being ambushed. Plus, he might feel more comfortable if it's just me and him. I'm hoping he'll tell me more about my biological father."

The difference between the father who helped make half my body and the father who helped make half my soul was divided by one thing, love. The father I grew up with didn't just share his soul with me. He shared his value system and love for the first seven years of my life. I knew nothing about the man with whom I shared DNA, and wondered what parts of me he helped create. I had to assume I had my father's hair, because my mother's hair was blonde. What else did we have in common? I hoped to solve those mysteries tonight during my talk with my grandfather.

"I'll call you when I'm through," Mason promises, kissing me on the lips lightly.

"Well, don't eat too much at lunch. I'm cooking you supper before we go see my grandfather."

"You cook?" Mason asks, sounding completely amazed by the fact.

"I might not like to cook, but, yes, I can cook." I stick my tongue out at Mason for asking such a question and sounding so surprised by it.

Mason laughs. "I apologize. I didn't mean it to come out like that. It's just… this is the first time you've cooked for me."

"Well, it won't be anything fancy," I warn, "probably just potato and sausage soup. I make it when it's cold out like today."

"Sounds wonderful," Mason says, a pleased smile on his face. I get the feeling not many people cook for him, and that this is a rare treat. "I'll try to make this meeting as short as possible. But he can be a bit long-winded sometimes. I hope to be back here in a couple of hours."

"That sounds good. It'll give me time to go shopping and start the soup."

Mason smiles and draws me into his arms. "I almost feel like a husband going off to work, with a loving wife at home cooking him supper."

I swallow hard at the analogy, and suddenly find myself hoping this isn't a preamble to a marriage proposal. The prospect of such a question makes me instantly nervous all of a sudden. It's only then I realize I don't want Mason to ask me to marry him, at least not yet.

Mason seems to sense the change in my mood at his remark, but doesn't comment on it.

"You'd better get going," I tell him, kissing him quickly on the lips. "You don't want to keep the leader of the free world waiting for too long. Who knows what he might do if you make him miss his regular lunchtime? Start a war? Raise taxes? I certainly don't want to be the reason for any of that."

"I love you," Mason says, not being fooled by my attempt to diffuse the situation.

I smile, but it feels like a smile you give out of politeness. "I love you too; now go."

After Mason phases, I let out a sigh of relief.

What would I have done if he'd asked me to marry him? Run? Hide? Neither option seemed the mature thing to do. The fact was that I wasn't ready for such a formal commitment. I loved Mason beyond all reason, but did that mean I had to marry him? Why couldn't we just live out our lives, loving one another? Did we really have to have the whole wedding and marriage license thing to prove our love?

I knew how old-fashioned Mason could be. He would want the wedding, the reception, the well-wishes from friends and family. He would probably be one of those men who framed their wedding vows and hung them on the wall so all the world could see just how devoted he was to me. I bury my face in my hands. Why did I have to fall in love with a gentleman?

At least there was one thing Mason didn't seem to have a problem with: sex before marriage. He wasn't so old-fashioned that we would have to endure that silly rule. It was only me and my hang-ups that were causing the problem in that area.

I sigh heavily and go change out of my T-shirt and back into the sweater I had on earlier. We weren't in an arid climate anymore, but in the cold of the Deep South; a cold that holds so much moisture in it your bones ache from its effects if you don't bundle up.

By the time I reach our local Piggly Wiggly, I decide to definitely make the soup I told Mason about, and pick up some pre-made garlic bread to eat with it. While I'm there, I pick up a few more items that my kitchen is lacking, like bread, milk, eggs, bacon… you know, the necessities of life.

I am searching through the red delicious apples, wondering if I have the culinary skills to try to make an apple pie for Mason. I've never made a pie before, but just thinking about baking one for Mason makes me happy.

I feel the bracelet Chandler and JoJo gave me begin to warm against my skin, warning me of danger. I look up across the display of apples, and see a rather handsome young man with short blond hair and a muscular physique wearing a black crew-neck sweater under a black double-breasted sweater jacket and black jeans. Too bad it's all ruined by the matching black aura surrounding him.

He's smiling at me. But, don't serial killers smile at their victims just before they lure them off somewhere to kill them? That's what I feel like he's doing, attempting to trap me with his smile, into a false sense of security. I'm suddenly glad I thought to wear my plasma pistol on my thigh before I came to the Piggly Wiggly, but I doubt it will be enough to hurt the prince of Hell standing across from me.

"Can I help you?" I ask the stranger, putting the apple in my hand back onto the pyramid of apples in front of me.

His smile deepens, and his blue eyes glisten with humor. Two perfectly symmetrical dimples appear in his cheeks, giving him that boy-next-door look.

"I was just admiring the display," he says smoothly.

He's beside me before I even realize it, picking up the same apple I'd just put down. He holds it up before my eyes and slowly spins it so the buffed red skin glistens under the fluorescent lights in the store.

"Now, why would you put back something so succulent, so juicy, you can almost taste its sweetness inside your mouth?"

I almost snatch the apple out of his hands and take a bite out of it because he makes the apple sound so good.

"Who are you?" I ask.

The man smiles. "You can call me Baal. I believe you've met my brothers," he says, bringing the apple to his full lips and taking a bite out of its tender flesh. "Asmodeus and Mammon said you were pretty, and I must say I'm pleasantly surprised they were right."

My hand instantly goes to the butt of my pistol out of habit, since I know I can't hurt him with it. I decide to see what game he's playing before I show him my whole deck of cards and bring out the flaming sword. A girl needs a few aces up her sleeve when dealing with a prince of Hell.

"Are you stalking me for a reason, or were you just hungry for an apple?" I ask.

Baal grins. "Irreverent, just like Lucifer said. I like that in my victims."

It's my turn to grin. "So, are you pretty and stupid, or just pretty stupid? Hasn't Lucifer told you I'm off-limits?"

"Yes, he made his protection of you abundantly clear to me when I got here. What he did to my brothers is not something I want to happen to me. I'm just too pretty for such torture. However, I wouldn't count on his protection forever if I were you. His fascination with you is bound to end." Baal folds his arms before him and stands with his legs slightly apart, like he's about to impart a fount of wisdom upon me.

"I've made it my mission to find out what spell you've cast over him."

"It's not like I'm a witch. I'm no one special, just a Watcher agent."

Baal's grin grows wider, deepening his dimples to craters.

"You and I both know you're not just that. And I promise you, when I find out, and tell Lucifer why he feels connected to you, he won't like it."

"How would you know that? Maybe he would."

"No. He doesn't like being played, and that's exactly what you're doing. No one likes looking like a fool, least of all him. Mind if I give you a bit of friendly advice?"

"I have a feeling you're going to give it to me whether I want it or not."

Baal smiles.

"You should be the one to tell Lucifer what you are before I figure it out. He might be willing to spare your life then. Otherwise, he'll feel betrayed by you, and that's not something you want to be on the receiving end of, I assure you."

"I'll take it under advisement," I reply. "Any other words of wisdom you would like to leave me with?"

"You should use the golden delicious apples if you want to make an apple pie, not the red."

Baal phases, and I'm left standing there wondering how he knew I wanted to make a pie.

Just as I'm putting my bags of groceries on the kitchen table, I feel my phone vibrate in my pocket.

My heart jumps when I see it's a text message from Mason.

Can I please come home now? I'm bored out of my mind here.

I smile at his use of the word 'home'. Does he feel like my home is his home? He did take a shower here this morning. Was I ready for that type of commitment? Only two words came to my mind: hell, yes.

When can you come home, and what are you doing now?

Listening to the President tell me about some sort of trouble in the Middle East. When isn't there trouble in the Middle East? It's been a perpetual war zone since the beginning of time.

Is he giving a speech?

To me, yes.

Alone?

Yes.

Are you telling me you are sitting with the President of the United States and texting me, while he's having a private conversation with you?

Yes. Is that bad?

I hang my head and shake it.

Yes it's bad! Isn't he offended you're texting while he's talking?

I don't think so. He seems rather into what he's saying. He's pacing back and forth in front of his desk. I'm not sure he's looked at me once the entire time he's been talking.

I giggle. It was often said the President liked to hear himself speak. His speeches in front of Congress were often cited as being the longest in recorded history.

Still, it's rude. You need to be listening to him.

What are you doing? Have you already gone grocery shopping?

Yes, I just got back. LISTEN TO THE PRESIDENT!

I can't concentrate on what he's saying anyway. All I can think about is kissing you.

I smile, and feel all warm and fuzzy inside.

I wish you were here kissing me too.

Then, can I come home, please? I'm begging you. Give me a good excuse to come home so I can be done with this for today. I need an emergency ASAP…

I was going to make you an apple pie…

Did you set the house on fire? I'm pretty sure that would be considered an emergency…

Lol, no. The house is still standing. I was rudely interrupted while I was trying to pick out apples at the Piggly Wiggly.

What aren't you telling me, Jess?

I take a deep breath because I know Mason is going to flip when he reads my answer.

Baal came to see me.

"Jess?" I hear Mason call to me from the living room.

I walk in, and he has me in his arms so quickly I don't even have a chance to blink.

Mason pulls away from me and looks me up and down, but not in the way I wish he would. He's more interested in making sure my body doesn't have any signs of injury.

"What did he want?" Mason asks. "What did he say to you?"

I recount my conversation with Baal.

"Do you think he's right?" I ask. "Do you think it would be better if Lucifer heard what I am from me, before the others find out?"

Mason sighs and runs his fingers through his hair. "I don't know. Maybe. But I think the timing would have to be right. He's going to be very mad when he learns the truth."

"But I thought he and Michael were best friends. Lucifer told me one of the only things he missed about Heaven was Michael."

Mason looks up at me sharply. "He told you that?"

I nod.

"That seems very uncharacteristic of him. He's not normally a heart-to-heart type of person, unless he's ripping out a heart."

"He's not like that with me," I say, almost feeling like I need to defend Lucifer. "The last time he was here, I felt what he feels for me."

I hold up my wrist so Mason pointedly sees the bracelet Chandler and JoJo made for me.

"I used this bracelet."

Mason looks at the bracelet, as if it's the first time he's noticed it.

"Where did you get that? What does it do?"

"I want you to know I never used it on you," I tell him. "I don't need to use it to know how you feel about me. But JoJo and Chandler thought I should have it in case I needed reassurance about your feelings for me. I haven't used it on you, but I did use it the other morning when Lucifer was here. Just before you came out onto the porch, he touched me on the cheek, and I used the bracelet to find out what he feels for me."

"And what did you discover?" Mason asks cautiously.

"He feels confused mostly," I say. "He wants to keep me protected, but I'm only his second priority. He desperately needs to perform whatever task he's laid out for himself to accomplish. He wants me to get to know him better, to fully understand who he is and why he does the things he does."

"Does he love you?"

I shake my head. "No, it's not love. But he needs to figure me out."

"And when he does, what do you think he'll do to you?"

I shrug. "I can't say for sure."

"Why aren't you more scared of him?" Mason asks. "I've never understood how you can be around him but not show fear."

"Because, deep down, I don't believe he would ever harm me. I honestly don't think he'll do it when he figures out, or when I tell him, what I am. I might even be safer if he knows Michael is inside me. I think Michael is the only person Lucifer ever truly thought of as a friend."

"God ordered Michael to bring Lucifer to Earth when he was exiled from Heaven. I'm not sure if Lucifer has ever forgiven him for that."

"Do you think Lucifer saw it as a betrayal?"

"Wouldn't you?" Mason asks.

"Maybe."

Mason lifts my hand with the bracelet.

"So what is this thing supposed to do exactly?"

"It warns me if I'm in danger, like at the grocery store, with Baal. And if I ask it to, it'll let me feel what someone else is feeling."

Mason places my hand over his heart.

"Ask it to tell you what I'm feeling."

"No."

Mason cocks his head at me.

"Why not? I want you to know."

"Because I don't need a bracelet to tell me what I already know."

Mason smiles. "And what do you know about my feelings for you?"

"That you love me beyond all reason. That you would do anything for me, whenever I wanted, and not care what it was. You would die for me if it came to that because you can't live without me, and you want me so bad it physically hurts you sometimes."

"And how do you know all that?"

"Because that's the way I feel about you."

Before I know it, Mason has me crushed against his body, kissing me fervently I wrap my fingers around the collar of his grey button-down shirt, knowing exactly what I want to do.

I pull back from the kiss, breathing heavily.

"I want to try something," I tell him.

He smiles. "Something pleasurable, I hope. What is it?"

"I want to undress you…and explore. Would you let me do that?"

"You can do anything you want with me, Jess. You know that."

"I think it might help me become more comfortable with you touching me."

Mason stands back a step and spreads his arms out wide. "Then, by all means, consider me your own personal playground. Do with me what you will, Jess Riley. I'm all yours."

His willingness at my proposed exploration makes me shy all of a sudden, but I know it's something I need to force myself to do. Poor me. Undressing the most handsome man on the planet and having free rein to do whatever I want to with his body. When did my life become so perfect?

"Don't get too excited," I tell him. "I just plan to take your shirt off, nothing more."

Mason pouts. I laugh.

"Stop," I say, trying to make myself stop giggling. "This is supposed to be serious."

"Well, I can't say I'm not disappointed, but, if that's all you want to do for now, please, feel free."

I walk up to Mason and start to unbutton his shirt. I feel his eyes watching me, and look up at his face.

"Stop staring," I order, lifting a stern eyebrow.

"Oh, are we doing that? Should I start saying 'yes, mistress'?"

I smile because I enjoy playful Mason's teasing. "No. I'm not into role-playing; at least, I don't think I am."

"And here I was imagining you in a skimpy nurse's uniform or perhaps a French maid's outfit."

"Stop," I order him again, trying to concentrate on undoing the buttons of his shirt. "This is supposed to be serious, and all you're doing is making me want to laugh."

"I know."

I look back at his face. "Why are you trying to make me laugh?"

"Because it relaxes you. I can feel the tension go out of you when I make you laugh. It means you're comfortable with me. And, right now, you need to be comfortable with me. You need to trust I won't do anything you don't want me to."

I feel tears sting my eyes because of Mason's efforts.

"Please don't start crying," he begs. "If you do, I might have to take you over my knee and give you something real to cry about, young lady."

I smile and stow the tears away for another time.

"Are you into that kind of thing?" I ask.

Mason cocks his head. "Spanking?"

I nod.

"Not particularly," he admits. "There are better and more pleasurable ways to excite a woman."

"And do you know many of these ways?"

"Wouldn't you like to know?"

I smile as I tug his shirt out of his slacks.

"Yes, I would; very much. I hope you can share your knowledge with me one day soon."

"If only you knew what I dream about at night…"

I lift one of Mason's cuffs to remove the cufflink he has there.

"What do you mean?"

"Watchers are able to dream whatever we want," he informs me as I move over to his other wrist and cufflink.

"Are you able to control what happens in these dreams?"

"Yes."

I lay Mason's cufflinks on the coffee table and stand in front of him, placing both of my hands on his chest, under his shirt.

"Do tell, Mr. Collier. What do you dream about?"

"You."

I slowly run my hands down Mason's chest and over his abdominal muscles to the waistband of his slacks.

"And what are we doing in these dreams of yours?" I ask, watching Mason's body react to my touch.

"Do you really want to know?" Mason asks, his voice growing hoarser. "Or would you rather wait until I'm able to demonstrate personally?"

I look up at Mason and see his eyes burn with the promise of pleasure. He wants to touch me, but knows he can't. For some reason, this knowledge makes me feel powerful. I have control, not him.

I lift my hands from his skin and hear him take a sharp breath, like me not touching him physically hurts. I walk behind him and lift his shirt from his shoulders, sliding it off his torso. I toss his shirt on the couch and let my eyes run down the length of him.

"I do like this side of you," I say.

"Yes," he replies, and I know he's wearing a smile, "I remember."

I rest my hands on Mason's shoulders and slowly slide them down his back to his slacks.

"You're more than welcome to investigate my assets," he says.

"Hmm," I say, taking my hands off him, staring at his assets. "I think it might be you who needs to go over *my* knee for a spanking, Mr. Collier."

"I am yours to discipline as you see fit," he replies. "I do look forward to your punishments."

I slide my arms between Mason's arms and torso until my chest is pressed against his back, and the palms of my hands are resting on his chest. He's taller than me, so I have to stand on the tips of my toes to whisper in his ear.

"Yes, Mr. Collier, you are all mine." I nip his ear lobe to punctuate my ownership.

I feel him tremble slightly under my touch.

"Do you like me touching you?" I ask.

Mason sighs. "You know I do."

"Turn around," I tell Mason, deciding on a course of action and taking advantage of it before I have a chance to change my mind.

Mason does as instructed, and I can tell he's wondering why I made such a request, but doesn't question me.

In one quick movement, I take my sweater off and toss it beside Mason's shirt on the couch.

I feel like I can barely breathe, and I'm finding it difficult to lift my gaze from Mason's chest to look at his face. I have a stray thought and am glad I put on my lacey bra from Victoria's Secret that morning. We're silent for a while, and I know Mason is letting me figure out if I want to put my sweater back on or not. I don't want to. I look into Mason's eyes and feel my heart melt at the love I see on his face.

He watches me, not moving, because I'm the one who is supposed to be making all the decisions. I walk up to Mason and reach for his right hand. I put it over my heart so he can feel its thunder.

"That's what you do to me," I tell him. "Sometimes, when I'm around you, I can barely breathe. And, sometimes, like now, my heart beats so fast I feel like I'm going to have a heart attack."

A small, pleased smile touches Mason's lips, but he remains silent, content to let me go at my own pace.

I close my eyes and slide Mason's hand down until he's cupping one of my breasts. I feel my body begin to tremble as years of buried memories bubble up to the surface, forcing me to remember another pair of hands touching, squeezing, probing in places they shouldn't have been, in places no man should ever touch a child.

I don't even realize I'm crying until I feel Mason cup the sides of my face and run his thumbs over my cheekbones to wipe away my tears. Silently, he brings me into his arms and just holds me, letting me cry away the memories I've buried so deep I didn't even remember half of them until now.

No wonder I'm so screwed up. No person, much less a child, should have memories so horrible. I don't want them. I want to get rid of them. I want them replaced with memories filled with love, not blind, unholy need, and selfishness.

I look up at Mason's face, and see that what he told me is true: he dies a little inside every time he sees me cry. And I'm tired of crying. I don't want to cry the tears of the child whose first sexual experience was corrupted by a man so far gone mentally he had to have been mad to force a little girl to do such vile things with him. I don't want those memories haunting me anymore. I want new ones, beautiful ones. And there's only one person I want to make those memories with.

I take a deep breath.

"Mason, I…"

The doorbell rings. At first, it doesn't register in my mind, but when Mason reaches for his shirt and my sweater, I have to snap myself out of the moment.

Mason is buttoning his shirt as he goes to the door.

I slip my sweater back on and try to wipe the remainder of my tears from my eyes. I sit down heavily on the couch and wait for Mason's return.

I hear low voices and then the door closes. Mason walks directly to the kitchen with something in his hands before coming back to sit with me on the couch.

"Who was at the door?" I ask.

"Your mother brought over some cookies for you to take to your grandfather," Mason tells me, pulling me into his arms.

"She didn't want to come in?"

"I told her you were resting. I didn't think you would want company right now."

I tighten my arms around Mason. "No, I don't want to be with anyone but you."

"What were you going to tell me before we were interrupted?"

I shake my head. "I'll tell you later; right now, I just want you to hold me."

We sit on the couch for a while, just holding one another. I decide to wait until the moment is right to show Mason I'm ready to make love. At least, I think I am. I hope I am, but I don't want to make a promise I can't keep.

After a while, Mason asks, "Have you started the soup yet?"

I shake my head against his chest. "No, in fact, the groceries are still sitting on the kitchen table."

Mason hugs me one last time before standing and helping me to my feet.

"Then let's go make supper. I can't take you to meet your grandfather on an empty stomach."

CHAPTER SEVENTEEN

As Mason and I work in the kitchen, I realize how natural it feels to be doing something so domestic with him. It makes me wonder what a normal life would feel like, one where all we had to worry about was cooking, shopping, watching TV, and raising children. The thought of having children with Mason makes me smile.

"What are you thinking that makes you smile so beautifully?" Mason asks, turning the gas stove burner down to let the soup simmer.

"Can we have children?" I ask. "Normal children?"

My question seems to catch Mason off-guard. He looks a little bit like a startled rabbit.

"Umm, yes," he says, running his fingers through his hair, "we can have normal children. The Watcher children aren't cursed anymore, and all of our offspring live out natural human lives. Why? Do you want to have a child?"

I shrug. "Eventually. Would you want to have another child?"

"To be honest, I haven't given it a lot of thought. I assumed we would have this conversation after we got married."

Crap. The 'm' word. Perhaps Mason wasn't quite as progressive as I thought.

"Is getting married important to you?" I ask him, needing to know if this is going to be a deal-breaker between us.

"I would like to marry you," he answers cautiously, "but, from the way you just asked that question, I get the feeling it's not something that's important to you."

"Not really," I tell him truthfully. "I don't see the point. You love me and I love you. Why do we have to have a piece of paper to make it official?"

"It's not just the paper, Jess," Mason says. "It's a declaration of our love for one another."

"But you know I love you," I tell him, not seeing the logic behind what he is trying to say, "and I know you love me. I don't need anything more than that."

"So, if I ask you to marry me," he says, "are you going to say no?"

I feel completely unprepared to answer his question, and begin to pray for some divine intervention to break the conversation off early. Unfortunately, all remains silent, and I'm forced to give him an answer.

"I don't know," I say to him. "If I said no, would you leave me?"

"There is nothing in this world or any other that would make me leave you. The only way I would leave you is if you asked me to."

"Well, there's no way that's ever happening," I assure him, relieved the whole marriage thing isn't going to cause a rift between us.

"But, I would like you to reconsider us getting married," Mason requests. "Just think about it. That's all I ask, for now."

I nod, letting him know I'll think about it. Though, I don't see me changing my mind anytime soon.

After we eat, I decide I should freshen up before I leave to meet my grandfather.

"Do you still want me to go get those croissants?" Mason asks me as I stand up to go change my clothes.

"No, I'll just take the cookies Mama Lynn made. I should probably call and thank her."

"I think she's worried."

"Worried about what?"

"Losing you to your real family."

"She *is* my real family."

"You know what I mean."

I sigh. "I know. I got that feeling, too, when I told her about him. I'll give her a call."

I take my phone out and call Mama Lynn. She picks up on the second ring.

"Hey, Jess."

She sounds happy to hear from me, and I suddenly feel badly for not calling her sooner.

"Mason said you were resting when I came by earlier. Are you all right? You're not sick again, are you?"

"No, I'm fine. I was just tired. Thank you for the cookies. I'm sure my grandfather will appreciate them."

"Well, you know when I get nervous, I cook."

Mama Lynn is silent, obviously waiting for me to continue the conversation.

"Why are you nervous?" I ask.

"Well, I'm just nervous about you going to meet him."

"I love you," I tell her, feeling the need to reassure her of my feelings. "You have nothing to be nervous about. It's he who should be nervous. I'm not sure he understands the family he's about to join."

Mama Lynn laughs. "That's true. Well, call me after you talk to him. I would like to know how it goes."

"Why don't I just come over to your house and stay the night instead?" I suggest, knowing this idea will bring a smile to Mama Lynn's face.

"Oh, that's a great idea! We can have a sleep-over. Faison should be back from work by then."

"Ok."

"Let's see, I've got chocolate ice cream, and I'll get Faison to bring home some snacks from the store. It'll be just like when you girls were kids."

"I shouldn't be longer than a couple of hours."

"Ok, Jess. See you soon."

When I get off the phone, I feel Mason come up behind me and wrap his arms around me.

"So, I guess I won't be getting you alone again this evening," he states, resigned to his fate.

"She needs me," I tell him.

He kisses me on the neck. "I know. You're a good daughter. Now, go get ready. I told your grandfather we would be there in half an hour."

I turn in Mason's arms and kiss him in a way that ensures he will be thinking about me for the rest of the night.

"You're sure you have to go to your mom's house afterwards?" he asks, breathless from the kiss.

I laugh and wiggle my way out of his arms.

"That's just a taste of what's in store for you, Mr. Collier. You'll have to wait for the rest, in a place and time of my choosing."

Mason crosses his arms and smiles. "You name the place and time, and I'll make sure I'm there."

"I'll have to get back to you on that," I say coyly, before turning and heading to my bedroom to change clothes.

When I close my bedroom door, I have to lean against it in order to catch my breath. The things kissing Mason does to my body just don't seem possible. I have a hard time imagining myself making love to him and coming out of the experience still in one piece.

As I stare at the clothes in my closet, I realize I don't have a clue what I'm going to wear. What do you wear to meet your estranged grandfather, the man who gave you so much money you would never have to work in your life again if you didn't want to?

I decide on something simple. I pull out a black faux-wrap cashmere sweater, black jeans, and black penny loafers. When I stand to look at myself in the mirror, I realize I look like I'm about to go to a funeral. I quickly dig out a long silver chain with small, glass, colored beads and put it on to at least add a little color to the ensemble. I grab my black wool coat and return to find Mason waiting for me in the living room.

"Ready?" he asks, holding the small basket of cookies Mama Lynn dropped off earlier.

"As I'll ever be, I guess," I reply, taking the basket and holding it tightly, feeling extremely nervous all of a sudden.

"Don't be nervous," Mason says; my feelings are transparent to him. "He's probably just as nervous as you are about this meeting."

"What's he like? You met him in person yesterday, right?"

"From what I could tell, he seems like a very nice man, and he truly wants to meet you and get to know you. I would know if he were lying about that."

I nod. "One advantage of being a walking lie-detector, I guess."

Mason holds his hand out to me. "Come on. Once you meet him, I don't think you'll be nervous anymore."

I place my hand in Mason's and instantly find myself standing in front of a mansion.

My grandfather's home is large, and I begin to wonder just how many brothers and sisters my father might have had. Although it's a mansion, it doesn't feel cold and impersonal. I can tell my grandfather spent a lot of time designing little touches here and there to make what is a palatial estate a home as well. In the distance, beyond the man-made lake with natural rock formations, is a breathtaking mountain view. The house itself looks like something you might find in Austria or Switzerland, with its dark wood detailing and turret-style extensions.

Mason leans in and kisses me on the cheek.

"Good luck; call me when you're ready to come home."

I nod and find myself biting the inside of my bottom lip.

"Don't be nervous," Mason says, kissing me one more time, but this time on the lips, forcing me to stop biting them.

He winks and phases away.

I press the button for the doorbell, and wait, absently tapping my right foot against the multi-colored stone step beneath my feet.

The door is almost instantly opened by a man in his late sixties/early seventies. He's tall, with short white hair, a white neatly-trimmed goatee and mustache, and a smile filled with happiness, making the wrinkles on his face crinkle.

"Jess?" he asks.

It's only then I realize I have no idea what his name is, or how to address him.

"Yes," I answer, "I'm Jess."

His smile broadens. "Please," he says, stepping away from the entrance and opening the door wider. "Come in."

I walk into the house and find myself standing in a grand entryway. There is a large circular staircase that seems to almost hang in midair, and leads to the second floor. Straight out from the doorway, I see a room of glass, which looks to be an arboretum.

"My mom sent these for you," I tell him, handing him the basket of cookies.

He takes them graciously and peeks underneath the red and white cloth.

"Oh, chocolate chip cookies," he croons, "my favorite."

He looks up at me and holds out his arm, bent at the elbow. Not seeing I have any other choice, unless I want to insult him, I loop my own arm through it.

"I thought we would go sit in the arboretum. Have you eaten?"

"Yes, I ate before I came. You didn't plan for me to eat here, did you?" I ask, suddenly worried he might have gone to some trouble to make a meal for me.

"No. But I do have a chef on standby. I was going to have her whip you up something if you were hungry."

"Then, no, definitely not hungry."

"Let's go sit and talk then," he says, leading me to the glass-enclosed room.

The arboretum looks out onto a well-manicured backyard. A large potted Ficus tree, which stands at least ten feet tall in the twenty-foot-high room, sits by a set of double doors leading out to the backyard. Neutral-colored wicker furniture sits angled towards the door. There are a couple of potted ferns scattered around the room. My grandfather sets the basket of cookies on an iron table with a glass top before leading me to one of the wicker sofas to sit down on.

"I guess I know a lot more about you than you know about me," my grandfather tells me.

"Mason said you found me years ago, but decided not to contact me. Why?"

"You had a family, and seemed happy enough with them. I didn't want to disrupt what you had by being selfish. Plus, you were almost through with high school, and I know what a trying time that can be in a teenager's life. You didn't need me. You had a life of your own. So, I did the next best thing, and sent that lawyer to give you some money. I wanted to make sure you didn't want for anything. You seemed like a level- headed young lady. I knew you wouldn't go wild with the money."

"I built a house," I tell him, looking around the room. "Nothing like this, of course, but it's nice. I like it."

We're quiet for a moment before my grandfather reaches beside him and pulls out a small photo album.

"I thought you might like to see some pictures of your father."

He opens the cover of the book, and staring back at me is a senior class portrait of a handsome man, with dark brown hair and eyes. He's not smiling, just staring at the camera, as if he's daring it to take his picture.

"Why does he look so mad?" I ask.

"Your father had a hard time after his mother passed away."

"She's dead?"

"Oh, I'm sorry," my grandfather says. "I thought Mason would have told you that already. Yes, she died of cancer when she was fifty. Your father took it hard. We both did. But watching his mother die like that did something to him. He simply couldn't cope, and turned to drugs to help ease his pain. I tried countless times to get him into a rehab program, but he just wouldn't do it."

"Is that when he met my mother?"

"It was during those years, yes. Your mother seemed to have demons of her own that she was trying to run away from. They clung to one another in their misery. When your father passed away, I tried to get your mother to move in here with me, because I knew she was pregnant with you. But she disappeared before I could persuade her. It was my hope that I could get her clean, and provide you both with a good life. From the moment she disappeared, I tried to find you, but it was like neither of you existed anymore. Not until almost your eighteenth birthday, anyway. A man came to me, and said he knew where you were. He gave me your name, address, the school you went to, everything."

"What man? What was his name?"

"He never told me his name. Just gave me the information and left as quickly as he came. He didn't even ask me for money for the information, which gave me hope that it was real."

"What did he look like?"

"Tall black man," my grandfather says, and his eyes scrunch up as he tries to remember the man. "He had a bald head, commanding voice. For some reason, I knew I could trust him and the information he gave me about you."

I didn't have a clue who my grandfather was talking about. At first, I thought it might have been my father who came and told him where to find me. Now, I just had one more mystery to add to an already long list.

My grandfather and I talk for well over an hour. I learn that the family name is Taylor, and that my grandmother used to be an O'Malley, which explains who I got my fiery temper from. Both my grandfather and grandmother were lawyers for the Hollywood elite, and invested their money wisely to afford the lifestyle my grandfather was now enjoying in retirement. They never had any more children after my father was born.

"That was a mistake," my grandfather tells me. "We should have had more kids so your father wouldn't have felt so alone. Both my wife and I worked long hours, and he ended up being by himself or with nannies most of the time. I often wondered if he would have still turned to drugs if he'd had some brothers or sisters to lean on."

"You can't change the past," I say. "Things happen for a reason."

"I suppose you wouldn't have been born if he'd had an easier life. Blessings come from heartache sometimes."

I smile, realizing how true his words are.

"Would you like to meet my family?" I ask him, not wanting him to think this will be our one and only meeting. Now that I know him a little better, I feel like I want him to become a real part of my life.

He smiles. "I would love that."

"We're having a party at my mother's house tomorrow night for a friend of ours. He's a tearer, and this will be his tenth year living in our neighborhood. I'd love it if you could come. I'm sure I can get Mason to come and get you, as long as you don't have a problem with letting him phase you there."

"They can do that?" My grandfather's eyes sparkle with excitement. "I didn't know Watchers could transport people."

"Don't tell anyone," I say in a conspiratorial voice. "They don't like to let many people know."

"Their secret is safe with me." My grandfather winks and I know I can trust him to keep a secret.

I call Mason when I'm ready to leave, and inform him of the plan to bring my grandfather to meet Mama Lynn and Faison the next evening.

Before I leave, my grandfather gives me a big hug. When I try to pull away from him, I feel him tighten the hug for just a fraction of a second longer before letting me go. I smile at the show of affection.

"See you tomorrow night," I tell him, before taking hold of Mason's hand.

"I look forward to seeing you tomorrow, Jess."

CHAPTER EIGHTEEN

Mason phases me to Mama Lynn's front door.

"It looked like you had a good visit with your grandfather," Mason says, coming to stand in front of me.

"I like him. I hope we get to spend more time together. I would like to get to know him better."

"See?" Mason says, smiling his knowing smile. "I told you there wasn't any reason to be nervous."

I wrap my arms around his waist and pull him to me until our bodies meet.

"I guess wisdom comes with age," I say.

Mason raises his eyebrows at me. "Are you calling me old?"

I shrug. "Well you are, aren't you?"

His mouth quirks up into a smile at my teasing. "Old enough."

"Kiss me before I have to say goodnight to you, old man. And make it good," I tell him. "The memory of it is going to have to last me the whole night."

"A good one, huh?" Mason says, planting small kisses on my forehead and working his way down to my neck. "And here I thought all of my kisses were memorable."

"They are," I say, restraining myself from throwing Mason down on the walkway and having my way with him right then and there. Why does he insist on driving me crazy with his lips? "But this is the last one we'll share until morning."

Mason stops his gentle torture and looks up at the house.

"Which room do you normally stay in?" he asks.

I follow his gaze and point to the second window on the left.

"That one," I tell him. "Why?"

Mason studies the tree nearest the window.

"I could make that jump."

"No," I say firmly.

"Why not?" he asks, almost pouting, which drives me crazy, and I have to kiss him before answering.

When I finally come up for air, I say, "Because we are not doing that in my mother's house."

"Doing what?" Mason asks, becoming serious.

I realize it's now or never.

"The next time we're alone, I don't plan for you to get out of my bed for a few hours at least."

"And what exactly will we be doing for these few hours at least?" he asks.

"Making love, of course," I tell him matter-of-factly.

"And you're telling me this now?" he asks flabbergasted. "When you're about to leave me for an entire night, a night we could be in your bed for these few hours?"

I nod.

"Are you sure?" he asks, all joking aside. "Are you sure you're ready?"

"Yes," I tell him. "I know I can't erase what happened in the past, but I *can* make beautiful memories with you, here in the present. All I know is what he did to me. And all I want now are memories of you making love to me to think about instead."

"And, I repeat, you're telling me this now?"

I laugh because Mason looks like he's in mortal pain.

"Yes, I'm telling you this now. Besides, you have work to do, anyway."

"What work?" he asks, suspicious of my motives.

"It's your job to make sure our first time making love is as special as the first time we kissed. It's a tall order. I thought you might need some time to prepare."

"Hmm, I suppose I do need some time to prepare."

Mason kisses me and drops his arms away from me.

"You should probably go now before I abscond with you. Your mother and sister might not ever see you again if I do."

I giggle and lean up for one more kiss.

"I love you," I tell him.

"And I adore and love you. Now, go, before I change my mind about you staying here tonight."

I wink at him, and he winks back just before he phases away.

"Sounds like I'm just in time with your little care package."

I whirl around and see Faison standing just down the sidewalk.

"How much of that did you hear?" I ask her, my cheeks burning.

"Enough to know I brought these condoms just in time," she says, a tease in her voice.

Besides the two Piggly Wiggly plastic bags, I also see a medium-sized brown paper sack in her hands. She walks up to me and hands me the bag.

"I can't take these in there," I say.

"Oh, Jess, Mama Lynn knows all about sex. She'll just be glad you're having it and using protection."

I lower my head and hide my face behind the bag.

"Now come on, my little grasshopper," Faison says, looping one of her arms around one of mine. "We have a lot to discuss."

"I do not want to discuss sex with you," I tell her resolutely.

"Why not?" Faison says, sounding offended. "I could give you some tips that'll drive Mason wild in bed. I know they do John Austin."

"Please," I beg, "stop. I don't need those mental pictures in my head. I have enough bad memories to get rid of without you adding to them."

Faison sticks her tongue out at me. "Fine, I won't share my extensive knowledge with you. Besides, I bet Mason's been around long enough to have a few tricks of his own."

"Not talking about this with you," I say in a singsong voice, heading for the door because I know only Mama Lynn's presence will keep Faison from trying to talk to me about sex.

Once I'm safely inside Mama Lynn's house, I sigh, relieved in the knowledge that I'm in a sex-talking-free zone.

"Jess is finally going to have sex, Mama Lynn!"

I turn to look at Faison in complete shock and horror. Have they been discussing my lack of a sex life behind my back? It sure sounds like it.

"Why don't you yell that a little louder?" I say through clenched teeth. "I don't think Ms. Margaret across the street heard you. I'm sure she'll be interested in knowing."

Mama Lynn walks into the living room from the kitchen area, a smile on her face.

"Oh, my baby is growing up," she says, coming to give me a kiss on the cheek and a brief hug. "Now, is there anything you need to know about it? Maybe I can help."

I stand dumbstruck. I have no words, only an irrational desire to turn around and run back to my house. Unfortunately, Faison cuts off my route of escape by closing and locking the front door behind her.

"I don't want to talk about it," I tell her. "Please. I am literally begging you. Can we just not talk about it?"

"Well, of course we don't have to talk about it," Mama Lynn says. "Come on. I made that cheese dip you love so much. You got the tortilla chips, right?" she asks Faison.

Faison holds up the bag they are presumably in.

"Now, come and tell us all about your grandfather. What's his name again?"

It's only then I realize I still don't know my grandfather's first name.

"One second."

I pull out my cell phone and text Mason.

Hey, what are you doing?

Wallowing in complete misery without you in my arms.

Dear Misery, what is my grandfather's name?

What do I get for answering the question? A midnight trip through a certain window?

LOL, No! My undying love and gratitude.

I already have your undying love…or so I was led to believe…

You know you do. Please. Just answer the question. I have two very curious onlookers staring holes at me.

Richard Taylor. And why are they staring holes at you?

Because they know we're going to be having sex soon.

Do the three of you share everything?

Faison overheard us talking outside. She brought me a rather large supply of condoms btw.

You don't say. And how long have you been scheming to take advantage of my body, Agent Riley?

Practically since the moment we met.

I didn't realize my chastity had been in danger for so long. You are full of surprises. I do hope she brought a lot for our few hours in your bed. You should know I have very good stamina.

"What?" Faison asks me. "Why do you look so confused all of a sudden?"

Thankfully, Mama Lynn is at the sink, washing out a pot. I show Faison Mason's last text message, and she starts to giggle.

She leans over to me and whispers in my ear, "That means he can do it more than once a night."

"Oh," I say, still not understanding why he feels the need to tell that to me. "Is that unusual, to do it more than just once a night?"

Faison shrugs. "Depends on the man. John Austin's only good for once a day. But I heard Shelby say her boyfriend can go three or four times a day. Just depends."

I am happy to hear you have good stamina. You will need it.

I wait for a response but don't get one. Worried, I text again.

Hello? Are you there?

Yes. I'm here. Just having an argument with myself about whether or not I should force my way into your window later tonight.

Please do not. I don't want our first time to be inside my mother's house.

I could always phase you out and phase you back in there in the morning.

I actually consider the proposition, but shake off the temptation.

No. Like I said, I want our first time together to be special. Hiding what we're doing does not scream special to me.

Fine. But you should know that I am pouting right now. My bottom lip is out and everything.

<sucks on Mason's pouty bottom lip> Stop pouting.

<kisses that tender spot right behind your ear>

Stop.

You started it…

And now I'm stopping it. I don't need to sit in my mother's kitchen and feel this way. Good night, Mr. Collier. I wish you the sweetest of dreams.

As you wish. And don't worry. I will have the sweetest dreams... about you... in your bed....underneath me...

Incorrigible...

Yes...very...but you love it.

I love you

And I love you. Good night.

I sigh and place my phone back in my pocket. When I look up, I see Mama Lynn and Faison staring at me.

"What?" I ask.

Mama Lynn just smiles. "Nothing; I just like seeing you happy. Now, come on. Let's play Jenga!"

I groan as Faison pulls me to the living room.

As I sit around the coffee table, a nervous wreck due to playing Mama Lynn's favorite game, I can't think about anything except what Mason might be planning for us. I pray the night passes quickly, because all I really want is for it to be the next day and in the arms of the man I love.

When I go to bed that evening, I hear a noise outside my window. I hurry over to see if it's Mason trying to climb through my window. I feel completely disappointed when I see John Austin climbing the tree and leaping over into Faison's window. I just smile and shake my head, knowing this probably isn't the first time he's made a midnight visit to my sister.

I grab my phone and text Mason.

I miss you...

I miss you too...get some sleep... I will see you tomorrow...

I crawl under my comforter and sigh, knowing it's going to be a long sleepless night.

CHAPTER NINETEEN

The next morning I slip out early, intent on taking a bath before I call Mason. I know we won't have time to make good on certain promises that morning, though. JoJo is sure to wake up today, and I promised I would be there when she did. In fact, it will probably be at least two days before we can do anything, since Chandler is due to wake up tomorrow. I sigh in disappointment, but know Mason and I will get our chance eventually.

As I'm walking up the sidewalk towards my house, I see George out in front of his home, looking up at the Tear. I decide to have an overdue talk with my friend and neighbor.

"Morning, George."

He looks down from the sky and at me. He smiles. "Good morning, Jess. How was the girls' night?"

"I think I gained ten pounds from all the junk food but, other than that, it was good."

George chuckles. "If there is one thing certain in this world, Lynn will never let you girls go hungry."

I'm not sure how to begin the conversation I have in mind with George, so I just blurt out what I want to ask.

"George, why did you want to leave your world?"

George looks at me in surprise. "How did you know that? I've never told anyone."

"I've…come to understand how tearers are chosen to go through the Tear. You have to want it. Why did you want to leave?"

"My wife cheated on me," George confides. "I just couldn't stand to be around her anymore, and I remember thinking that maybe my life would be better if I went through the tear and started over."

"But what about your kids?"

"I only saw them once a year. They had families of their own and not a lot of time for me. It's just the way things work on my planet. Once you leave your parents' home, you're gone for good. We never feel the need to visit our parents, except when we celebrate our birthday."

"Why on your birthday?"

"Because that's the day they gave us life. Here, birthdays are completely opposite. It's the person who was born who gets to celebrate. Back on my planet, it's the parents who are given a party."

"Then why haven't you made your move on Mama Lynn?"

"I didn't want to get involved and then disappear on her. You know some tearers get sent back home."

"Only if they want to go."

George stares at me hard before asking, "You know this for a fact? I won't be sent back unless I want to go?"

"Yes, George, I know that for a fact."

The relief I see in George's eyes makes me smile.

"Well, hot damn," he says, as if I've just lifted the weight of the world off his shoulders. "Do you think she'll go out with me?"

"George, she's been waiting ten years for you to ask. Yes, I think she'll go out with you."

George makes like he's going to walk over to Mama Lynn's house that instant.

"Why don't you let her wake up first?" I suggest. "Last I saw, she was still in bed."

George chuckles. Even out of his Santa Clause suit, he still reminds me of Old Saint Nick when he laughs.

"Maybe you're right. I'll go get some donuts for her and Faison. Maybe by then they'll be up. You want some?"

"No, I'll be fine. I have a busy day planned. I might not even be here when you get back."

George leans in and kisses me on the cheek. "You gave me the best gift ever, Jess. Thank you."

When I make it back into my house, I head straight to the bathroom and take a shower. Thirty minutes later I'm dressed and groomed for the day. I text Mason.

Can you come and get me?

Almost instantly, Mason is standing in my living room.
He looks at me, somewhat disappointed.

"What's wrong?" I ask, walking up to him.

"I was hoping you literally meant I could come and get you and have my way with you, but you have clothes on."

I drape my arms over his shoulders. "Not today. Probably not tomorrow either. I need to be with JoJo and Chandler when they wake up. It's important."

Mason sighs. "I know. And I will wait. But, just so you know, I don't like it."

He pouts and purposely sticks out his bottom lip.

I nip his pouty lip with my teeth, which leads to a full-on kiss.

Finally, I break the kiss and take two steps back.

"I am not going to let you seduce me right now," I say to him imperiously. "I've waited a long time, and I won't be rushed the first time we make love. So, take me to JoJo now, please; I have work to do."

"You do realize," Mason says, "that she might not wake up for a few hours. A few hours we *could* be putting to good use."

"And she could wake up in the next minute. No," I say firmly, "we do it my way. You'll just have to rein in your urges for two days."

"Two days?" he laments. "Are you trying to kill me?"

I didn't want to admit it, but I felt like I might die as well. So, I simply hold out my hand to him and say, "JoJo."

Mason grabs my hand and pulls me roughly to him, kissing me so hard I don't have time to breathe. When he decides to let me go, he looks very pleased with himself.

"Just a small taste," he says, and smiles before phasing us to his villa. Mason ends up being right. JoJo doesn't wake up until almost five hours later. When she finally does begin to stir, Mason smirks at me in an 'I told you so' fashion.

"I know, I know," I say, but stand behind my decision. There really was no way of telling when she would wake up. And I promised Chandler I would be at both their bedsides when they finally did awaken from their first encounter with their archangels.

When JoJo opens her eyes, a warm yellow aura only I can see surrounds her. I assume its presence means she and her archangel are indeed connected.

"Hey," I say to her, sitting on the bed at her side, looking into her jubilant face.

"*Bonjour,*" she says, smiling happily up at me.

"How do you feel?"

JoJo pats her stomach. "Famished."

"Come with me, then. Mason made his famous chicken soup for you. It's down in the kitchen."

After JoJo eats her first bowl of soup, I ask, "So, who is your archangel?"

"Jophiel," JoJo beams. "Ah, she is so beautiful and sweet."

"Did she explain to you that she looks the way you think she should look?"

"*Oui, oui,* she told me that."

"Did she tell you anything useful?"

"Not anything more than what you said Michael told you. We mostly played."

I feel sure I misunderstood what JoJo said, so I repeat, "Played?"

"Played dress-up! I could dress her in anything my mind imagined. I cannot tell you how much fun that was for me! And we danced," JoJo says with a smile, hugging herself as she relives the memory. "We had so much fun together!"

I have a hard time imagining Michael and me ever dancing. Maybe the archangels really were matched perfectly to their human hosts.

"When will Chandler wake up?" JoJo asks me

"Theoretically, tomorrow some time."

JoJo finishes her second bowl of soup in record time.

"Another?" Mason asks her.

"*Non,* I've had enough." JoJo yawns. "I think I need to sleep again."

"You should only sleep for one more day," I tell her from my own experience.

"I do not mind. Jophiel is so much fun to be with. I can't wait to see her all the time!"

"All the time?" I ask.

"*Oui*, when the connections are made," JoJo says, spinning her index fingers around her head. "Then I can see her when I am awake, *oui*?"

"Yes, then you can see her when you're awake."

"Do you see Michael all the time now?"

"Uh, no. I only talk to him when I have to."

"Why?"

"I don't see any reason to bring him out unless I need to ask a question."

JoJo looks at me like she doesn't understand me. I thought I was pretty plain in my explanation. But she just shrugs and doesn't ask any more questions.

After I tuck JoJo into bed with Chandler again, she instantly goes back to sleep.

I turn to face Mason, who has a wicked look in his eyes that makes me very aware of his needs.

I sigh.

"No, not now," I say. I swear to God I feel like I'm dealing with a teenage boy instead of an angel. "I need to go to Mama Lynn's and help her prepare for the party."

"You...are...killing....me."

I can't help but laugh at his plight.

"Ok, let's make a date. Be in my house at five tomorrow night. I'll even cook."

Mason growls and tugs me to him. "I don't need food."

I melt against him. "Then I'll make something that can be eaten afterwards. I assume we'll be hungry?"

"For food? Probably."

Mason's phone vibrates.

"I have to take this," he says, kissing me before he pulls the phone out of his pocket.

"Yes?" he says to the caller but keeps me in his arms. "All right. I have the afternoon free. Ask Isaiah to come back to the villa to watch over JoJo and Chandler."

Isaiah appears almost instantly in the room. I try to pull away from Mason, but he doesn't let me.

"See you in a minute, Nick." Mason ends the call. "Isaiah, would you mind turning your back to us for a minute?"

Isaiah grins knowingly and turns his back to us.

"I have to go apologize to your President for leaving so abruptly yesterday," Mason tells me, "but I will be back for the party tonight."

"Was he mad that you left without saying anything?"

Mason shrugs. "Miffed would be a better word. But it was definitely worth it. I just need to go stroke his ego some. Make him feel like I think he's important."

"You don't think he's important?"

"He's a blip in time, as far as I'm concerned."

"Am I a blip too?"

"No, you're the reason time exists for me."

I glance in Isaiah's direction to make sure his back is still turned before showing Mason with my lips how much his words mean to me.

When I finally pull away, I tell Mason, "Please take me to Mama Lynn's before I lose my willpower to wait until tomorrow night."

"We're leaving, Isaiah. Call if you need anything, or if there is a change in their condition."

Mason phases me to Mama Lynn's front door.

"I'll try to be quick," he tells me.

"Play nice."

Mason grins. "I always play nice."

"And don't forget you're supposed to bring my grandfather to the party tonight."

He winks at me.

"I won't forget," he says before phasing to apologize to the President of the United States.

Mama Lynn is practically beaming with joy when I walk into her house.

"I guess George made it by here this morning?" I say to her.

Mama Lynn smiles brightly. "Yes, he did. He finally asked me out after ten years of waiting. He told me you helped him finally get the courage to do it. What did you say to him?"

"Yeah," Faison asks as she and John Austin are blowing up balloons with a helium tank in the living room. "What did you tell him?"

I explain to them about how the Tear works, but swear them to secrecy. It's not knowledge the public has, but neither is it top-secret information.

"So everyone who goes through *wants* to go through?" Faison summarizes.

"Yes. Apparently, that's the way it works."

"Then it isn't exactly a bad thing," she goes on to say. "If it just takes people who want to leave the lives they have to start over fresh, maybe it's actually good."

"For them maybe, but I don't think it's always good for the people they leave behind. It's selfish of them to just want a new life and leave their families and friends to pick up the pieces when they're gone."

"Yeah, I guess you're right," Faison agrees.

We spend most of the afternoon cooking and preparing for George's party. Beau is the first to arrive, with the much-anticipated stack of cinnamon rolls. Faison and I both sneak one because we know they will be the first things to be eaten.

Our friends and neighbors slowly start to trickle in at around five, and Mama Lynn sends John Austin out to get some more crushed ice.

By the time George arrives, the party is in full-swing and Mama Lynn has already pulled out the Pictionary game.

"Where're Mason and your grandfather?" Faison asks me. "I thought they were going to come."

"Mason had to go talk to the President. I'm not sure what's keeping him. I thought he would be here by now."

"The president of what?"

"The United States."

Faison's mouth forms a silent 'O'.

"Of course he's talking to *the* President; should have known."

I pull out my phone to text Mason.

Are you all right?

I get a response almost immediately.

Sorry. I should have texted or called. I am fine. He wanted me to stay for supper. I am on my way to get your grandfather right now. Love you.

Love you too. See you soon.

"He had to eat supper with the President. He's going to get my grandfather now and be right over," I tell Faison.

"Wow, do you think you'll get to meet him one day? The President?"

"Apparently, it's not as exciting as you might think," I tell her, hating to burst her bubble.

The doorbell rings and Faison gets up to answer it, since she's on door duty until John Austin gets back.

When Faison opens the door, there is a highway police officer standing on the other side.

"I'm sorry," Faison says. "Are we making too much noise? You know how rowdy kids can get nowadays."

The patrol officer looks at the group of middle-aged and elderly people gathered in the living room, but doesn't seem to be in the mood for Faison's joke.

"Are you Faison Mills?" he asks instead.

"Yes," she answers hesitantly. "Am I in trouble?"

"Ma'am, I was asked by the family of a John Austin Allen to inform you of their son's death. Please accept my deepest condolences."

I walk over to the door. Faison is still standing there, a pleasant smile on her face like she's frozen in time.

"You must be mistaken," she tells him, shaking her head. "John Austin just went to get some crushed ice. He'll be back in just a minute."

It's only then I realize it's been almost an hour since John Austin left to get the ice. I'd been so concerned about Mason I didn't even realize John Austin had been gone for so long.

"What happened?" I ask the trooper.

"An eighteen-wheeler side swiped his truck as he was crossing Hwy 61. He died instantly, from what I know. It was a quick death. He didn't feel any pain."

"That wasn't John Austin," Faison tells the policeman. "He'll be back any minute."

The officer looks to me for help in the situation.

"Thank you for coming, Officer," I tell him. "I'll take it from here."

He nods his understanding. I'm sure he's dealt with people refusing to believe him before.

Faison stands stock-still. I take her hand off the doorknob and close the door.

All has turned quiet in the house, and everyone is staring at Faison. Mama Lynn comes up to Faison and tries to put her arms around her, but Faison shrugs them off.

"Don't," she says, turning to walk into the kitchen.

Mama Lynn and I follow her. Faison starts to pull every drinking glass in the cabinets out, and sets them on the counter in a straight line.

"Faison," I say, but she holds up her hand silently, telling me not to talk.

"When John Austin gets back, we'll need to fill all these glasses with the ice he's bringing."

I watch my sister count the glasses over and over again, as if she's making sure we have enough. I look to Mama Lynn, but see she's fighting back tears, watching her daughter helplessly as Faison completely refuses to accept what has happened to the love of her life.

I walk up to Faison and try to put my hands on her shoulders, but she just knocks them off.

"Don't touch me while I'm counting. He'll be here any minute, and I need to make sure we have enough glasses."

"He's not coming, Faison," I say, not trying to be mean or cruel, but needing her to face the reality of the situation.

"He'll be here any minute," she argues. "Now, leave me alone."

I put both my hands on her shoulders and force her to turn around and face me. She fights me, but eventually I win.

"He's dead, Faison," I say.

Her eyes look glazed over, like she's trapped in a world where John Austin is only a few minutes away. I can't let her wall herself off in that world, because I know I will lose her for good if I do.

"John Austin is dead," I say again, trying to shock her system into accepting that fundamental truth. "He is not coming back. He is not bringing ice. He is dead, Faison."

I watch as her eyes start to refocus on my face, and know she's coming back from whatever fantasy world she was creating.

A mask of grief contorts her features.

"He's dead," she says aloud, forcing the words to sink into the cracks of her broken heart. "He's dead!"

Faison collapses into my arms in a fit of sorrow, and I bear the brunt of her weight.

I feel a pair of strong hands grab my shoulders, keeping me steady so I don't topple over. Without even looking behind me, I know it's Mason. He comes up closer behind me so my back is pressed against his chest, allowing me to use him as my center while my sister, my best friend, dissolves in my arms.

CHAPTER TWENTY

For the next three days, I am constantly by Faison's side. I've never seen grief like hers, and it breaks my heart to watch such a genteel soul suffer the way she is. Chandler and JoJo come to offer their support to me, and I wish Faison could draw some strength from the connection we feel with one another. I ask my friends if there's anything they can do for Faison to ease her pain, but they pretty much tell me whatever they did would only stop her suffering for a moment. She would still have to work through it naturally to ever find true peace and be whole again. I know they're right, but the torment I see Faison going through seems beyond a human's capability to deal with.

I'm not even sure she wants to be alive, which worries me more than anything else. I try to put myself in her position. How would I feel if I lost Mason? Would I want to go on? I don't see how. I would probably be just like Faison, alive but not really living.

I feel torn between my need to continue my work with Chandler and JoJo and my desire to be there for Faison anytime she needs me. Even though all I want to do is take care of Faison, I know I have work, which is just as important.

Mason was my rock after John Austin's death. He not only helped me deal with Faison and her grief, but he also helped me cope with my own feelings of loss. John Austin had been in my life just as long as he'd been in Faison's, albeit not as intimately. We all grew up together, and all I can think about is the little freckle-nosed boy who used to pull on Faison's bright red pigtails in second grade, trying to get her attention.

I always envied the two of them. To be able to find your soul mate at such a young age seemed like a small miracle. Now, it just seems like a cruel twist of fate. They finally reached a point in their lives where they could fulfill their dream of getting married and starting a family. Now, one of them was gone forever, never to return except in the world of dreams.

Mason held me when I needed to cry over the loss of my friend, and he held me when I needed to cry because I felt like I was losing Faison too.

There are times I look at Faison and see nothing behind her eyes, like her body is with me but her mind is trapped somewhere else. I have no idea how to help her, and am clueless as to how to ease her pain.

"Grief passes," Mason told me late one night, after Faison went to bed. "She just needs time."

"I'm not sure she's strong enough to get past John Austin's death," I replied. "She'll never be the same again."

"No, she won't be the same. She'll either grow from the experience or shrink from it. There isn't much you can do except be there for her. She has to find a reason to live again. You can't give it to her."

On the fourth day after John Austin's passing, I ask Mason to bring JoJo and Chandler to my house. We need to at least try to connect with the fourth vessel, even though I fear my mental state might block our efforts, like it has before.

Faison and I are working on a puzzle of Vincent van Gogh's *Starry Night* painting at my kitchen table when Mason phases to my house with JoJo and Chandler. I'm usually not one to do puzzles, but it seems to help Faison concentrate on something else besides her unending grief.

Faison looks up from the puzzle and notices JoJo and Chandler standing awkwardly in my living room, waiting for me as Mason walks into the kitchen.

"I'm going to step outside for a little while," she tells me, standing from her chair.

"You can stay in here while we work," I urge her. "It's cold out there, Fai."

"No, I think some fresh night air will do me good. I won't stay out long."

"Don't forget to put your coat on."

She nods and heads to her room to get her coat.

Since John Austin's death, Faison has been staying with me. A part of her blames Mama Lynn for his death, because she's the one who asked him to go get the ice. I know Faison realizes it wasn't Mama

Lynn's fault, but, in her desolation, she seems to need someone real to blame, besides fate.

"Did she do any better today?" Mason asks me.

I stand and hug him, drawing strength from his nearness while I can. I asked Mason only to come to the house once during the day while Faison was awake. I didn't want her to feel like a third wheel around us. Plus, I feared our love would just remind her of the love she lost, and throw her over the deep end.

At night, Mason would come back and sleep with me because I needed his comfort. I needed him like I needed air or food. It just made me understand even more the pain Faison was suffering through. How was I supposed to help her find a way to live again, when I wasn't sure if *I* could under the same circumstances?

"She's talking," I say, resting my head on his shoulder, wishing we lived in a world where grief didn't exist. "That's an improvement."

I see Chandler and JoJo watching us from the living room. I wasn't able to be there for Chandler when he woke up after connecting with Chamuel. He understood, but I still felt bad about it. Now Chandler has a perpetual pink glow around him. I asked Michael why Chandler and JoJo had different-colored auras, and he told me each of the archangels would have their own special aura that only I would be able to see. When I told Chandler he glowed pink to my eyes, he seemed a bit disappointed, saying it wasn't a very manly color.

I squeeze Mason tightly before letting him go to walk over to my friends.

JoJo hands me a bag with her designing company's signature 'A' on the front.

"Mason said this would help you," she tells me.

I open the bag, expecting to see a piece of clothing, but find a soft black leather sheath for my sword instead.

"Thank you," I tell her, setting the bag aside.

"Is there anything we can do for you, Jess?" Chandler asked.

"Let's just find the next vessel," I tell them both. "I don't know how much time we have left, considering Lucifer only has to find three more princes. We're falling behind."

Faison walks out of her room, putting her arms through her coat. She attempts to smile at my friends but fails miserably. I'm just happy to see her make the effort. It shows me that a small bit of my sister is trying to resurface. I hear her go out the front door, and I sigh.

"She'll be all right," Chandler reassures me, seeing my distress and most likely feeling it as well.

"*Oui*," JoJo agrees. "You will both survive this tragedy and come out stronger for it."

"I'll just be happy to take the survive part of that sentence for now," I say weakly.

"Do you want me to build a fire?" Mason asks me, knowing the sound of a fire helps me concentrate.

I nod, and he sets to work.

Once the fire is built, we move the coffee table out of the way and sit in a circle on the floor. Holding hands, we close our eyes and try to concentrate on the location of the fourth vessel.

After a while, I almost give up, but something happens. I start to smell something burning, but know it isn't coming from the fire we're sitting by or anything inside my house. I concentrate on the smell until a picture forms in my mind.

A girl, maybe fifteen or sixteen, stands in front of a building going up in a blazing inferno. On the side of the building, I see a 'W' and an 'A', marking it as Watcher property. I can see the girl's face clearly, like she's standing right in front of me. Her beautiful facial features are Asian in origin. Her long black hair hangs almost down to her waist, and she's dressed shabbily in an old green coat and threadbare green knit cap. Her face is streaked with either soot or dirt; it's hard to tell which. She stands completely still and stares at the building, as if the dancing flames have hypnotized her.

I hear the blare of sirens in the distance and so does she. She looks frightened and runs down a darkened street before disappearing from my mind.

When I open my eyes, I see Chandler and JoJo open theirs too.

"We have to find a Watcher building on fire right now," Chandler says.

Mason immediately gets on his phone and makes inquiries about the fire, but no Watcher building in the world is on fire at that moment.

"What do we do now?" Chandler asks.

"We connected with her," I tell him. "That's all that matters for the moment. The rest will come."

I decide that's enough for one night, and suggest we just relax and visit with one another for the rest of the evening. I grab my coat and go out onto the porch to find Faison, intent on bringing her back inside to be with the rest of us.

When I get out there, she's sitting on the top step, looking up at the stars in the sky.

Without saying a word, I sit down beside her.

"I wonder if he's in Heaven, watching me," she finally says.

"Maybe," I concede, not knowing if people in Heaven actually do look down and watch over the lives of the people they've left behind.

Faison breaks down into sobs, and I pull her to me, cradling her in my arms as her heart continues to break.

"I can't live like this," she wails, shaking her head against my chest, bereft of hope.

"You just need time," I tell her. "Your heart needs time to heal. You'll get through this, I promise. I'll help you."

As I'm holding her, I see a flash of white light out of the corner of my eye. When I turn my head, I see the Tear is open.

Involuntarily, I gasp. Faison raises her head and follows my gaze to the Tear in the sky.

Through the opening, we see a planet that looks a lot like Earth, but there's something off about it. I can't quiet put my finger on what's different, but there is definitely something wrong with this alternate Earth. It seems darker for some reason.

As we both stare at the Tear, I hear Faison say, "I don't want to be here."

I look over at her. "We could always go stay at Mason's villa for a while. I'm sure he wouldn't mind. We can go anywhere you want."

Her eyes remain steady on the Tear.

"I don't want to be here," she says again, with more force behind her words.

It's only then I realize what she's trying to do. Quickly, I stand up so I'm blocking her view of the Tear, forcing her to look at me.

"No," I tell her, as if that one word will stop her.

"I don't want to be here," she repeats, breaking down into a heart-wrenching sob.

I kneel down in front of her and grab her by the shoulders, shaking her.

"Faison, look at me!"

She refuses, and continues to repeat her sentence like a litany, all the while staring past me to the Tear.

I scream at her again, but she's too far gone. She just keeps repeating the same sentence over and over. Finally, I slap her hard across the face, hoping to break her concentration and bring her back to reality.

Her eyes, mad with grief, finally focus on me as she screams, "I don't want to be here!"

Before I know it, I'm not holding Faison anymore.

In her place sits a half-formed creature I've only seen once before. It looks like a Watcher child in the midst of its transformation into a werewolf. It seems startled by its new surroundings, but still hungry for human flesh. It snaps its protruding jaw in my face, causing me to fall back onto the sidewalk.

Without even having to think about it, my sword appears in my hand just as the creature lunges toward me, intent on tearing out my throat. As I lift the sword to ward off the attack, the blade bursts into flames as the end of it pierces the werewolf through its gut. The creature disintegrates into a cloud of black ash around me.

I drop the sword onto the ground, trying to wrap my head around what just happened. The reality of what Faison has done finally hits home. In her grief over John Austin's death, she used the information I gave her about how the Tear chooses its travelers, and abandoned me like most of the people in my life have at one time or another.

She's gone.

Before I know it, Mason is by my side, helping me stand up.

"Jess, what happened? Where is Faison?" he asks, but I can't find a voice to answer with. My own grief has all but closed my throat, and my body is wracked with wave after wave of unbearable pain.

I feel Mason's arms hold me tight as he tries to reassure me everything will be all right, but I know it won't. I know there will be no way to get Faison back, because she won't willingly ask to come home through the tear again. Why return to a place that only holds heartache? She has a chance to start fresh in another world. She'll never ask to come back.

I see Lucifer phase in, a few feet behind Mason. Our connection has brought him to me in my time of grief. Strangely enough, his presence makes me stop crying because I instantly know what I have to do next. I have to bring Faison back home. I vow to myself that I will see her again, no matter the cost.

Even if I have to make a deal with the devil himself…

CHAPTER TWENTY-ONE

Abandoned...

As I look at Lucifer over Mason's shoulder, I wonder if that word entered Lucifer's mind when Michael left him on Earth for his exile. Strangely enough, the thought makes me feel like I understand Lucifer a little better. If there was one thing we both had in common, it was the pain of having those we love and trust abandon us when we need them the most.

"Jess, what's happened?" Mason asks again, since I didn't answer him the first time.

"Faison went through the Tear," I tell him, pulling myself out of his arms and wiping the tears from my eyes, filled with a new determination.

When I look at Mason's face, I see how worried he is about me.

"Don't worry," I tell him, "I have a plan."

"A plan? A plan to do what, exactly?"

"A plan to bring her back."

Before he can ask how I intend to perform such a miracle, I walk around him and head straight towards Lucifer.

"What's happened to make you so upset?" Lucifer asks me, sounding truly concerned, but I can never tell how true his sincerity is.

"My sister just went through the Tear," I say, coming to stand in front of him.

"I'm sorry to hear that. Why did she want to go?"

"Her fiancé just died. She's grieving, not thinking."

I remain silent, waiting to see if he says anything. Will he offer me his help, out of this growing friendship he seems to think we have? It doesn't seem like it. I have a feeling nothing comes free from Lucifer.

I feel Mason come up behind me, but don't turn around. I know he'll disapprove of what I'm about to do, but I just don't care. The only thing I can think about is getting Faison back. If a Watcher child came through the tear to replace her, then she might be in mortal danger. I just pray there aren't any more of those things where she was sent.

"Can you help me get her back?" I ask Lucifer directly.

"Jess…" Mason says, and I hear the warning in his voice. He knows as well as I do that Lucifer won't just help me out of the goodness of his heart… if there *is* any goodness left in him.

Lucifer smiles, and I feel like a mouse about to be eaten by a cat.

"And if I help you, what do you offer me in return?"

"Jess, don't," I hear a familiar voice say beside me.

I look to my right and see Michael standing beside me. I faintly wonder what Lucifer would give to speak to Michael.

"You can't trust him to help you," Michael tells me. "He'll get the information he wants from you, but he won't help you get Faison back."

"How can you be so sure?" I ask him.

"Because I know him better than anyone; please, Jess, trust me. He can't help you get her back."

I feel my heart sink into the pit of my stomach, because I know Michael is telling me the truth. I can feel his certainty within my soul in this matter, but I also feel a spark of hope.

"You know how I can get her back," I say to him, not having to ask for verification because I know the answer is yes.

"Excuse me," Lucifer says, "but I feel like I'm only hearing one side of a conversation here. Who are you talking to, Jessica?"

I look back at Lucifer, ignoring his question and asking one of my own.

"Can you help me get my sister back or not?"

"Perhaps, but you haven't told me what I get in return for my help yet."

I look between Lucifer and Michael and know which of the two can actually offer me a real chance at hope.

I turn to Michael.

"What do I have to do?"

"You have to ask for help."

"Isn't that what I'm doing?" I ask, becoming irritated with what sounds like a run- around answer.

"I can't help you, but my father can."

I let out a harsh laugh. "When has God ever helped me with anything?"

"Have you ever asked for His help?"

I realize I haven't. I've never tried to directly speak with God because I didn't believe in His existence until a few weeks ago.

"Why would He help me? Because of you?"

Michael shakes his head. "No, Jess. He'll help you because you ask."

I shake my head in disbelief and look down at the ground. I'm not sure what's crazier: seeking help from Lucifer or praying to God, someone who's stayed in the shadows of my life, never bothering to directly interfere for better or worse.

"Jess," Mason says, trying to draw my attention.

I turn around to face him.

"Ask for His help," Mason urges me, obviously understanding the advice Michael is giving me from what I've said on my side of the conversation.

"Praying really isn't my thing," I admit, not even knowing how to start a prayer.

"There's no guarantee He'll answer it anyway," Lucifer says behind me, casting doubt. "He's not exactly the most responsive. I've been talking to Him for years and haven't heard a peep."

"And we're supposed to be surprised by that?" Mason questions sarcastically. "I would imagine it's because of what you say."

Lucifer shrugs.

"Either way," Lucifer says looking me straight in the eyes, "not a peep. Your prayer will probably fall on deaf ears too. If Faison was meant to go through the Tear, He won't interfere with her fate. You, of anyone here, should know that fact. If it's part of your destiny to suffer by the hands of others or events in your life, He won't lift a finger to make your life any easier."

"You aren't Jess," Mason tells Lucifer. "He'll listen to her."

"How can you be so sure?" I ask, my voice almost a whisper.

Mason takes both of my hands into his and looks at me.

"Because I think He's been waiting for you to talk to Him for a very long time. However, Lucifer is right about one thing: If it's Faison's destiny to stay on that alternate Earth, He won't interfere. The only way you'll know for sure though is if you ask."

"How do I do that?" I ask, desperate enough to try anything. "How do I talk to Him so He hears me?"

"Just ask Him for help," Mason says, making it sound so simple.

"Out loud?"

Mason smiles at me indulgently. "It doesn't matter. He'll hear a silent prayer just as well as a voiced one."

I take a deep breath and squeeze Mason's hands even tighter.

"Here goes nothing," I mumble.

I feel somewhat stupid, so I decide to just talk to God in my head and hope He hears my first attempt at a prayer. I close my eyes.

Dear God,

Jess here. Need your help if you have time.

Not exactly eloquent, but surely He knows what's going on. Isn't He, like, omniscient or something?

Mason lets go of my hands, turns his back to me, and kneels on one knee with his head bowed. Out of the corner of my eye, I see my vision of Michael do the same. Lucifer snorts behind me, but I don't feel any movement telling me he feels compelled to fall to his knees.

I lift my gaze from Mason's kneeling figure, and look straight ahead.

I see a tall, bald, black man in his forties, standing where I left my sword on the sidewalk. He's dressed all in black, from his turtleneck sweater underneath a black leather jacket to his non-descript shoes. Even in the dark, His eyes are piercing, like they could burn a hole in my soul if that's what He wanted to do.

He leans down and picks my sword up off the ground by the hilt.

"You may want to be more careful where you leave this," he admonishes lightly, looking from the sword to me.

"I usually leave it on my dresser," I tell him.

The man nods and twists his wrist, making the sword spin through the air towards the house. I watch as it disappears.

"Then that's where you'll find it," the man tells me.

I see the man's eyes shift from me to Lucifer, who is still standing directly behind me.

"I've heard your prayers to me, Lucifer. I'm simply waiting to hear one that isn't selfish and demanding."

"What's the saying the monkeys like to use?" Lucifer says. "Ah, yes. That'll happen when Hell freezes over."

"I still have hope for you," God says, His gaze steady on Lucifer. "It's not too late."

Lucifer burst into harsh laughter. "Then who would take care of all the bad little monkey souls? Isn't that what you made me for? Isn't that my purpose for existing?"

"You chose your own path, My son," God says.

"Like I had much of a choice," Lucifer scoffs. "You've always loved them more than us. Jessica prays to you once, and You give her a visit in person. I've prayed to You millions of times and nary a word."

"If it had been the right prayer," God says, "I would have answered you."

"If You're looking for me to ask for forgiveness, then You have a long wait ahead of you."

"Like I said, I still have hope for you."

"Well, while I always love these little heart to heart talks with You, Father, I think I'll be leaving now. You're not here to talk to me anyway. Good luck, Jessica," Lucifer says to me. I turn my head to look at Lucifer. "I hope you get more out of Him than I ever have."

Lucifer phases, and I'm left to face God with my two kneeling angels.

God walks over to Michael first and places His hand on his curly black hair. I faintly wonder how He's able to touch Michael like he's real, but quickly set such a question aside. He's God; of course He can touch a figment of my imagination.

"It's been a long time, My son," God says to Michael. "Please stand."

Michael stands and lifts his gaze to God.

"Thank You for asking me to come here," Michael tells Him. "I was able to hold my daughter for the first time because of Jess' generosity."

God nods. "I know. I was watching. Lilly was extremely moved by the visit. She needed to know how much you love her."

God turns to look at Mason, who is still kneeling on one knee.

God walks over and places His hand on Mason's head.

"Please stand, Mason."

Mason stands and shifts slightly, so he's not standing in front of me but beside me.

God raises His hand and traces His fingers over Mason's scar.

"Not as deep as it once was," God says approvingly, letting His hand drop back to His side. "I'm glad to see that."

"Meeting Jess has given me hope we can seal the Tear," Mason tells Him.

"And her love is helping you see yourself the way I see you."

"Yes," Mason says, taking one of my hands into his. "Her love has helped a great deal. It's the main reason that I would like to accept the offer You gave us the night the Tear was made, but only after we've sealed it."

"You can have it now if you want," God says. "Any of you can have it at any time."

"No, not yet," Mason says with a definite shake of his head. "I wouldn't be as effective that way. When it's sealed and all of this is over, I will ask You to do it."

"And I will grant it."

I have no idea what they're talking about, but it sounds important. I make a mental sticky note to ask Mason about it later.

God turns his full attention to me, and it's almost like we're the only two people in the world at that moment.

"Would the two of you mind giving me some time alone with Jess?" God asks.

I think Mason feels my nervousness, because he squeezes my hand in reassurance.

"I'll be in the house with JoJo and Chandler," he tells me, letting me know he'll only be a few feet away.

I nod, finding strength in his closeness before he phases.

Michael simply disappears back into the recesses of my mind.

I'm left standing in front of God. Alone.

"It's been a long time since we last spoke," God says to me.

"Has it?" I ask. "When was the first time, because I thought this was it?"

"Of course," God grins, "you wouldn't remember the first time. Your soul and I had a lengthy discussion before you melded with Michael's soul."

"Oh, that. My father told me about that. I don't remember it, though. Thanks for letting my dad come back, by the way. I needed him that night."

"Yes, I know."

I stand there quietly staring at God, not knowing how to ask for what I want.

"Just ask, Jess," He says to me, like He knows exactly what I'm thinking.

And maybe He does. Hell if I know. This isn't exactly something I ever thought I would be doing: asking God for a favor while He's standing in my front yard. Not one of those life moments I ever planned to have.

"Will You help me get Faison back?" I finally ask, holding my breath while I wait for the answer.

"Only she has the power to bring herself back home," He tells me.

"Then You won't help me?"

"I didn't say that. I will help you, but you won't be able to drag her back here against her will. She has to decide to come back on her own."

"How are You going to help me then?"

"I will open the tear to where she went. Only you and Mason will be allowed to travel through it, though. You will find her in that world and be able to plead your case to her, but, ultimately, it has to be her decision to come back here."

"Why are You letting Mason go with me?"

"Because I believe he needs to see this particular alternate reality."

"Why? What's different there?"

"Everything."

"Is he there, a different version of Mason?"

"That's something you and he will have to discover on your own. But I do hope seeing what has happened on this alternate Earth will prove to him he has nothing to feel guilty about anymore."

"Why does he keep blaming himself for something that happened so long ago?"

"Because he's a good and honorable man, but I believe you know that already."

I nod. "Yes. I do. I just wish he understood that about himself."

"He will in time."

"Can I ask You to do something else for me?" I question.

"Yes, you can ask."

"Can Lucifer really send Uncle Dan to the Void?"

God's gaze never falters, and He continues to look at me even at the mention of the man who tormented my childhood.

"Yes, he can."

"Could You do it? Could You send him there, instead of me asking Lucifer to do it? I would rather not owe him a favor."

"I can do it for you, if that is what you want."

"Then do it."

"It's done."

I take a deep breath and nod my head. "Thank You."

"Do you mind Me asking why you've freed him?"

"I had to. If I didn't, I would always feel guilt for letting him stay in a place where Lucifer could get to him. It's more for my peace of mind than for his. Now I can leave what happened with him behind, and not look back. I guess you could say it's my form of closure. I'm closing the door on what happened in my childhood. If I don't do it now, I can't move forward with Mason. And I need to move forward. It's time."

"I agree."

"So," I say, not quite sure how you end a conversation with God, "when do You plan to open the Tear, and how do Mason and I go through it together?"

"I will give you an hour to get things together. I suggest you take the sword with you. It might come in handy where you're going."

"Should I take the crown?"

"No, it's not meant to leave this Earth just yet. You're only allowed to take the sword and Mason."

"I have a feeling Chandler and JoJo will want to go with me."

"They need to stay here."

"And look for the fourth vessel?"

"Not exactly."

Wow, God really was an obtuse talker, just like Lilly said.

"Ok, I'll tell them that You said they can't go. They might not argue about it as much."

"Let them know I intend to speak with them myself when I come back to open the Tear for you."

"Ok, I'll tell them. So You'll be back in an hour?"

"Yes. I'll see you then."

God disappears, and I feel my shoulders relax.

When I go back into the house, Chandler and JoJo end up asking me a million questions. I tell them God's plan and, as I suspected, they aren't very happy about it.

"He said he would explain things to the two of you when He comes back," I tell them. "But right now, I need to get ready to go through the Tear and bring Faison back."

I pick up the bag with the sheath JoJo made me for my sword, grab Mason's hand, and head to my bedroom.

Once I close the door, I drop the bag and wrap my arms around Mason's waist, burying my head in his chest and taking a deep cleansing breath.

"Everything will work out fine," Mason reassures me, rubbing his hands up and down my back. "He wouldn't be sending us to Faison if He didn't think you had a chance of convincing her to come back."

I lift my head and look into Mason's eyes. I can see he's not just telling me this to give me hope. He truly believes it.

"He seems to think this trip will help you in some way," I say to Mason. "But He didn't say how."

Mason smiles. "I'm surprised He told you that much, to be honest. I guess we'll just have to wait and find out the reason for ourselves."

"I'm scared," I confess. "I'm scared I won't be able to convince her to come back with us."

"She will," Mason says confidently.

"How do you know that? God doesn't even know that."

"Because she loves you; when she sees what you're willing to do for her, I believe it will break through her grief and make her want to come back home to be with you."

"I hope you're right," I say.

Mason grins. "Trust me."

I change into my Watcher uniform, plasma pistol and all. I strap the black leather baldric JoJo made for me on over my jacket. Strangely enough, the sword isn't as cumbersome to pull from the sheath on my back as I thought it would be.

"I'm not sure I should take you to this alternate Earth," Mason says, eyeing me up and down. "You look far too sexy with that pistol strapped to your thigh and the sword peeking out from behind your back."

I smile. "I'll have you there to protect my chastity."

"Hmm, I'm not so sure I'm the best candidate for that job, since I'm the one who plans to take it from you one day."

"Not take," I correct. "I'll freely give it to you when the time is right. We just haven't had the right time."

Mason sighs. "I knew I shouldn't have listened to you that night at your mother's house. I should have snuck in through your window and had my way with you then and there."

I giggle. "Incorrigible."

Mason takes me into his arms and kisses me soundly. "Only where you're concerned. Now let's go get your sister. Then maybe we can continue this conversation."

God comes back exactly one hour later. We're all waiting for Him out on my porch.

"Are you ready?" He asks me, not wasting time.

I nod, and Mason takes hold of my hand.

Chandler puts an arm around the shoulders of a distraught JoJo as they watch us walk off the porch to stand in front of God.

"We'll be waiting for you!" Chandler calls out to me.

Chandler's statement brings up a good question.

"How will we get back?" I ask God.

"I will open the Tear when it's time for you to come back home. Don't worry. I will be watching."

God lifts His hand and snaps His fingers. The Tear opens, showing the same Earth Faison traveled to.

"Why does it look different?" I ask God, still not able to pinpoint why this other Earth seems so dark.

"It looks different to you because you can see what's there. Stay close to one another," God tells us, and I hear a warning in His voice.

"How do we go through?" Mason asks.

"Concentrate on your need to find Faison," He tells us.

I picture my sister's grief stricken face just before she went through the Tear. I feel a great pressure on my chest, and hold Mason's hand even tighter as we go through the Tear.

I have no idea what awaits us on this alternate Earth. I only know I'm glad to have Mason by my side to face whatever challenges await us.

Even though I only started to believe in Him, I also feel better knowing God will be watching over us. Maybe, with His help, we'll all make it back home.

Maybe…

Author's Note

I hope you enjoyed the second book in *The Watcher Chronicles* series.

The third book in the series, *Oblivion*, is now available.

Sincerely,

S.J. West

FB Book Page:
https://www.facebook.com/ReadTheWatchersTrilogy/timeline/

FB Author Page: https://www.facebook.com/sandra.west.585112

Website: www.sjwest.com

Email: sandrawest481@gmail.com

Newsletter Sign-up:
https://confirmsubscription.com/h/i/51B24C1DB7A7908B

Instagram: sandrawest481

Twitter: @SJWest2013